An Act of Devotion

A. M. Leibowitz

Supposed Crimes LLC • Matthews, North Carolina

Published in the United States.

ISBN: 978-1-938108-87-7

www.supposedcrimes.com

This book is typeset in Goudy Old Style, licensed by Ascender Corporation.

For my big, beautiful bi family.

CHAPTER ONE

ADAM LANSING sauntered into the campus health center. A new year, a new school, a new job—he'd been there less than a week, and the feeling of good things to come hadn't left him yet. He'd already managed to secure a date with the other graduate assistant in his department, which necessitated the trip to the health center. Not that he always expected a date to end the same way—all right, maybe he usually did—but odds were better than fifty-fifty a good time would be had by all. He didn't want to be caught out unprepared.

Inside the one-floor building there were half a dozen other students. Two of them were going through boxes; they looked like undergraduates on work study. Two were sitting in chairs in the waiting area, probably to see the nurse practitioner in the back offices. One was flipping through brochures in the rack on the wall, and the last one was behind the desk. When Adam saw him, his jaw nearly hit the floor.

The man—because this was absolutely not one of the gangly, barely-adult boys in abundance on campus—was gorgeous. No, not merely gorgeous. God-like in his stunning beauty. He was practically a work of art. His skin was bronze, and he had a mass of thick, almost black hair that lay in heavy waves. Under long lashes, his dark eyes shone, and his lips were full and pink. He wasn't quite clean-shaven, and the light, purposeful stubble oozed attractive masculinity. Even seeing only his upper body, it was obvious he was muscular and toned in a way Adam barely aspired to be.

Adam wasn't one to be overly concerned about the packaging when it came to love—or lust, as the case might be. Hot people were hot people, in his opinion. As long as everyone was on the same page with what they wanted, the particulars of hes or shes or theys were only as important to him as they were to his partners. In all the years he'd been practicing the science of mate selection, he was certain he'd never met anyone who had melted his insides as fast as the man at the desk.

While Adam was busy staring, the young woman who had been browsing pamphlets stepped up to the counter. She leaned against it, and The Sexy One bent toward her. They talked quietly for a few minutes, interspersing words with light laughter. Eventually, she straightened up, accepted something the man produced from under the counter, and turned to leave. As she did so, Adam caught her profile and recognized her as an undergraduate from one of his swing classes. She smiled at him in passing before exiting the center.

Adam returned his attention to the counter, but he stood rooted to the spot, having forgotten why he was there in the first place. The low throat-clearing startled him, and he shifted his gaze from Sexy's torso to his face. The man's lips twitched, but he didn't smile.

"May I help you?" he asked.

"Uh..." Adam mentally slapped himself. He was not one to lose his words over anyone, no matter how attractive. Time to take control back. He stepped up to the counter. "Yeah. I need a couple of things." He lowered his voice and put on what he hoped was his sexiest expression. "I came in to get condoms."

Once again, amusement flashed on the other man's face. "No problem. You can leave a donation here." He shoved a jar forward on the counter.

Adam almost laughed at the pink paper label taped to the front. It read, *Condoms—Tip Jar.* Still feeling off-kilter, he snipped, "They're not free?"

"They are. We're asking for donations because we offer a lot of free stuff here, and it helps offset the cost when people give a little." He looked Adam up and down. "I'm guessing you're non-traditional or a graduate student, so maybe you can spare some change."

Adam sneered, but he reached into his pocket for his wallet. He withdrew a dollar and stuck it in the jar then held out his hand. The other man reached under the counter and came back up with one condom, which he slapped into Adam's palm.

"You have got to be kidding me. You want me to pay a dollar per condom? I'm going to need more than one," Adam huffed. "For less than that price, I could buy them at the drug store."

The man laughed. "I'm messing with you. You're being a huge dick about making a small donation to the health center, so payback is fair." He snorted. "Although, look who thinks he's such a stud. If you need that many, why *not* buy them at the store?"

"Because I live in student housing, and this is more convenient. If you must know, yes, I have an important date."

"I'm sure." The man's smile was condescending. "Fine." He reached under the counter again and came up with a handful of condoms. "Enjoy them, with my blessing."

"Whatever."

Adam stuffed them in his pockets, turned around, and stalked out of the health center. No matter how hot that guy was, he was an ass, and Adam didn't want to stick around for any more of his attitude. He had a date to get ready for, and guaranteed she would be much better company than the self-righteous jerk in the center. Which, of course, was exactly why Adam couldn't get his handsome face and toned body out of his head.

In the morning, Adam stretched, his arm brushing against the hair half-hidden under the blanket. Renee had stayed the night, which had turned out to be fun for both of them. At first, Adam had been a little annoyed—the man in the health center had clearly wanted to mess with his head. He'd given Adam an assortment of condoms ranging from glow-in-the-dark to neon colors to decorated varieties. Adam had worried how Renee would take it. Other than the one marked with a ruler, he didn't mind, but it wasn't like they'd had a big conversation about weird condoms before making out on his couch. She'd been a good sport, though, especially with the glow version. Those hadn't been as interesting as they sounded; they were a bit too thick for the sex to be enjoyable. However, Renee had seemed to like watching him strut around in the dark with his hard, glowing dick on display for her.

He grinned at the memory. There was no real relationship going on between them; Renee was as down for no-strings sex as he was, and they weren't likely to hook up often. It had been a good time, though. He watched her stir then ran his hand under the covers to tickle her side. She giggled and squirmed before shoving off the blanket and sitting up.

"What time is it?" she asked. She stretched and yawned, her perfect breasts rising as she lifted her arms over her head.

Distracted, Adam replied, "Hm? Oh. Eight-ish?"

Renee stood up and gathered her clothes. "Mind if I use your shower? I need to go over to the library. Boss-lady has me looking for research articles, and I've got my own work to do."

"Yeah, sure."

While she stepped out to shower, Adam lay back in bed, eyes closed and hands laced behind his head. He'd been hoping for a wake-up something with Renee, but she was the driven sort who spent nearly all her time on work—present situation excepted. He heard the shower turn on, and he let himself drift back off for a few minutes.

In the dim space between awake and asleep, Adam was half-dreaming, his mind wandering to the beautiful man at the health clinic. The man was saying something, but Adam couldn't understand. He tried to ask what it was, but his mouth wasn't working because the other man was too close, too sensual. His cock twitched, and Adam gasped as his eyes flew open.

"I said, do you have any milk?" Renee was standing in the doorway, fully dressed and with her hands on her hips, her damp hair hanging down her back.

Adam almost groaned. "No, sorry. I'm out. I need to get to the store."

"I'll make do." Renee shrugged and turned around. "Coffee?"

she asked over her shoulder.

"Please."

Rising from the bed, Adam looked down at his not-quite-aroused state and really did groan. Regardless of how hot Mr. Health Center was or how good a night he'd ensured with his ridiculous condom assortment, that man had no business whatsoever haunting Adam's dreams. He was not allowed in any way, shape, or form to reduce Adam to a bumbling mess of incoherent words. Adam was going to have to go right back there the minute the health center opened to return the unused condoms and demand normal ones instead, just in case his next date wasn't as cool as Renee. It had absolutely nothing to do with needing a better look at the fine specimen of manhood stationed at the desk. Nope.

Adam dragged on a pair of sweats and padded out to the kitchen, where he said a proper good morning to Renee with a kiss on her temple. She grinned and handed him a mug of coffee.

"Up and at 'em," she said. She kissed him quickly on the lips. "I had a great time last night. Nice way to unwind from work. See you around the department?"

"Sure," he said. "Maybe we can do this again sometime."

Renee smiled. "That would be fun. We didn't get to try out the political-themed condoms, after all."

She winked then took off, and Adam leaned against the counter, blowing on his coffee. He sighed. The health center opened in an hour, which gave him plenty of time to gather what he needed and walk over. He hoped there was someone else working the shift so he wouldn't have to deal with...oh, who was he kidding? He prayed to whatever Sex Gods existed that the hottest man he'd ever seen would be there, followed by an equally fervent prayer he wouldn't screw it up with his lack of adequate communication skills.

By the time Adam reached the health center, he'd made up his mind not to be swayed by Mr. Dark and Handsome. Adam was an effective communicator—that was his job. Not since middle school had he been at such a loss for how to speak to another human being. The only reason he'd ever been rendered silent, his mouth opening and closing like a fish, had been his eighth grade English teacher. Ms. Figueroa had been the single most gorgeous woman he'd ever seen, and the combination of puberty hormonal overload and awkward, geeky middle schooler had left him incapable of anything but sitting in class staring dreamily at her. No matter how attractive the guy in the health center was, he was not allowed to have the same effect on a grown-ass man with years' worth of experience in the fine arts of dating and sex.

He walked in, and he was immediately disappointed to see a short young woman with a magenta pixie cut at the desk. The same student he'd seen the day before from his swing class—he remembered now her name was Lauryn—was in again, talking to the person behind the counter.

"Is AJ in?" she asked. "I had a question for him."

"Sure," Pixie Cut said. "He's in back. Hang on." She disappeared from view.

A moment later, Mr. Sexy emerged. Adam realized he must be the AJ in question. Hovering in the doorway, Adam watched AJ converse with Lauryn. He scowled at the way they exchanged comfortable banter, and he nearly growled when he saw her put her hand on his arm. He smiled at her then straightened up. When he turned his head, his eyes locked with Adam's and he raised his eyebrows briefly. With a tiny shake of his head, he returned his attention to Lauryn. Their discussion appeared to be over because he handed her a small booklet, and she turned away from the counter.

Once again, she smiled at Adam on her way past, and he managed to return it. He knew he had no claim on AJ, but it still annoyed him to see her flirting. That was *his* job. Shoving away his poor attitude, he approached the counter. He was there to give AJ a piece of his mind and exchange the unused condoms; that was all.

"You're AJ?" Adam asked. At his nod, he continued. "I'm Adam. I was in yesterday."

"I remember." AJ's smile was knowing, as though he'd expected to see Adam again. "Back for more? I guess your date went well."

"Not that well," Adam replied. "We didn't use all of them." He dumped the packets on the counter. "Normal ones, please."

"I see. Well, we don't do refunds. This isn't customer service here."

Adam threw his hands up. "Seriously? You're the one who gave me the wrong kind!"

"Oh, please. Don't tell me you didn't enjoy them." AJ laughed, and the sound of it made Adam's head buzz; it wasn't unpleasant. "You said yourself you didn't use *all* of them, which means you did use *some* of them."

"They were fine for me," Adam corrected. "I don't like to scare my partners the first time around with a picture of the President's face. You're lucky my date last night was understanding. If it were up to me, wouldn't be a problem." He lowered his voice. "I have plenty of experience."

"Hm," AJ said. "I'm sure you do." He surprised Adam by looking him up and down, assessing. Before Adam could enjoy the attention, AJ chuckled and said, "I'll bet you think you could teach our staff a thing or two."

This was more like it. Adam possessed a wealth of knowledge. "I could." He leaned in to stage-whisper, "I know how to make my lover scream. I've done it all, baby."

AJ coughed. His mouth twisted into a partial smile. "Oh, really?" He ticked off on his fingers. "Coprophilia, axillism, nasolingus."

Inside, Adam seethed. He didn't know any of the words, given that AJ was using technical terms and not slang, and it raised his hackles. He'd always considered himself well-versed, even when it came to unusual practices. Scowling at AJ he said, "Fine. You win. I have no idea what any of those are."

"Uh huh." AJ looked thoughtful. "Well, you do seem like the type to shit on people, but probably not literally or during sex." He leaned in. "The others are armpit fucking and sucking your partner's nose to get off."

There was no way Adam would let this guy get the better of him. He dropped his voice to a sultry pitch, half-closed his eyes, and said, "Are you offering?"

AJ put his face closer, his mouth next to Adam's cheek. He kept his dark eyes focused on Adam, and his breath tickled Adam's skin. So quietly it was hard to hear, he said, "You. Wish." Abruptly, he pulled away and straightened up.

Holy fuck, Adam thought. Despite the fact that AJ hadn't been serious and was probably screwing with Adam's head, the whole exchange left Adam hot all over and partially aroused. AJ was sexy as hell, regardless of whether he was being a nozzle. The ire he felt at being shown up by AJ was matched only by the degree to which he found AJ's intelligence equally as attractive as his body.

Adam covered his reaction with a sneer. "No thanks. Can I get my condom exchange now?"

AJ dropped the attitude and turned professional. "Already told you we don't do that. Go ahead and keep them, and I'll see if I can find you some 'normal' ones, as you put it." AJ disappeared for a couple of minutes under the counter, finally reemerging with a few more condoms. He set them on top of the pile. "Is that all?"

Adam paused. As long as he was there, he figured he might as well fish a little to see how much of a chance he had if he put his mind to it. AJ was obviously pretty liberated; he'd accepted Lauryn's flirting, and he hadn't backed off at the idea of offering to exchange sexual favors with another man. His comfort in his own skin was intimidating, but it was a turn-on. Adam didn't want to give AJ the satisfaction of being hit on, though. During his internal debate, his rational mind won out, and he opted to gather information directly instead. Besides, he was curious. He was probably out of luck if AJ was involved with Lauryn.

"You like her?" he asked, jerking his thumb at the door Lauryn had gone through.

"Who?"

"The student who left a few minutes ago. I saw you flirt—talking to her."

"Hm? Oh, Lauryn?" AJ shrugged. "We're just friends at this time." He frowned. "Why?"

"You know she's a—" Adam started.

The reaction was swift and ferocious. AJ leaned in and put his angry face right up next to Adam's. "She's a what, asshole?"

"Jesus fucking Christ, calm down. I was going to say she's an undergrad. What did you think I meant?"

AJ backed off, and his face relaxed. "Sorry. Thought you were going to say something else, like maybe a slur. She's a pretty outspoken trans activist, and it's gotten her some heat."

"Yeah, I know. She's in one of my classes," Adam replied. "I'm not like that. I'm a lot more open-minded than you think."

Rolling his eyes, AJ muttered, "Could've fooled me." Louder, he said, "Unless you need something else, I have to get back to work." He arched an eyebrow as though challenging Adam to make any further requests.

Adam shook his head. "Nope." He gathered the condoms from the counter and tossed them into his bag. He turned toward the door, but he still felt AJ's eyes on him. He glanced over his shoulder. "See you around," he said.

AJ didn't respond, so Adam walked out of the center. He wanted to turn around again, but he resisted, hitching his bag higher on his shoulder and walking away from the building. Maybe he would meet Renee in the library to study. If he was lucky, she might want a repeat performance so he could entertain her with the President's face on his dick.

CHAPTER TWO

AJ WATCHED Adam walk out of the campus health center then waited a few minutes to make sure he was gone for good. He'd rarely met anyone with such an entitled attitude. It made no difference that he was also ridiculously adorable, with his unruly red-orange hair, his lanky frame, and his handful of freckles. He was like an oversized elf. If he hadn't been so damn self-righteous and smug, AJ would have liked to get to know him better. It had surprised him to find Adam knew Lauryn and was cool with her. He'd eyed AJ up and down and then styled himself as God's sex gift to humanity, which left a bad taste in AJ's mouth. He'd been hit on by men like Adam a few times in gay clubs—certain guys who were so full of themselves they thought they could teach him a thing or two. Usually, they assumed he'd spent too much time with women or that he only needed the right man to achieve his full gay potential.

After Adam had been so obnoxious, AJ had thoroughly enjoyed baiting him, throwing him off with scientific terms for sex acts he was pretty sure Adam wouldn't find appealing. His reaction had surprised AJ, accepting the challenge and pushing back with as good as he got. It was all bravado, and AJ wasn't interested in someone faking confidence he didn't have. Yet there was something appealing about him. If his reaction to AJ's anger over Lauryn was any indication, there was more under the surface if AJ cared to dig for it.

Satisfied Adam wasn't coming back, AJ retreated to the other room to let Carrie take over desk duty again. He needed to get the pamphlets sorted and stacked for the campus health fair. Now in his second year as one of the graduate assistants on the job, AJ was familiar with how everything ran. He could do it without a road map from the center's health director this time around. While he sorted, he distracted himself from thinking about Adam by recalling his conversation with Lauryn. In spite of his effort, Adam managed to intrude on his thoughts. He'd asked if AJ liked her, and AJ couldn't deny he found her attractive. Adam was right, though. She was an undergraduate, and he would be moving back home in the spring when he finished his program. He would have to think about whether he wanted a serious relationship with anybody, particularly given how long it had been since he'd had one.

Carrie interrupted his brain trail. "Do we still have all those laminated recipe cards for non-alcoholic cocktails?" she called from up front.

AJ straightened his back and stood up from where he'd been crouched. "I think so. Try the stock room, cabinet on the left. They're probably in the box on the bottom. What do you need them for?"

She appeared in the doorway. "My curriculum development professor is having us run a mini program in the residence halls to practice before the health fair. We took a class survey, and most of us wanted to do it on alcohol consumption. We're using the mocktails as a jumping off point." She stepped past AJ and into the stock room.

"Do you need other stuff, too?" he asked. "There's a bunch of good materials."

Carrie emerged with the laminated cards in hand. "For the fair, yeah. I'll want the beer glasses and the dick model."

AJ snickered. "I should find the guy I gave the glow-condoms to. He didn't want them after all. You could use them for the demonstration instead of wasting decent ones."

"Oh, those are the worst!" Carrie said then clapped a hand over her mouth. She slowly lowered her fingers. "Not that I would know, of course."

"Of course," AJ said. "They'd be fine for the demo, though. I doubt Drive Shaft cares what you put on him."

Carrie cackled at the nickname for the penis model they kept in the health center. They'd had it for years, and one of the former graduate assistants had named it. AJ suspected the student who christened it had not been entirely sober at the time. The name had stuck over all the years they'd been using the model, and now they referred to it with affection.

"Drive Shaft is always up for anything." Carrie grinned. "Speaking of things being up, what was with Condom Man, anyway?"

"He wanted to exchange the ones I gave him." AJ shrugged.

Carrie gave him her best *what-the-hell* look. "Something wrong with them?"

"Besides the glow ones, I may have given him a random assortment he wasn't pleased with." At her raised eyebrows, he said, "What? He deserved it. He was being an ass."

"A cute ass. I might like to—"

AJ scoffed. "I'd say he's all yours, but I think he's gay. He was laying it on a bit thick with me."

"Assume things much? You should know better. Too bad if he is, though," Carrie said. "Anyway, I'm about to head out for lunch. Can I bring you back something?"

"Nah. I'll go when you're done. I have a few errands to run anyway."

Carrie nodded. She knew what AJ meant when he said "errands"; it was an open secret between them. He was going to check on a friend, but he had to be careful not to be overt about it. Luke was in a precarious position, and if anyone tried to intervene before Luke was ready, it wouldn't go well for him or the well-meaning person who got in the middle. For the time being, AJ was comfortable catching him when he knew it was safe.

As the door closed behind Carrie, AJ returned to his filing, listening for anyone coming into the center. Another hour or two and he was off work, and he could head to the library to catch up on researching for his thesis. It was never-ending. *Just two more semesters*, he told himself as he wound a rubber band around a stack of pamphlets and tossed them in the box.

Once Carrie was back and taking care of the people in and out of the health center, AJ ducked out. In his car, he debated whether or not to text Luke and decided against it. Luke sometimes forgot to delete messages, and AJ wasn't up for another confrontation with Luke's volatile boyfriend when he saw a message from another man. AJ sighed. Without having witnessed Greg's vicious side directly—other than the time he called to scream into the phone at AJ—there was little he could do. Luke had to make that call himself, and thus far, he'd never done it.

At least Luke had work, a local place called Taco King. It was run by a family, and they were good to Luke. He deserved it, after all he'd been through. AJ knew Luke hid a lot from them, too. If they'd known even half of what AJ did—or had ever seen it—they'd have called someone, not that it would have done any good. AJ pulled up out front and got out of his car, scanning the lot to make sure Greg's compact wasn't parked anywhere before he entered the tiny counter-service restaurant.

Luke was finishing up with a customer. AJ studied him from the doorway, while Luke wasn't paying attention to him, and was relieved to see nothing immediately worrisome. His surfer-blond hair had been trimmed short and spiked, and he had faux-diamond studs in both ears. AJ wondered if the new look was Greg's doing. Luke looked tired, and he was still too thin, but his face wasn't a mess like it had been last time. Satisfied, AJ approached the counter as soon as the previous customer was gone.

"Hey," he said.

Luke's eyes lit up. "AJ!" He grinned. "I have news."

AJ's eyebrows rose. "Okay. Tell me over lunch."

"The usual?"

"You know it."

Luke entered the order and took AJ's money. He'd always

offered—courtesy of the owners, who knew AJ looked out for him—to give AJ a discount, but he wouldn't take it. People running a business deserved to be paid for the work they did, and despite its cheesy name, the food at Taco King was outstanding. When the order arrived, AJ took it to a booth. He'd ordered enough for both of them, and Luke hollered in Spanish that he was taking a lunch break. Señora Guzman poked her head out and waved to AJ then nodded at Luke.

The minute Luke's butt hit the seat, AJ said, "You're in a great mood. What's this big news?"

Luke glanced over his shoulder and leaned in close. In a whisper he said, "I'm going to school."

"What?" AJ said. Realizing he was too loud, he also leaned in and said more quietly, "You are?"

Nodding, Luke said, "I'm getting out. I've been saving up, a little at a time. I have enough for a security deposit and first month's rent, and I already got a scholarship." His cheeks flushed red. "I didn't think they'd give it to me. I'm not real smart like you."

"The hell you're not," AJ countered. "This is great! Does Connor know?" Connor was another of their friends, the only other person who had any idea about Luke's situation.

Luke shook his head. "I was planning to tell you both when we went out, but..." He bit his lip.

AJ knew what he meant. The last time they'd gone out together, Greg had kept Luke at his side the whole time. He wasn't even allowed to have a pee alone, and AJ and Connor couldn't separate him to find out how he was doing. It was a big deal that he'd found a way to apply for school and tuck money away on his own. Even six months ago he wouldn't have been in a frame of mind to manage it.

"Are you going to tell him?" AJ asked.

"Can you?" The anxiety hadn't left Luke's light blue eyes. "I would, but I don't think I should call him."

"Sure. Is there anything I can do?"

"Mm-mm." Luke grinned again, the joy returning as suddenly as it had left. It came complete with Luke's charming dimples, which only appeared when his smile was genuine. "I can't wait!"

"I'll bet," AJ agreed. "What are you studying?"

"Liberal arts, for now," Luke said with a shrug. "I don't know what I want to do. Maybe something in food service. I really like my job, even if it is just serving fast tacos."

AJ laughed. "There's no such thing as 'just.' If you love your job, who cares?"

"Maybe. Anyway, I'll figure it out. For now, I want to know what else is out there. Señor Hierra and Señora Guzman have said they'll let me work around my classes. They're the best." He blushed again, bright scarlet on his pale cheeks.

"They are," AJ said.

Conversation moved on while they finished eating. When Luke was done, he checked the time. "I should get back to work." He crumpled his trash and stood up.

"Me too." AJ stole another look around, hoping Luke wouldn't notice, and then gave him a hug.

To his dismay, Luke had seen. "He's not here," he said.

"I know. I'm sorry."

"Don't be." Luke squeezed AJ's hand and put his mouth up to AJ's ear. "I'm okay. I'm getting out for real this time."

"I know," AJ repeated. "Love you, Lukey."

"You too."

One last smile and Luke retreated to the service counter, slipping back in through the employee door. AJ waved to him on his way back out, saying a silent prayer for Saint Monica to intervene on behalf of Luke's safety.

Saturday nights were for Piet and Donny. The three of them had been inseparable for as long as AJ could remember, from their Catholic secondary school days to living together during their undergraduate years. Piet had moved in with his girlfriend at the beginning of summer, and Donny's work required a commute during the week. They only saw each other for their regular nights out. AJ reserved Saturdays for them and kept Fridays for Connor and Luke, though getting Luke to come with them had been a stretch after the night Greg had kept him so close.

AJ intentionally kept these two parts of his life separate. It made it easier on everyone. He wasn't lying or pretending, exactly. He'd never made his couple of relationships with people other than women a secret with Piet or Donny. Piet got it; his brother and sister-in-law were both bisexual, so it didn't faze him. Donny was good enough to keep his mouth shut. He preferred to pretend AJ was going to settle down with a woman eventually because anything else didn't quite register.

Piet suggested bowling, which AJ thought might have been because he wanted to ask his girlfriend to join them. That wasn't going to fly for two reasons: One, it was guys' night out. Two, Dara was better than all of them. She bowled on a league and was a top scorer. No way did AJ want to suffer through her critique of his skills. When AJ called Piet back, he said he'd only go if Dara stayed home. Piet laughed, but he agreed.

They met up at the alley a mile from campus. Piet looked better than he had the previous spring. He'd put back on some of the weight he'd lost when he was sick, and his skin was no longer gray. He'd cut his thick mop of blond hair, and he resembled his older brother much more closely. Donny looked fantastic as always, with his short dreads, small, neat beard, and well-defined muscles which were obvious even under his casual clothes. The slight strain around his dark eyes was hardly noticeable when he grabbed AJ in a fierce bro hug.

A couple of shared pizzas, a pitcher of so-so beer, and a game and a half later, AJ was finally beginning to relax. It had taken him almost the whole time to turn his brain off and enjoy. Up until then, he'd been distracted with thoughts of Adam the Annoying and Luke's future plans. It was bad enough Piet had asked three separate times what his problem was, and his score reflected his distraction.

AJ was broken out of his fog by the sound of Piet's voice. In response, he said, "Huh?"

"Dude," Piet said. "You're up." He frowned at AJ. "You are all kinds of not with us tonight. I know I've already asked, but come on. This isn't fun."

"Sorry," AJ muttered. "Issues at work."

He didn't like to talk about Luke with the guys. It made Donny uncomfortable, and Piet was never sure what to say. It was the same when he went out with Luke and Connor—they couldn't have cared less about what AJ's straight friends were up to. He'd never tried spending time with all of them in the same place, in much the same way he compartmentalized, organized, and sorted everything else. It was a special talent, keeping all the boxes in his life tidy.

It made sense, really, that AJ should be the hub. He was the go-to guy, the one who could handle everyone else's issues: Luke's violent boyfriend, Connor's family problems, Donny's brother and his mental health, and Piet's cancer treatments. If AJ had no one at the moment to lay his own troubles on, it was all right—he wasn't in the midst of anything big himself, and it was better than dwelling on the stress of his last year of school or why he was now heading for a life different than the one he'd imagined. Earning his degree in Public Health was a reasonable compromise between following his heart and the vast departure he might have preferred.

Donny sat down, a plastic cup half full of beer in his hand. "What's this about problems at work?"

AJ ran his fingers through his hair. "Nothing serious. Getting ready for the health fair, which is a ton of work, and—" He paused then decided he could tell the guys something to get them off his back. "There's this guy who keeps coming in to interrupt me. One of those types who thinks he's God's gift to the universe."

"Oh, man," Piet said. "I know the sort. Thinks he's going to tell you how to do your job, right?"

"Something like that," AJ agreed. The others were not to know he'd found Adam interesting despite his obnoxious streak. "It's not as if I can do anything. I'm there to help whoever comes in, so I can't tell him where to go."

"Is it really as bad as all that?" Donny asked. "It's one guy, and it's less than two weeks into the semester. He'll stop eventually."

AJ shrugged. He didn't want the others to know Adam was the least of his current worries. "Yeah, probably."

"C'mon," Piet suggested. "Let's get back to the game. Take your mind off it."

Nodding, AJ got up to take his turn. He pushed out all thoughts but having a good time with Piet and Donny. As he finally began to unwind, laughing and talking with the guys, some of the other students from campus walked in. Lauryn was there, surrounded by her friends. AJ watched her, and terrific as she was, he didn't find himself wanting to approach her. He looked over and saw Donny eying the group, though.

"They're undergrads," he said.

Donny tore his gaze away. "Too bad. The one in the middle—the tall one who leaves her hair natural—is definitely my type."

AJ wasn't sure what to think. Donny wasn't the most open-minded of his friends, and he might flip about Lauryn. On the other hand, Donny sometimes surprised him. Lauryn was out, but without having her permission, AJ didn't want to explain to Donny on her behalf. The best he could do was introduce them and hope for the best. He might be able to talk to Lauryn at some point; she was in and out of the health center regularly. If she liked Donny, a double or triple date would be a good ice breaker, provided AJ could come up with someone to bring along for the ride.

"I know her," he said. "Do you want to meet her?"

Donny grinned. "Hell, yes."

While Piet reset the electronic score sheet for another round, AJ contemplated how to get Lauryn and Donny in the same space. Out of the corner of his eye, AJ spotted Donny focusing on Lauryn, and when she glanced over at them, he didn't look away. She raised an eyebrow, and Donny gave her a sheepish smile. Her answering grin was enough to startle him. He turned to AJ, who shrugged.

"Bowl first, or meet the woman of your dreams first?" he asked.

Chapter Three

Adam lugged an old computer monitor up the stairs of the Communications building and to the departmental office. Behind him, Renee had the tower. They'd had to carry everything halfway across campus or risk losing their parking spots. He groaned as he hit the top step, nearly toppling backwards. He caught himself and hauled the monitor onto the landing. His arms felt like jelly when he set the thing down to open the door to the office he and Renee shared with three adjunct professors.

It was nothing but a long room with a built-in desk taking up each wall. There were cupboards above the desks, and four of the six stations already had computers. The adjuncts all shared one desk, and the graduate assistants shared the other. There was an empty station at the far end of the room on the same desk Adam shared with Renee. The two of them had been given chairs from the department. They weren't horrible, but they were hardly comfortable. Judging by the work he'd already been assigned, however, Adam suspected he wouldn't have to spend much time sitting in his. Renee, in her second year, was the research assistant, so most of her work was in the library or the main department offices. As the newbie, Adam was mainly there to fetch and carry.

Good thing Renee had been amenable to helping him retrieve his "new" computer, or he'd have had two trips to get it. The thought alone made him wilt.

Renee plunked the tower down, and Adam slid it under the desk. He began attaching the cords. Dr. Weinstock, the head of the Communications department, had already had an extra mouse and keyboard in her desk. Adam had no idea why. He hoped they still worked. Everything about the computer was ancient—the monitor looked like it belonged in the last century. When everything was connected, he pressed the button on the tower to turn it all on. To his relief, it booted up in under ten minutes.

"All set?" Renee asked. "I have to go back to the library to find some case studies. Dr. Weinstock wants to use them in class."

"Yeah." Adam waved his hand at her. "I'm going to go see what other errands they want me to run. At this rate, I'm not even going to need to use the student gym."

Renee laughed. "I put in my time last year. Don't worry—you'll survive." She patted his shoulder then turned around and disappeared through the doorway.

Adam sighed, and one of the adjuncts glared at him. Cringing, Adam backed out of the room and shut the door. He headed down the hall to the departmental offices, a large space at the junction of the two long hallways on the second floor. Inside, there were five offices for the professors and one for the department administrative assistant. In the center of the room, there were two student desks for the work study undergraduates. The copier was on one side. A plump young woman stood beside it, pressing buttons. Her pink-, purple-, and blue-streaked hair was secured in a high ponytail which swung as she worked.

She turned around and stared at Adam as the office door clicked shut. "Can I help you?"

"Is Dr. Weinstock in? I was supposed to meet with her after I came back with the computer."

"I'll check to see if she has an appointment."

The young woman obviously relished her authority to deny access to the professors. Adam tried not to look impatient while he waited for her to pull up the calendar. He knew Dr. Weinstock's class schedule because he had to work around it. However, he had to rely on the student employees to fill him in on the rest of her commitments since she hadn't given him any information. He wondered if it was her way of making sure graduate assistants knew their place.

There was definitely a hierarchy Adam had discovered within his first day on the job. The full professors shared the beautifully remodeled new office and the administrative assistant. The assistant professors had the old office down the hall, which wasn't much more than a collection of closets put together. The adjuncts and graduate assistants shared the long human storage room. As a first-year graduate assistant, Adam was lower even than the undergrad work study students. Renee had officially earned the right to boss them around, though, and he wished she were there to defend him.

At last the woman turned to him and said, "Go ahead. She's got you in for this morning already."

"Thanks." Adam knew it was probably a terrible idea to get on her bad side so early in the semester, so he flashed a grin and a wink at her. She blushed and waved him off.

He knocked on Dr. Weinstock's door and opened it at the muffled, "Come in." Her office was a paradise of books, professional journals, stacks of papers, and artwork done by her three-year-old. Amid the clutter, Dr. Weinstock sat behind her desk, which was miraculously devoid of anything but a paper calendar and her computer. She looked up at Adam and smiled. Despite her gruff exterior, Dr. Weinstock seemed to genuinely care about her students, and it showed in her classes. Adam appreciated any small gesture she offered him.

"The computer works fine," he told her.

"Fantastic! I was hoping you'd say that. We'll get the wireless printer software installed, and you'll be off and running. Good thing, since you have a major task ahead of you." She handed him a flyer.

Adam glanced down at it. The paper was an advert for the previous year's health fair. "What's this for?"

"You'll be helping with the PR for this year's fair." She peered up at him over the top of her glasses. "You can use the old flyer as a guide for designing the new one. Check in with the students working in the health center to get the details you'll need."

That meant potentially having to talk to Mr. Know-It-All again, and he was undecided whether that was a good thing or a bad thing. Unable to help himself, Adam choked out, "Why?"

Dr. Weinstock arched an eyebrow at him. "Interdepartmental cooperation. The faculty and deans have determined we've become too isolated in our disciplines, especially when it comes to campus-wide events. This year, the health fair has several new components. The School of Nursing will be running a flu shot and basic wellness clinic. The Health Science department is providing free materials and brochures on a range of topics, and Physical Education is hosting a variety of classes. Several other disciplines are stepping in as well. Even the Music department is sending students for a demonstration on guided imagery for stress relief. Since we're not in the business of health or education, our contribution is the promotional materials."

Adam held back a snide comment about wondering how the Math department fit into it all. Instead, he said, "All right. What exactly do I need to do?"

"I'm glad you asked. You won't be doing all the promotion, of course—volunteer students will be involved. You're going to design this year's adverts, and you're going to collect information from the student health center on the services offered at the fair. You'll be putting together a menu of options as a brochure. The student volunteers will copy and distribute them."

"Is there a menu from last year I can look at?" he asked.

Dr. Weinstock pulled out a tri-fold and handed it to him. "Here you go. Have a preliminary design to me by the end of next week. In the meantime, I already have some papers for you to sort. I need these alphabetized, and I want you to create a spreadsheet of student information." She set several stacks of half-sheets on her desk, each paper clipped and laying sideways on top of each other.

Adam nodded and picked up the pile. "No problem," he said.

On his way out, he passed the student with the multi-colored hair. She glanced up from her desk and smiled flirtatiously at him. He twitched his eyebrows and breezed past her without a second look.

By lunch time, Adam had completed the spreadsheet of new students for each of Dr. Weinstock's classes. He emailed them to her then stood up, stretching. None of the adjuncts were in the office at the moment, and Renee wasn't back from the library. He drummed his fingers on the desk, debating. His two options were to go back to the office and get the directory so he could call the health center or walk over there himself and speak to someone. It would be faster to get the directory, but he'd have to deal with whichever student was on duty in there. The undergraduates wouldn't be able to give him what he needed anyway. If he went over to the center, he ran the risk of running into AJ. Or *not* running into him, which Adam told himself would definitely not be disappointing in the least.

Before he could stop himself, he pictured AJ's dark hair and eyes, his full lips, and his broad but lean build. He could almost smell the woodsy scent of whatever soap he used—it was too mellow to have been aftershave. Adam had noticed it when AJ leaned in close to taunt him the last time he'd been in the health center. Thinking about that brought him back to the present. AJ had been angry with him at the end of their conversation, making assumptions about what kind of person Adam was. The memory made him scowl, and he thumped his fist against the desk.

An adjunct returning with his lunch jumped at the sound and nearly dropped the container of soup he was carrying. He frowned at Adam and plunked his food on the desk. Adam sighed and tried to appear dignified as he strode past the man on his way out. On principle, he decided against returning to the room to make phone calls while the professor sat there with his lunch. Instead, he exited the building, squinting in the early afternoon sunlight.

On the way, he reminded himself how unlikely he was to run into AJ again during the day. Most of the graduate classes were at night, to accommodate students' work hours, so it was possible AJ was on his shift. But he'd been there Saturday, which meant he might have time off during the week. The whole walk across campus, Adam vacillated between wanting and not wanting to see him.

He couldn't decide if he was disappointed to find only the magenta-haired student at the desk. She smiled at him when he entered, and he managed to return it. No need to antagonize her if he was going to have to depend on her for the information he needed; time to turn up the charm.

"Hi," she said, and her smile brightened. "I remember you from the other day."

"Yeah?" he asked, resting his arms on the counter and leaning in. "I'm Adam."

"Carrie," she said. "Nice to put a name with a face." She giggled. "I was secretly calling you Condom Man."

"Sounds like a superhero. Has my reputation preceded me?" He laughed, but it quickly faded. "Oh, because AJ gave me the wrong ones."

"Yep. Sorry about that. Anyway, what can I do for you?"

Carrie was definitely cute, even if Adam wasn't specifically interested in her. It wouldn't be so bad discussing his task with her, and maybe he wouldn't end up having to worry about AJ at all. He smiled again and said, "I'm here to talk to someone about the health fair. Do you think you could help me out?"

"Sure," she said. "It's not until the first week of November, though. What did you want to talk about?"

Adam put the flyer on the counter. "I'm creating a new one of these as well as a menu of options for the health fair. I need some details."

"Ah, okay," she said, sounding disappointed. "Well, you'll want to talk to AJ about it. He's got the information."

He almost snarled at her. *Of course* only AJ had the information because that was the kind of day Adam was having. He stood there at the counter, wondering what he was going to do about it.

When he didn't make a move to leave or provide her with anything else, she prompted, "So...is there something else I can do for you?"

Adam made his mouth formulate words. "No, I obviously need to speak with AJ."

"He's out right now," she replied. "He'll be back after lunch."

Adam glanced at the clock. "It's almost one."

"Then he should be back any time. Is that all?" By this point, her expression had morphed from sunny to confused, probably because Adam was still standing there motionless.

"Not really. Is it okay to wait there?" He pointed to the chairs.

"Suit yourself." She turned away and busied herself with something other than speaking to Adam, though she did give him one last amused glance.

He huffed. There was no telling how long he'd have to wait, so he plunked down in one of the plastic chairs and looked for something to keep himself occupied. He had just picked up a magazine from the table to read about "ten ways to manage stress" when the door opened and AJ walked in.

It took everything in Adam not to show any signs of reacting. AJ looked every bit as good as he had the first two times. He had on a white polo shirt and a pair of dark trousers, and as he walked in, he pushed his sunglasses onto the top of his head. Adam braced himself for the moment AJ turned his attention to the waiting area. His best effort wasn't enough. AJ's gorgeous dark eyes shone in the dim lighting, and he looked utterly delicious—so far out of Adam's league it was painful. His gaze came to rest on Adam. If he was surprised to see him, he didn't show it.

"You again," he said.

Adam pursed his lips while bringing himself under control, all hopes dashed. There had been no need to be unfriendly. "Yes, me again," he replied.

"Back for more condoms already?"

"No." Adam stood up, glad he had a couple of inches in height on AJ. "I came to get information."

AJ's soft hum sounded condescending. "Apparently you don't know everything already. What a surprise."

"Oh, my God. What is your problem?" Adam stepped closer. "All I did was come here to ask you about the health fair because my department is apparently responsible for your PR. You're not exactly making this easier, you know." The combination of ire and excitement at being so near AJ made his heart pound.

The smile on AJ's face slipped, and he backed away. "I'm sorry," he said, and he genuinely sounded contrite. He straightened his shoulders and took on a professional tone. "Come on in back and I'll help you out."

Well, that was easy, Adam thought. *Maybe too easy.* He followed AJ around behind the counter into a small room with a table and chairs. AJ waved him into a seat and disappeared out the other door. He was back in a minute with a stack of papers in his hand. After handing them over, he sat down across from Adam. When he saw the faint tremor in AJ's hand, Adam frowned, not sure what to make of the change in posture.

"I'm sorry again," AJ said. "You were kind of obnoxious last time you were here, so I assumed I was in for more of the same. If it's for the health fair, I'm happy to give you whatever you need." His nose wrinkled in disdain. "In the interest of 'interdepartmental cooperation,' of course."

Adam didn't bother concealing his laughter. "You've got that right. I don't have a problem with this, really, but it seems a little forced."

For a moment, AJ remained tense, as though he was trying to regain control. Then his mouth twitched, and he dropped the businesslike demeanor. "It is," he agreed. "We did everything ourselves last year, and now it seems like everyone wants in on it. This was our baby up until now. Other disciplines have their own events, so I'm not sure why we have to share ours."

Grabbing the top paper from the pile, Adam said, "I see why they want us, though. This is kind of boring."

"What? Let me see." AJ snatched the paper back. "It's informative! Why does it need to be exciting?"

"You actually want people to show up, right?" Adam asked.

"They did show up last year."

"Uh huh. How many people came?"

AJ cringed visibly. "Fine. Not that many, and most of them only wanted what they could have gotten by stopping in here anyway. If I'd had my way, we'd have publicized it better—put up the information sooner, that kind of thing."

"Right," Adam agreed. "Which I guess is why they asked us to step in." He paused. "So, this is what Dr. Weinstock meant. She said this is what we do. Well, here I am. Tell me what you're thinking, and I'll make it happen."

AJ's eyebrows rose. "What department?"

"Communications," AJ said.

"Not marketing or business?"

"Nope. Trust me, you do not want an MBA doing your PR for you." Adam grinned. "I may have made a bad first impression on you, but I can be smooth when I want to be. Want to start over?" He held out his hand. "Adam Lansing. Pleasure to meet you."

Accepting the handshake, AJ replied, "AJ Mancuso. Likewise."

"Well, that wasn't so hard." Adam couldn't resist teasing a little. He gave AJ a sly smile and said, "Yet."

"Oh, dear God. You're dreadful." AJ laughed. "Do you actually pick people up with those lines?"

Adam shrugged, playing it cool. "Among other things. I tend to read the situation and get what we both want from it."

AJ leaned in. "I'll bet. Sometime, you'll have to tell me exactly how you managed to make your date appreciate those God-awful glow condoms."

If Adam had been drinking, he'd have spewed his mouthful everywhere. As it was, his spit went down the wrong pipe, and he wound up coughing. "I can't believe you just said that."

"You were kind of asking for it."

"Not yet I wasn't. We haven't even had a date." Adam winked and took the paper from AJ. "Back to business. If you give me an idea of what you want, I'll email you within a couple days with some mock-ups."

"All right." AJ tapped the stack of papers. "You've got copies of the information sheets provided by each department, and you've seen last year's flyer. Let me give you my email address, and you can send me what you've got." He scrawled his address on the top of the old flyer.

"Here's mine, in case you want to ask me anything." Adam wrote his down and traded it, glancing at AJ's in the process. "Your full name is Antonio?" He grinned. "Does that mean I can call you Tony?"

"God, no," AJ said, chuckling. "That's my father. I'm Antonio

Junior, and no one calls me anything but AJ except my mother. She calls me Tonino, and she's the only person who can get away with it."

"Tonino?"

AJ nodded. "It means 'little Tony.'" He curled his lip.

"No kidding?" Adam gaped at him. When AJ nodded, he roared with laughter. "That's...wow."

"Which is why no one else calls me that." AJ shook his head and laughed quietly.

"Can you speak Italian?" Adam asked.

"A bit, yeah." AJ gave Adam a crooked smile. "My Nonna—that's my grandmother—came to the U. S. right before my mom was born. My mother grew up speaking both languages, and she passed some of it on to me." He snorted. "She wanted me to learn 'proper' Italian, but at least fifty percent of what I know is dirty."

"Cool," Adam said, and it made him feel good when AJ's smile expanded and his eyes crinkled a little. "Wait...you learned raunchy Italian from your mother?"

"No, from Nonna." AJ snickered. "I can say the equivalent of 'fuck you' several different ways."

"Oh, my God." Adam grinned. "You'll have to teach me."

"Maybe that'll be your reward for giving me a good set of mock-ups. For now, I'd better get back to work. Send me whatever you've got, and let me know if there's anything else you need."

AJ stood up, making it clear their conversation was over. Reluctantly, Adam rose from his seat as well to follow AJ out to the front. He offered a cheerful wave to the magenta-haired student on his way out. Maybe working with AJ wouldn't turn out half bad after all.

Chapter Four

AJ AVOIDED watching Adam leave the health center. For one thing, he didn't need Carrie to catch him staring. For another, he didn't want Adam to turn around at the last minute and catch him staring. For all his arrogance, he'd proved to be all right once they'd sat down. AJ had noticed the change in attitude when he was in his element. Creating good content was clearly something he enjoyed, even if he didn't seem to want to say it outright. For a few minutes, AJ allowed himself to dwell on exactly how sexy real confidence–rather than bravado–looked on Adam.

Before his thoughts could stray too far, he dragged himself away to focus on a different set of worries. He'd gone to see Connor over lunch this time, meeting up in the campus dining hall. Connor was the only other one of AJ's friends in graduate school. Piet's education had been derailed by his illness, and he was only just beginning to regain his health. Donny had never planned to continue. Connor, however, had started classes in the graduate Nursing division.

AJ had told Connor what was going on with Luke, and unsurprisingly, Connor was skeptical. Still, he didn't outright say it, and AJ held onto hope that Luke was ready for a change. His classes didn't start until spring, so he had time to plan ahead and figure out what he was going to do in the meantime. It also gave AJ time to convince Connor to lend a hand in getting Luke on his feet.

Connor's lack of faith troubled AJ, but he pushed it into the heap of "things not to be distracted by." He had work to do. In between his classwork and his tasks at the health center, he focused on other concerns. His current pet project was petitioning the local LGBT center to spread their funding more equitably. They devoted almost all their time and money to some causes while leaving others to flounder. They'd been heavily invested in supporting organizations pushing for marriage equality, and now that it was reality, AJ feared they might back off or ignore other community needs. They also didn't offer enough information for bisexual and transgender people, which AJ found equally frustrating. He suspected he poured too much energy into his side projects—he did have classes, after all—but it was easy to get sucked in once he'd started.

He sat down with his laptop to continue an email correspondence with the director. He'd been at it only a few minutes when Carrie peered over his shoulder. He glanced up at her briefly before hitting send on his message.

"Saving the world one email at a time, I see," Carrie remarked. She often told him he needed to let things go, but it wasn't in his nature to give up when he felt passionately about something.

He waved her off. "I'm only trying to do my part."

"Right," she said. "By wearing yourself out. Babe, I see what you do. Do you ever sleep?"

"Of course!" AJ shot back, choosing not to disclose an exact figure on his minimal hours.

"In between emailing people and reading up on the latest issues and flirting with cute but full-of-themselves guys?"

"Exactly!" AJ replied. "Hold on...not that last one, no."

Carrie laughed. "Oh, yes, you do. I've never seen you apologize so fast to anyone, let alone someone you complained was being a jerk."

AJ tried to glare up at her, but his expression faltered. Carrie meant well, but she was being nosier than he preferred. "I suppose.

That was work, though. I don't want to get fired for failing to promote—"

"—interdepartmental cooperation," they chorused together.

"I know," Carrie concluded. She made a dramatic production out of her sigh. "Lucky you, though. At least you have eye candy to enjoy while you work."

"You'll find someone," AJ assured her. "Now shoo, so I can go back to saving the world."

Still giggling, Carrie pranced back up to the front desk to keep an eye on the pair of freshmen staffing it. AJ checked for any other messages before turning to his online group. There were a couple of posts there he responded to, and then he closed everything out. Like it or not, Carrie wasn't far off the mark. He decided to put his efforts into sorting the pile of books in the bin by the door instead of dwelling on Adam.

The student health center was one of a dozen book exchange locations on campus. Students took a book off the shelf and in return dropped one in the bin. Every so often, some wiseass put a library book in there, necessitating a trip to return it for real. This week's offerings included several copies of the same few books, so AJ had the option of looking in the other drop boxes or trading them in at the used bookstore downtown. He tended to prefer trading them because there were some great finds at the store. He took it as his personal responsibility to bring back books on controversial topics students might not feel comfortable borrowing from the library.

He set the extra copies aside, separate from the three campus library books at the bottom of the bin. He needed to get to the library at some point later in the week anyway, so he could return them then. When he was through bagging everything, he returned to the desk and pulled Carrie aside.

"My turn," he said.

"Good," she replied. Tilting her head at the students, she said, "They're really starting to annoy me. Apparently, they've started dating. That's not going to be awkward at all when they break up."

AJ snorted. "I'll keep my eye on it."

Shaking his head, he watched Carrie retreat into the back with her bag before turning his attention to the students at the desk. They were engaged in playful banter, but one serious look from AJ and they were right back to work without another word.

When AJ stopped by the library later in the week with his stack of books to return, it was nearly empty. It was a gorgeous day, the majority of undergraduate classes were done until seven, and most people not trying to put together a thesis were out enjoying the late afternoon sunshine. He, on the other hand, wanted to get as much done as possible, especially since it wasn't a night he had class. Finishing by May wasn't an option—he needed to wrap it up so he could go back home. He wasn't sure working in the youth services center there was what he wanted to do forever, but it was a sure thing. After six years of school, a guaranteed job was exactly what he needed, especially if it meant escaping the college town and everything it represented to AJ.

He walked through the first floor cafe, past the circulation desk, and toward the spiral staircase in the center leading to the computers and the quiet section. If it had been a search for scholarly articles, he'd have gone to his apartment and worked there. Instead, he needed several books, only half of which were owned by the library. He would need to put in a request to have the others sent. Adjusting his bag, he ascended the stairs toward the shelves he needed.

When he arrived at the top, he nearly groaned. Sitting at the first computer table was Adam, right next to a woman with long, brown hair. He pointed something out to her, and they both muffled their laughter. AJ tried sneak past. He and Adam had made temporary peace, but AJ wasn't ready to be best friends, and he was already having a hard time reconciling the two versions of Adam he'd seen. There was no guarantee he would get the decent side rather than the arrogant prick.

Unfortunately, AJ must have made some kind of noise because Adam looked up. So briefly it almost didn't register, a look of pleased surprise swept across his face. Within a few seconds, he composed himself, and his mouth spread into a wide grin accompanied by a suggestive twitch of his eyebrows. AJ stifled a growl. Clearly it was going to be Overconfident Adam; he was probably showing off for his study buddy.

"Hey, AJ," he said, waving him over.

Stepping up to their table, AJ attempted a smile. "Hey."

"Hi!" the brown-haired woman said. "I'm Renee." She stuck out her hand.

AJ accepted it. "Nice to meet you. I'm AJ."

She held on for an extended moment, eying him before giving a sideways glance at Adam and winking. She was the type of woman AJ avoided at all costs—very feminine, all soft curves and long hair and a heavy dose of flirting. His nose twitched at her delicate perfume, and his stomach churned from the familiar scent. Everything about her was too much like his ex. All he could think about was being away from her. His face was hot, and he wanted his hand back. He tried to keep it steady, controlling his anxiety as best he could. When she let go, she put her fingers on Adam's arm. The familiarity and possessiveness of the gesture bothered AJ on the same level her handshake had, and AJ had to breathe slowly for a minute.

As if she could read AJ's thoughts, Renee's eyes crinkled when she peered up at him. A moment later, her features relaxed into a warm smile, and she said, "I work with Adam. I'm the other Communications graduate assistant."

"Oh, I see," AJ responded, unnerved by his own worries over whether she was part of the deal when it came to planning with Adam for the health fair. Working with women like her was unavoidable, and he would need to learn to manage it sometime. He had to pull himself together. Squaring his shoulders, he took a step back from their table, keeping his eyes on Renee and reminding himself she was not Michelle.

Offering a sly half-smile, Adam said, "You're welcome to join us. I'm open to a three-way."

Pulled out of his reverie by Adam's innuendo and embarrassed by his reaction to Renee, AJ almost made a rude reply. He knew that was what Adam wanted—to get a rise out of him. Refusing to give him the satisfaction, AJ leaned closer and adopted a matching suggestive tone. "So sorry, *mio bambino*. Not tonight. I have a hot date with my research."

Adam laughed, and he looked AJ up and down with approval, making him warm again for a different reason than before. "Prefer to fly solo, eh?"

"If only," AJ replied. "I need to go find an enormous stack of books and pretend I can carry them all back home, where they'll keep me company for the rest of the night."

Once again, Adam's eyes swept over him. "You look like you can manage fine, but if you want, we'll help."

"We will?" Renee asked.

"Y-you will?" AJ stammered, unsure whether Adam was still referring to something library-related. "I mean, that is...you don't have to. I'm good." He kept his eyes on Adam.

For several long seconds, they stared at each other. He was glad his skin was too dark to make a blush obvious. Even so, he was sure both of them were aware of how his whole face and neck had gone hot. Out of the corner of his eye, he saw Renee looking from one to the other as though enjoying a particularly exciting tennis match. She laughed and nudged Adam, who jumped and snapped out of his daze.

She grinned. "Of course we'll help. Pass me the list."

AJ blinked and turned his head. He cleared his throat to give himself a minute to recover. "That would be great. Thanks."

Less than thirty minutes later, he was armed with most of the books on his list. After parting ways with the others, he checked them out, ordered the last handful the library didn't own, and was on his way, relieved to be out of there. Before he'd gone ten steps out the door, he heard someone behind him.

"Wait!" It was Adam.

AJ turned around. "Yeah?"

Adam twisted his mouth to the side and scratched his neck before speaking. "I know we had kind of a rough start, but...did you want to, you know, hang out?" When AJ didn't respond right away, he added, "We can work on the stuff for the health fair. I could show you some of the ideas I came up with."

"Oh." AJ didn't want to admit he was disappointed Adam hadn't meant it as a date after all. "Sure, I suppose. I don't have anything after dinner."

It made no real sense to him that he wanted to see Adam in another context. No matter how much fun he was having with their teasing, AJ's current reality meant it wouldn't be anything more than hooking up. Adam seemed like he'd be fine with that arrangement, but AJ hadn't ever been the one-night sort. He was far too intense in every definition of the word. It was best to keep their relationship to business only. So why was he still standing there thinking about Adam in a decidedly unprofessional way?

"Ah, damn. I have class tonight," Adam said, interrupting AJ's mass of confused thoughts. "What about Friday?"

AJ shook his head. "No, I have plans." It didn't matter that he probably wouldn't see Luke. Connor would still want to go somewhere. "Maybe Saturday morning."

"You're not working?"

"Nope. I don't usually work Saturdays—they have student employees for that. I was only there because we were sorting supplies last weekend."

Adam relaxed. "You could come over to my place." He leaned in closer. "Speaking of supplies, I still have those glow-condoms. Maybe we can work out a way to use them in the health fair."

"Actually, I already told Carrie—the other graduate student in the health center—she should use those for her demonstration."

"Ooh, a demonstration? Count me in." Adam grinned. "We should test them ourselves first," he suggested, waggling his eyebrows.

A deep belly laugh erupted out of AJ at how forward Adam was being, especially since he couldn't possibly be serious. "*Bambino*, you say the sexiest things to me. I usually like to take things a little slower, get to know people before we try out the health center products. Maybe a rain check on lighting up our dicks. How about we go over those mock-ups first?"

"O-okay," Adam answered, jumping back a little as though AJ had shocked him with his answer. "Well, what did you have in mind?"

AJ shrugged, and an idea occurred to him, something of a casual compromise. Making Adam work for it a bit wouldn't necessarily be a bad thing, and he might be able to draw out the real Adam—the one he'd glimpsed the other day, which he suspected lurked under the surface. That person was worth knowing, maybe in multiple ways.

"I'll tell you what—let's meet up Saturday morning, and we'll go from there. Work first, then fun."

With that, he turned around and walked away, leaving Adam to wonder what he'd meant.

CHAPTER FIVE

THE HAND on Adam's arm startled him, and he whirled around to face a grinning Renee. He took a step back from her and tried to sound casual when he said, "Hello there."

"Did you score a date with Hot Stuff?" she asked.

"What makes you think that's what we were talking about? I still need to give him my mock-ups for the flyers." Adam crossed his arms and gave her a pointed look.

"You have them done already? Damn, you're quick."

"That's not what you said the other night." Adam grinned.

"I didn't want to bruise your fragile ego," she shot back. "But seriously, you already have the mock-ups?"

He dropped his smile. "Not exactly. It was an excuse, okay? I like talking to him."

Renee mimicked his pose. "And that's all you talked about? For real?"

Adam deflated. "Yeah. We're meeting up on Saturday, if I can get them finished."

Her eyebrows shot up. "You didn't even try for a date?"

"Maybe he's not my type." Adam tried to look as though he thought she were uninformed. "Maybe being friends is enough."

It didn't work; Renee laughed. "I've only known you a few weeks, and so far, I've seen you flirt with anyone who shows even the most mild interest. And in case you hadn't noticed, AJ is probably the hottest thing on two legs this campus has right now."

Annoyed, Adam snipped, "I've seen some attractive pigeons."

"Right. But none of them are sexy Italians." She put her hands on her hips. "You also haven't used finishing your work as an excuse to talk to them. I'm glad not all men are as clueless and immature as you are. You're an adult—feel free to ask him to go for coffee or drinks. Jesus. It didn't take nearly this much effort for you to get me to agree to go back to your place." Making a show of gesturing between them, she said, "Have we gone back to middle school? Adam, you might as well send him a note saying 'Do you like me? Check yes or no.'"

Adam glared at her and followed with the same mocking tone. "Have we gone back to two thousand four? I don't need you to woman-splain my feelings at me like an emotionally stuck toddler. AJ is now a colleague because we're working on the health fair. Something else develops, I'll be sure to send you an engraved invitation to our first date. Oh, wait—no, I won't because it's none of your business. This is all a result of the push for interdepartmental—"

"—cooperation," Renee finished. "I know, I know. But 'woman-splain'? Are you for real? Anyway, fine. I can see you don't want my help. Go, do your thing." She shooed him with her hands.

Adam grunted. "I need to finish the damn flyers anyway." He fixed his gaze on Renee and gave her a hard stare. "I don't need your help."

"In any sense of the word," she agreed. "You've made that clear."

With a heavy sigh, Adam rubbed his chin. "Look," he said. "You've been great, and I'm not trying to be an ass. I'm not used to having a friend be so...in my face about my relationships." *If you can call them that,* he thought. "I've made my share of mistakes, but my nearest and dearest usually know enough to let me handle it myself. I know you mean well, but back the hell off, okay? The whole point is this *isn't* middle school anymore."

Renee had the sense to look embarrassed. "All right," she said. "You'll let me know if you need anything?" Her question was timid.

Adam relaxed. "I promise. For now, I'm going to go back home and mess around with the designs. I have a few ideas, but I need to work things out so I'm ready for Saturday." He huffed. "That's one thing you got right—I did use them as an excuse, and now I'm in a pinch because I promised them to AJ by then."

A smile spread across Renee's face. "Which brings me back to what I said earlier regarding why you would feel it necessary to have a story to talk to him."

Adam contemplated her words; he didn't have a good answer. Something about AJ compelled Adam to want to know more about him beyond his good looks. Adam wasn't content to proposition him, get him in bed, and wish him well the next day. He craved more of what they'd already shared—sexy banter and an exchange of ideas. AJ didn't talk down to him or assume his only skill was what he could do with his dick. Not that he didn't want to try that out, too; Adam was convinced AJ would be equally capable sexually as he was verbally. The problem was how Adam's usual tactics weren't working on AJ, and he didn't have anything to fall back on to interest someone as gorgeous and brilliant as AJ.

"I don't want him to see me as a slacker," Adam told Renee. "The health fair means a lot to AJ and his department, and I want to do a good job."

"You could have told him that instead," Renee replied.

"I suppose." He shrugged. "I'm on it now. Besides, I like working on a tight deadline. I'll have the designs done."

He leaned in and kissed Renee on the cheek then bid her goodbye. Time to turn his attention to creating a good campaign to draw students in for the health fair. How hard could it be?

Out of sheer adrenaline, Adam flew through work on the flyers for the campus health fair. He chose a carnival design, taking each aspect of the fair and plugging it into the theme. The nutrition panels became food vendors; the fitness booths became carnival games; other information tables and demonstrations were rides. It was borderline cheesy, but Adam did it with flair, and he tried to make it as visually appealing as possible. If AJ liked it and Dr. Weinstock approved, the undergraduate volunteers could work on designing banners and posters. Adam relished the idea of supervising them rather than being under the watchful eye of the other departmental employees.

When he was done with the mock-ups, he emailed AJ to ask for his feedback then set to work on grading Dr. Weinstock's multiple choice quizzes. He'd gotten halfway done when AJ emailed back.

Love the design, but I have some concerns about the font you used. It may not be visually accessible to some students. The placement of the text could be an issue too. Talk about it on Saturday morning?

Adam replied, *Sure. We could meet up in the library again.*

Sounds great. 10am okay? If we're still at it by lunchtime, I'll take you to my favorite place for a quick bite.

Adam wondered what sort of place AJ liked. First he pictured him in a classy, upscale restaurant, the kind that didn't list their prices on the menu. It seemed a little far-fetched, so he tried thinking about AJ in a casual Italian kitchen, possibly with a chef whose actual name was Luigi. That didn't seem quite right either, so he gave up and focused on what the offer meant. Rereading the email, his stomach clenched. Was he asking for a date? Sure, they'd engaged in some flirting, and the whole Saturday meeting was AJ's idea. Hell, he'd even thrown in a comment about having fun, but that's as far as it went. AJ wasn't interested in taking Adam up on any of his multiple offers or he'd have said so. Adam couldn't read tone of voice in the email, so his imagination wandered to what else AJ might be after.

As much as AJ got his blood moving, there was no denying the man was far, far out of Adam's league, at least in terms of the physical. Probably everything else, too. AJ was confident, smart, and hard-working. What could he possibly want to do with a former schoolyard target who'd spent the previous year goofing off and trying to figure out what to do with the rest of his life? AJ was the kind of man who had to have been one of the cool, popular guys in school, the type who became 70-hour-a-week professionals with a million connections made long before he stepped off the stage at graduation. When it came to work, he was smooth and polished and outwardly mature beyond what any twenty-three-year-old should be. Adam's only marketable skill was his mouth, and AJ didn't appear to want it for any of its many uses.

The thought made Adam swallow. He had to be misreading it. Their forced closeness was the only reason someone like AJ would associate with anyone like Adam if he wasn't going to take advantage of the offer to enjoy his body. Whatever lunch plans he'd made were nothing more than a token gesture. Adam shook himself. When he met with AJ, he would politely turn down the proposed meal. He would never again bear the humiliation of the last time he'd gone after someone miles away from his zone.

He ran his hand down his face and tugged on his chin, sighing. This would be the first time he'd refused anyone in as long as he could remember. What he would tell Renee in the aftermath was anyone's guess. Maybe he could make something up, if she didn't see right through it and ask him what the real deal was. Either way, there was no chance he was going to let AJ make a fool of him, especially not when they still had to work together on the project.

He sent an email back. *Work first, then fun,* he typed, echoing AJ's words the last time they'd seen each other. *See you Saturday at 10 in the library.*

Saturday morning, Adam changed his clothes three times. He felt like a teenager, going through his closet and examining every shirt for its potential. There wasn't any reason to bother; after working on their project, he was going to firmly but nicely tell AJ he was too busy for lunch. He wanted to look good but not too good while doing it, though. After standing shirtless in his off-black jeans for fifteen minutes following the second wardrobe change, he selected a white tee and a black-and-white checked short-sleeve button-down, left halfway open and untucked. He liked the way it looked on him, but more importantly, it was the last thing he would wear if he were trying to get someone like AJ to notice him.

Satisfied, he gelled his hair, and peered at himself in the mirror. Thank God his skin was almost clear now, not that it mattered at the moment. He twisted his face, examining for anything he might have missed in his grooming. Glancing down at the spray bottle of his favorite cologne, he decided not to use any. No sense in making any special effort just to reject AJ before the reverse happened.

He wasn't aiming to be cruel, only to protect his own interests. If AJ had really been interested, he'd have taken one of the several offers Adam had already made—much like everyone else did. He'd made it clear they wouldn't be hooking up, that day or any other.

It was still hot out, so Adam drove to the library. It was a short distance from his section of student housing—where the married and graduate students lived—to the campus proper, and he could easily have walked. He'd have been beyond merely sweaty, though, so despite the hot car, it made more sense. Adam was surprised to find the library lot nearly full, since it wasn't anywhere near exam or term paper time. He pulled into one of the last three remaining spots.

Inside, the library was busier than he'd expected. He realized although they'd set a time, he and AJ hadn't agreed on a location. He glanced at the wall clock, noting he was a few minutes early. Unless AJ was also the sort to show up early—which he might well have been, given everything Adam had seen so far—he probably wasn't there yet. Adam stationed himself in the small lounge by the large front window to watch for him.

He lost himself in thought, staring out the window without really seeing. Aside from being anxious about declining a potential date with AJ, he was excited to show off the new ideas he had. He'd brought printed copies for AJ to look at in case he wanted to see the live versions before they made changes on his laptop. While he waited, he went over the details in his mind. He was so immersed in picturing how he would pitch it that he jumped at the light tap to his shoulder.

He looked up to see AJ standing over him, smiling, and he was rendered speechless. AJ looked fantastic. Like Adam, he was casual, wearing jeans. He had on a gray v-neck t-shirt, and a thin, gold chain peeked out from underneath it. The shirt was just tight enough to make his muscles more pronounced. He wasn't one of those guys who looked like he spent twenty-four-seven in the gym; it was more like he was naturally well-defined in all the right ways. Not too lean, but not a bulky hulk, either. If he wasn't careful, Adam would start drooling. He stood up and tried to look nonchalant.

"AJ. *Ciao?*" he tried, hoping he had both the right word and the right inflection.

"*Ciao.*" AJ laughed quietly. "I'm guessing that's the only Italian you know, but I'm impressed you bothered." His smile softened, as did his eyes. His gaze traveled up and down Adam. "You look good," he said, his voice catching slightly at the end.

Those three words nearly undid all of Adam's resolve. He hadn't meant to "look good." He'd meant to give the impression of not caring so he could pretend he hadn't gone to any effort and didn't want anything other than to finish their project. AJ had upended everything with a single sentence. Adam couldn't lose what little control he still possessed, so he said, "All part of my charm."

"No doubt," AJ agreed. "On the subject of Italian, how about we get started? The sooner we finish, the sooner I can coach you on how to sound sexy while you tell people to get bent."

"That's right," Adam replied, snickering. "You did promise me you'd teach me some of your grandmother's dirty words."

"It all depends on how much I like your work," AJ informed him. "Show me the goods, and I'll keep my vow."

They made their way deeper into the library to the study desks at the back of the first floor. Adam set down his bag, pulled out his laptop, and plugged it in. Once he'd pulled up the pages he'd created, he turned it for AJ to see. They spent the next two hours going over everything, AJ making changes and Adam testing them out. AJ was nothing if not thorough. He went over the details meticulously, offering information on the program's topics and pausing to give his opinion. To his relief, Adam was able to let AJ do most of the talking. It was easier to focus on the work and silence the inner war raging between what he knew he needed to do and what he increasingly wanted to do. It was also easier to ignore all the warnings in his head in favor of simply staring at AJ while he worked.

When they were through, they had what Adam felt was a good product. They'd kept the carnival theme, but it was far more accessible and the cheesy factor was greatly reduced. AJ had come up with the idea of collecting stamps or signatures on a card for each part of the fair students attended and turning in completed cards to enter a drawing. They could offer a chance to win a door prize, provided the health director was agreeable to it and they had the budget. For the final change, AJ agreed to ask his boss about opening the health fair outside of the student population so the general public could benefit as well. A small donation would offset the extra expenses on typically free items such as the condoms.

AJ sat back and looked at what they had. "This is fantastic. I'm sure Kira—she's the health director—will agree to this. Do you need Dr. Weinstock's approval?"

"Yes, for the flyers and brochures, but I can't see her saying no. She left them for me to design. The student volunteers will take it from here, printing and posting the signs and distributing information in campus mail." Adam grinned. "Now, about that promise you made..."

AJ's dark eyes lit up. "Fair's fair," he said. "So, the first one I'll teach you I heard when I was about ten. Nonna was on the phone with someone, and I have no idea who it was or what they were arguing about. Right before she hung up, she hollered, '*Vaffanculo!*' at whoever it was. I was sitting on the floor at my mother's feet, and she reached down and covered my ears, but it was too late."

Adam's eyebrows rose. "What's it mean?"

"Roughly? 'Go fuck yourself.'"

"Say it again?"

"*Vaffanculo*," AJ repeated, drawing it out so Adam could hear the syllables.

"*Vaffanculo*." Adam tried to imitate AJ's inflection. "You're right, it does sound sexier. Well, I suppose not if you're screaming it at someone."

AJ laughed. "No, not then. I wondered why my mother was upset, so I tried looking it up. Needless to say, it wasn't in my grandmother's Italian-English dictionary. I was thirteen before I found out what it meant."

"Are you going to teach me any more?"

"Not today, *tesoro*," AJ replied. "You'll have to earn it."

"Aw, shit. I was hoping you'd give me a few more." Adam grinned. "And what did you call me? I hope it wasn't an insult."

"I think you mean, '*ah, merda,*'" AJ corrected him. "I promise, I didn't insult you. If you stick around, you'll find out what it means. I know you were only responsible for the flyers and advertising, but maybe you'd like to stop by and help us out with some of the other work." He took a deep breath, and it looked like it took a lot for him to say, "You can ask your friend Renee, too."

Adam wondered what it was AJ didn't like about her. He'd been icy to her the last time they'd seen each other too. "Renee's the research assistant, which will be my job next year. I do Dr. Weinstock's grunt work."

"You're not—she's not—"

Catching on, Adam rescued AJ. "My girlfriend? Nope, just a friend. I guess it would be fun to work on the health fair, but I'm warning you, I don't know much about the kinds of things you do. At least, not the ones that don't involve sex."

AJ shook his head, smiling. "Right. I'd forgotten you're an expert on sex. It's mostly a matter of organizing people and programs, but since the theme was your idea, I thought you might like to help us make it work. We'll need to meet with the various student groups involved and explain it to everyone."

"All right," Adam said. "I could at least do that much." He slid his laptop and folder away.

Before he finished packing up his bag, AJ put a hand on his arm. "Did you still want to have lunch with me? I know a decent place. It's not fancy, but the owners are great and the food is good." He left his fingers on Adam's skin, and despite how warm they were, Adam shivered.

All his resolve melted when his gaze connected with AJ's. He blew out his breath. "Can I be honest with you?"

AJ drew his brows together. "Of course."

"When I got your email, I was going to tell you I had plans for this afternoon." Adam sat back and fiddled with the strap on his bag.

Withdrawing his hand, AJ mimicked his posture. "Why?"

"We didn't get off to the best start, and I wasn't sure how well our meeting would go." That was as much as Adam was willing to admit to for the time being.

"Oh." AJ put his hand back on Adam's wrist and slid it upwards, wrapping his fingers a little. The touch felt good. "You're right. It wasn't the best start. But we've worked pretty well as professional colleagues so far. You've done a lot of work, and I thought we could both use some time to relax." His eyes narrowed. "As long as we treat each other respectfully. No games. All right?"

Adam took his time answering, letting the pressure and texture of AJ's fingers linger against his skin. He wanted to say yes, to agree to this one small thing. No obligations.

He took a deep breath, looked AJ dead-on, and said, "Yes."

CHAPTER SIX

AJ HELD open the door at Taco King. Luke waved to them when he finished ringing out the previous customer. "You brought a friend! Hi, AJ's friend," he joked.

"Hi," Adam replied. His breath tickled AJ's ear as he leaned in to whisper, "You brought me to a fast food taco joint?"

AJ laughed. "Were you expecting a five-star steak house? It's not quite fast food, and everything is fresh. Wait till you try it. You're going to thank me." Louder, he said, "Luke, this is Adam."

Luke grinned, and it made AJ's chest tight to see him so happy. It had been far too long since Luke's face had been anything but drawn and pinched. They hadn't seen each other in a few days due to mismatched schedules, and AJ had been right; Luke hadn't gone out with them the night before. No doubt he'd stayed home to appease Greg, hopefully throwing him off the trail. Connor had taken it as a bad sign, but Luke's expression now told a different story.

"What can I get you?" Luke asked.

They placed their order and retreated to a booth in the corner. Within a few minutes, Luke brought their tray, along with a slip of paper.

"Courtesy of Señora Guzman," he explained. "For dessert." He winked at AJ. "Bring it up to the counter when you're done, and I'll get it for you." He pressed his fingers into AJ's shoulder before he walked away.

"What was that all about?" Adam asked. His gaze was fixed on Luke's back, and his brows were drawn together.

AJ put a hand on top of Adam's. "Nothing. Señora Guzman must have assumed we're here on a date, so she's giving us a little treat. She likes me," he added.

"Can't see why," Adam said, but he grinned.

"Jerk." AJ withdrew his hand and reached across the table to smack Adam in the head.

Adam looked over his shoulder at the counter. "Is surfer boy your boyfriend?"

AJ almost choked on a sip of his water. "Who?"

"The cute blond taking orders."

"Oh, Lukey...uh, Luke? No, he's just a good friend." AJ needed to move the conversation to something else before Adam asked any other questions about him. "Speaking of boyfriends, I have to ask. Did I ruin your chances with your last date by giving you those unorthodox supplies?"

"No," Adam replied. "She and I were agreed it was a one-off. Nothing serious." He snorted a laugh. "She thought the condoms were funny, actually."

"She?" AJ's eyebrows shot up. "Ah, crap."

"'Ah, crap' because now you think I'm straight?"

"No. 'Ah, crap' because Carrie was right. I jumped to conclusions, especially after you said you're not dating Renee. It's not something I do often, and I ought to know better." AJ chuckled. "Maybe I didn't like thinking you play for my team."

"You're bi?"

"Yeah. Is that going to be a problem?" AJ bit his tongue. "Sorry. I mean, clearly it's not, since you...well...never mind."

"No, not an issue." Adam shrugged one shoulder. "I made assumptions too."

AJ sat back in his seat, more at ease than he had been. "Well, then, we're even. How about we enjoy this food?"

Adam dug in and groaned at his first taste. AJ didn't bother covering up his laughter as he watched Adam eat. It was sinful the way his mouth curled around each bite, relishing it. Realizing he was staring, AJ shifted his attention to his own plate. He wasn't sure how he would make it through dessert if Adam was like this every time. He'd wanted to get to know him without quite so much sexual energy between them and work up to something else, but it would take a lot more self-control than he'd realized.

Eventually, Adam slowed down, and they talked between mouthfuls. He asked, "So, are you Health Science?"

AJ shook his head. "Public Health Admin. Same building, and there's overlap between our departments, but the program is different. Carrie's Health Science, with a focus on community education. You're strictly Communications?"

"Yeah, for now. Same as my undergrad, but I minored in Econ too. I haven't chosen a narrower focus yet, but I will next semester when I pick electives. What about you?"

"Oh, my undergrad?" AJ fidgeted. He didn't need to tell Adam the whole truth. "Social Work, with a double minor in Health Sci and...Psychology," he lied. It didn't make a difference what his real minor had been or how he hadn't ended up completing it and why. No need to give Adam his life story; it wasn't as though they were in a relationship. "I'm finishing up my certificate of non-profit management as well as getting my MPH."

"Geez," Adam said and whistled. "Would you like fries with that?"

Forcing a laugh, AJ replied, "My father is on the board of a non-profit. That's where I'm headed when I'm done here—go back home, work for them. It's all lined up." Exactly like everything else in his life. It was better that way.

Adam nodded. "What kind of work?"

"It's a network of homeless shelters, each with a different focus. Dad mostly manages work at the youth shelter, which is where I'll be placed." AJ didn't tell Adam how most of the work he would be doing involved filing reams and reams of papers and begging donors for more money.

"And that's what you want to do?" Adam tilted his head, and

his intense focus made AJ sweat.

AJ wiped his clammy hands on his jeans. "Sure. I mean, it's a guaranteed job, right? Not everyone can say the same after six years of school."

A slight frown crossed Adam's face, but it was gone as quickly as it had come. "Sounds like you've got it all figured out."

"I suppose I do. Better than flying by the seat of my pants." AJ tensed, waiting for Adam's answer to mirror the same things most of his friends said to him.

All Adam said was, "Hm," and he left it there. Through with his meal, he wiped his mouth and changed the subject. "Why the hell have I never eaten here before? I thought it was just some dingy hole in the wall. Damn."

"I told you so," AJ said, relaxing now that the topic of his future was off the table. "I'll go get our dessert."

He brought the slip of paper up to the counter, and when Luke took it, he bent across the counter to say quietly, "He's real cute. It's about time." He straightened his back and headed for the kitchen.

AJ sighed. Luke meant well, and unlike Connor and Piet and Donny, he knew the truth about Michelle. The others mostly accepted AJ's claims about needing to focus on school and not on his love life or lack thereof. Luke was convinced Michelle was the problem. In a sense she was, but not for the reasons Luke imagined. He thought AJ only needed the right guy to make him happy, as though Michelle had been the last woman he would ever go out with.

When Luke returned with the dessert plates, AJ decided not to push him on it. He was only trying to help, and God knew AJ had done that enough for him in exchange. "Thanks," he said and gave Luke a smile he hoped implied a few things.

He sat back down at the table, placing one plate in front of each of them. Adam stuck his spoon in the creamy triangle and brought it to his mouth. Once again, AJ found himself watching Adam instead of taking a bite. He tried to pass it off as wanting to find out Adam's reaction, but he wasn't sure if he successfully convinced Adam that's all it was.

"Well?" AJ said.

"Fantastic. What is it?"

"Vanilla orange flan. I guess it's Señora Guzman's family recipe. I'll tell her you liked it."

Adam waved his spoon at AJ's plate. "What about you? You haven't tried it."

AJ took a bite, and the whole sensation was intensely pleasurable. It was cool and creamy, sweet with a hint of tart spiciness. He closed his eyes in bliss, not even caring what Adam thought of the look on his face.

"Oh, my God."

"Guess it's my turn to tell you I told you so, huh?" Adam teased.

They finished in silence, and at last AJ popped the sugar flower into his mouth, letting it dissolve on his tongue. He swallowed and grinned at Adam. His smile faded when he thought about ending their time together, but an idea popped into his head for a way to see him again. It would be the first time he'd ever brought another man on their nights out. He wasn't sure what the guys would make of it, but Dara and Lauryn would be cool. AJ sighed, causing Adam to look up at him.

"What?" Adam asked.

"Oh, just thinking it's about time to go so I can get some work done. What would you say to dinner later tonight, though?"

A look of confusion and then wariness passed across Adam's face, but it was replaced by a grin. His eyes sparked. "Say the word, and I'm there. Wasn't it supposed to be my turn to treat you to a meal, though?"

AJ shrugged. He took a deep breath and let it out slowly. "The truth is, I have ulterior motives."

Adam laughed. "You clearly don't know me well. Hell, I'd have gone back to your place this afternoon if you'd asked. No need to be formal."

Just like that, Arrogant Jackass Version 2.0 was back in place. At least it was familiar territory, and AJ knew how to handle it. He resigned himself to admitting he enjoyed their back and forth. "Not sex, you dog. You know Lauryn, who was in the health center the first day you came in?"

A puzzled look crossed Adam's face. "Sure."

"My friend Donny asked her out, but he's...not always open-minded. I thought a group date might break the ice. Would you be willing to come with us?" He coughed. "As my date, I mean."

For a moment, Adam sat with his mouth open. Eventually, he pulled himself together and said, "Yeah, okay."

Relieved, AJ sat back against the booth. "Great," he said. "I'll let you know as soon as I talk to the guys when I'll pick you up and where we're going." He pulled out his phone and handed it over. "Put your number in there so I don't have to go over to your building and throw rocks at windows until someone answers."

Adam entered his information and handed the phone back. "So, tonight, then?"

A slow smile spread across AJ's face. "You got it."

They stood up to throw away their trash. AJ returned the plates to the counter, and Luke gave him a thumbs up before carting them into the kitchen. AJ ignored it and followed Adam to the parking lot. For a moment, he debated how to end their time together. While he pondered, Adam solved the problem for him. He pulled AJ into a half-hug and put his mouth up to AJ's ear, causing AJ to tense.

"Next time, you can teach me more of your grandmother's vocabulary," he said.

AJ relaxed and shoved him away. "I told you, you owe me help with the health fair first."

"I can think of better ways to repay me," Adam teased, putting a hand on AJ's arm.

The touch sent a shiver through AJ. "I'm sure you can," he said. "But let's be friends without the benefits first."

"First?" Adam stood still, and all traces of joking left his face. "Is that an offer?" he asked, low.

"I'll let you know after tonight." AJ stepped back and took a more casual tone to let Adam know that part of their conversation was over. "Get me those flyers and I'll say it *in Italiano*."

"Yeah, yeah. I got it." Adam grinned and turned around. "See you!" he called over his shoulder, leaving AJ standing next to his car and wondering what Adam's next move was—or his own, for that matter.

AJ and Adam met the others outside the bar-and-grill restaurant for their triple date. Piet looked tired, and when AJ asked how he was doing, he said he'd had a doctor appointment the previous day. AJ understood; those always took so much out of him, largely at an emotional level, and it took days to recover. Every appointment for the next several years would be an exercise in tension. AJ was glad he had Dara to help him through it. Seeing how close they were gave him a faint pang of jealousy which he shook off.

"This is Adam," he said. "Adam, you've met Lauryn already. The others are Piet, his girlfriend, Dara, and Donny." He pointed to each of them in turn.

Everyone was friendly toward Adam, but AJ had the prickling feeling he'd crossed a line. It wouldn't be the first time. If Piet ever discovered a few details about his brother, Garritt, and his wife—details AJ was intimately familiar with—it would strain their friendship. One of the ways he kept Piet from finding out exactly how close Garritt and AJ had been was by sticking strictly to bringing women when they met up and dismissing his relationships with anyone else as something he did privately.

Despite AJ's worries, the evening was pleasant. Adam kept the others entertained with stories about working for his department chair and some of the ridiculous tasks she assigned. At one point, Adam had been required to make a list of all the possible conferences in the U.S. she might be interested in over the next year, prioritizing them in order of how likely she was to attend.

They lingered over their food, but at last they received the check and conversation wound down. Donny stood up, and Lauryn followed, slipping her fingers into his. He didn't smile, but the way he relaxed at her touch and the shine in his eyes made it clear how he felt. AJ, however, tensed. If Donny was going to grow attached, it could end badly for both of them. He rose to his feet as well.

"We're gonna take off," Donny said. He reached over and fist-bumped Piet then nodded at Dara and Adam. "There's a movie we both wanted to see—that new action film."

Lauryn giggled. "I can't remember the title, but it's basically hot people blowing things up. Actually, maybe that *is* the title."

Piet, Dara, and Adam all chuckled, and Donny grinned. "Beautiful, smart, and always up for explosions. What more could a guy want?"

"Are you sure?" AJ asked.

Donny curled his lip in distaste. "For real? You're asking if I'm sure we want some alone time?"

Piet cleared his throat. "We should get home anyway." He touched Dara's hand. "I'm not feeling great tonight."

"I'll take care of the bill," Adam offered. "Ante up, everyone."

He collected the money, and Lauryn excused herself to the restroom to freshen up. Dara accompanied her while Piet and AJ followed Donny to the parking lot. When they were away from the restaurant, Donny rounded on AJ.

"What's your problem, man?" he demanded.

"Nothing, I—"

"You've been all weird since the night you introduced me to Lauryn. I don't know what's up with you, but you gotta stop. First you told me to ask her out. Now you're trynna mess it up. You better start explaining."

AJ sighed. "I don't want to see either of you hurt."

"You and Lauryn are that tight, huh?" Donny scowled. "Or is it 'cause she's transgender?"

AJ's eyebrows shot up. "You knew?"

"Aw, hell. So that's it. Yeah, I knew. She told me when I called to ask her out. Who were you protecting—me or her?"

"Her," AJ muttered. Louder, he said, "You can be kind of an ass about stuff sometimes. You're uncomfortable if I talk about Luke, and you don't want me to mention guys I'm going out with. I saw how you looked at Adam earlier. How was I supposed to know how you'd feel about someone like Lauryn?"

Donny stepped closer so their faces almost touched. His face was hard. "You don't know shit, man. Do you know why my brother's been so fucked up? I wasn't gonna say anything, but you've known him since he was a little kid." He huffed and stepped back, pulling out his phone. "Look," he said, holding it out to AJ.

The picture was Donny's brother, Jaxon. Donny and all five of his siblings were adopted at different times and in different ways, so the brothers bore no resemblance. Jaxon sported a hot pink tank and gold hoop earrings, and his long, black hair was tied back from his face. With his delicate features and shimmering makeup, he was exceptionally pretty. AJ looked from the photo to Donny.

"I didn't know," he said.

"He says sometimes he's a boy and sometimes he's a girl. I don't exactly get it, but I'm trying." Donny's shoulders slumped. "Our parents aren't cool with it. They told Jaxon he can't wear that shit in the house, so he sneaks it. Soon as he turns eighteen, they're planning on kicking him out of the house, but I gotta get him outta there sooner or he's gonna die. I've been working extra hours just so I can get him here before he kills himself."

"Why didn't you tell me? I could have helped you," AJ said. He reached out for Donny, but Donny pulled away.

"Naw, man. You'd have tried to fix it, just like you do with everything else." Donny shoved his phone back in his pocket. "You know why I hate when you talk about Luke? It's 'cause I saw what happened to him. His parents did the same thing mine are doing. And goddamnit, I feel so fucking helpless!" Donny yelled.

"AJ?" The soft voice broke the moment.

AJ turned around to see Adam and the women standing there watching the whole thing. Dara stepped around him to where Piet stood, and he wrapped his arm around her shoulders. Lauryn looked between AJ and Donny, a puzzled expression on her face. Adam hung back, his hands in his pockets.

"We're done," Donny said, and AJ wasn't sure if he was referring to the conversation or their friendship. "I'm gonna take this fine woman here on a date to watch hot people blow things up, if she'll still have me." He glanced at Lauryn, offering her a half-smile.

Lauryn relaxed visibly. "Well, I do like explosions, after all." She turned to the rest of the group. "It was nice meeting you all. AJ, I'll see you around, okay?"

"Sure." He tried to smile at her, but he knew he didn't make it, and her own expression faltered. AJ looked at Donny. "I'm sorry."

Donny shrugged. "We'll talk," he said, and AJ was grateful he was willing to give that much.

Piet and Dara bid the others an awkward goodnight, and AJ watched all four of them walk to their cars. The hand on his shoulder made him jump and spin around; he'd almost forgotten Adam was still there.

"Sorry," Adam said, stepping away.

AJ clenched his teeth and waited for the lingering shame for his behavior to pass. "Don't worry about it. I'm sorry for how dinner ended."

"You okay?" Adam's brow was creased.

"I don't think I'm the one you should be asking." He leaned against his car. "Let's just go back to campus."

They drove in silence. AJ could tell from his posture Adam wanted to say something, but there wasn't anything that could fix what had been lost between himself and Donny. He'd overstepped this time, and once Donny told Lauryn, she wouldn't be thrilled with him either. He'd known it wasn't his best idea, but he hadn't been able to stay out of it. If he was lucky, Piet wouldn't go too hard on him.

At Adam's building, AJ pulled up to the door. "Thanks for coming with me."

Adam nodded and exited the car. He started toward the door, but he paused and turned around. He circled the car to AJ's side and motioned for him to roll down the window.

"I had a good time, even if it did get weird for a minute there." He paused. "Did you want to come in?" he asked, sounding hopeful.

His meaning was clear, and AJ did want to go in. He wanted to let Adam do anything to erase the argument with Donny from his mind. But the desire to forget probably wasn't the right reason. He wouldn't be able to explain to Adam why he couldn't spend the whole night, and once he left, he'd be back to thinking about Donny again.

AJ put his hand on Adam's. "Not this time. I'll see you this week to work on the health fair." He wanted to let Adam know he hadn't forgotten what he'd said after lunch the previous day. "We'll talk then."

Adam nodded. For a moment, it looked like he might pull his hand back and go inside, but instead, he leaned into the car. "Can

I?" he asked.

"Can you what?"

"Kiss you."

His hesitant tone and the way he chewed his lower lip was so unlike how he usually was that AJ inhaled sharply in surprise. It negated everything he'd mapped out about how their non-relationship was supposed to go. Yet when he locked eyes with Adam, it was all he could think about.

When he had recovered, he said, "I would like that."

Adam bent closer, and AJ tilted his head. It was only a soft brush of their lips, but it was enough to make AJ sigh. Adam chuckled under his breath, and something about the sound relaxed AJ. He reached up and drew Adam closer so he could kiss him again. It was a bad idea, he knew, and if he didn't stop, he would change his mind and go inside with Adam.

As though reading his thoughts, Adam withdrew, both from AJ's lips and from his window. "I'll stop by the health center this week," he said. "See you."

This time, he went straight into his building without even a glance back. It didn't matter; AJ had what he needed to stop the endless loop of his fight with Donny. Maybe he would be able to sleep well after all.

Chapter Seven

From the safety of his building, Adam watched through the window as AJ drove away. The minute his headlights rounded the corner, Adam dashed up two flights of stairs to his apartment. Once inside, he leaned against his door, catching his breath and fighting to keep the shaking in his knees and arms under control. The kiss he'd shared with AJ had left him lightheaded and caused a whole fleet of jellyfish to take up residence in his stomach.

After a minute or two, he stepped away from the door and headed for the bedroom. He flopped onto the bed and flung an arm over his eyes, replaying the previous ten minutes over and over. A ripple of child-like excitement overtook him, and he drummed his feet on the bed as he pumped his fist in the air. He'd initiated the kiss—wasn't it AJ who was supposed to feel all the magic? Yet here Adam was, recalling the way AJ had pulled him closer and made him feel wanted but in a different way than he was used to.

It was a rush, and not merely arousal. Adam was giddy—happy, nervous, excited, and yes, pleasantly turned on but not to the point he needed relief. This was nothing like the way he felt when he'd simply encountered someone who interested him. This was something else entirely, even if he couldn't put his finger on what it was. He wanted to burn off the energy by running around campus or jumping on his mattress. He curled his knees toward his chest then rocked until he was upright. Swinging his legs over the side of the bed, he bounced for a few minutes on the edge then bounded up. He couldn't focus on anything but AJ, and he couldn't keep still.

In the kitchen, he poured a glass of milk and sat down at the kitchen table, hoping that would relax him. He hadn't felt this good in a long time, and there was no reasonable explanation for it. He barely knew AJ, but one thing was clear—he *liked* AJ. And possibly, just maybe, AJ liked him, too. Not in the way most people liked him, with flirting and casual dates and even more casual sex. AJ had turned down his offer to come up, yet he had not only accepted a kiss but delivered a better one in return. It meant something, even if Adam wasn't sure what it was.

His fingers twitched, itching to text AJ and see if the spark was still there. He pulled out his phone, stared at it for a few seconds, then typed his message.

Hey, you. Sorry it was weird at the end, but I like your friends. I had a good time.

He hit send, and then he panicked. What if AJ didn't want to hear from him so soon? He'd been so upset about whatever happened with his friend Donny. Maybe their kiss hadn't meant as much to him as it had to Adam—he could have been too distracted to enjoy it. Even worse, maybe telling Adam he would see him to work on the health fair meant business only. Maybe AJ wanted to limit their contact. This was all new territory; the last time he'd felt this way had ended badly, and he couldn't keep the tension at bay. The more time went by without a response from AJ, the more Adam worried.

His phone vibrated against the table, causing Adam to jerk in his seat. He ran a shaking hand through his hair and picked it up, hopeful and eager.

I'm sorry too.

Adam deflated a little; it wasn't the response he'd hoped for. Maybe he'd been right about it meaning more to him than to AJ. His phone vibrated again.

I want to kiss you again, preferably as soon as possible.

Sucking in his breath, Adam stared at his phone. Another thrill spiked through him, and he trembled enough he almost dropped the phone. *You could come back, you know. I'm still here.* He set the phone down and took a swig from his glass.

It took several minutes for AJ to send another message. *If I do that, it won't end well.*

Why not?

I don't do casual. Told you, friends first. Benefits later. I hope you're not disappointed.

Adam thought about it. Was he disappointed? He might have been a little, but only because he didn't want the night to end yet. The memory of their kiss lingered. He typed, *It's okay. You must have superpowers, though.*

A moment later, a series of question marks popped up on the screen. Adam laughed out loud, though it was shaky.

You left me weak-kneed, and I'm not even mad you won't come back and fuck me into the mattress.

AJ's reply was faster this time. *Avete un debole per me?*

It was Adam's turn to reply with a question mark. He was torn between hoping whatever AJ had said was dirty and hoping it wasn't.

It means "Do you have a weakness (or a soft spot) for me?"

Adam's heart pounded as he typed, *How do I tell you I think maybe I do?*

Several minutes passed, and worry gnawed Adam's stomach that he'd said the wrong thing. At last AJ responded. *Sorry, had another text. You can say "Si è vero."*

After copying the text, Adam pasted it into the message. *Si è vero.*

Anch'io. Me too, AJ sent back. *Buona notte, tesoro.*

That one even Adam could figure out. *Good night, though I still don't know what you're calling me.*

He pictured AJ's soft laughter when the reply came through. *Behave while we're working, and I'll think about telling you.*

Hey! You'd better. Get some rest.

You too, tesoro.

Adam closed out his texts and set the phone back on the table next to his half-full glass. He wrapped his arms around himself, trying to hold in the warmth from their brief conversation. Closing his eyes, he let out a sigh. If Renee had seen him, she would have mocked him for behaving like a kid with a first crush, but he didn't care about her opinion. She'd only known him for a short time, and she was already geared up to interfere. There was one person whose opinion he did care about, however, and he knew he could count on her not to make fun of him. He picked the phone back up and pulled up his frequent contacts.

He'd sworn six ways from Sunday he wasn't going to do this anywhere near as often as he wanted, but guilt stole over him for not having called his best friend, Ainsley, sooner. They'd talked the first day he'd arrived on campus and once the following week, but not since then because he'd gotten so wrapped up in class, work, and the health fair. It didn't matter whether she was busy with her own classes and still trying to balance a relationship. She was going to listen and not judge him for maybe-possibly-almost-definitely falling for someone so different from his usual string of partners. He hit her digits, crossing his fingers like he had, indeed, gone back to middle school.

She answered on the first ring. "Knew you'd call sooner or later." He could hear the mix of sarcasm and warmth in her voice.

"Not even a hi or how are you?"

"Nope. There are only two reasons why you would be calling me. I'm guessing you haven't broken up with anyone recently"—she snorted—"so it must be the other one. You've met someone you can't live without, and they won't give you the time of day."

"That only happened once." Adam growled into the phone. "And it's neither. Or, well, maybe it's a version of the second one, but I kind of..." He paused. "...have the opposite problem."

"Oh?" Ainsley's voice brightened considerably. "That's new."

"Well, yeah. This has never happened to me before! It's...weird. You know me—I am not a hearts and flowers kind of person, but..." He paused.

"But this guy makes you wish you were," Ainsley mused, picking up on his thoughts. "You might not be romantic, but you know how to charm the pants off just about anyone."

"Usually literally," he agreed. "This is different. We've been on two sort of dates, and I think he's into me, but he didn't come up to my apartment for sex. I mean, not even blowies or a hand job or hell, making out in my car."

There was a long pause, and he knew exactly what her face looked like; she was frowning and biting her lower lip. When he couldn't stand it anymore, she said, "Wait. This isn't one of your professors, is it? Because you were pretty hard on me about that with Meredith. It would be the definition of irony if you were now in the same position."

Adam thought about Dr. Weinstock and shuddered. "Ugh. Not at all. He works in the student health center."

"An undergrad?" she asked.

"No. He's one of the graduate assistants." Adam closed his eyes, picturing AJ's gorgeous face. His eyes popped back open, and without meaning to, he said, "Shit."

"What?"

Adam swallowed several times to clear the lump of anxiety in his throat. He didn't want to admit why it didn't bother him when AJ opted not to join him inside. He didn't answer Ainsley, unsure how to explain to her why this was different. He'd tried so hard to have a spark with his ex—or whatever term was appropriate for a relationship so one-sided—and never achieved the level of excitement he had over AJ.

"Adam?" Ainsley broke him out of his trance. "What's wrong?"

"I'm not—" He drew in a deep breath. "I'm not just trying to get him into bed."

"Oh," Ainsley said. Her tone softened. "*Oh.* You've finally met someone for real, haven't you?"

"Maybe," he said.

"Only maybe?" Ainsley teased. Adam pictured her sitting up on her knees, her eyes bright. "Sounds like more than maybe."

Adam sighed. "It is. Only I usually fuck first, ask questions later. I don't know how to do this the old-fashioned way."

Her laugh was a sudden burst of joy. "You'll learn." Another chuckle. "Bring him a dozen roses."

"What if he doesn't like flowers? Also, cheesy. Do guys even give each other flowers?" He'd never considered the possibility. Of course, he'd never brought *anyone* flowers—they weren't necessary for hooking up or friends with benefits or almost-relationships that should have ended before they started.

"Then bring him something else. Seriously, this is not as hard as you're making it. You are a grown-ass man acting like you're back in seventh grade. Did you also slip him a note asking him if he liked you?"

Adam glowered, even though he knew she couldn't see him. "That's what Renee said, too."

"Who's Renee?"

"The other grad assistant. I told you about her." Except for the part where they'd already slept together, as he hadn't talked to Ainsley since classes started.

"Right. Well, she's smart, and so are you. I guarantee you'll figure it out. Listen, I have to go—work to do. Keep me posted, okay?"

"Yeah, okay," Adam grumbled. "You were no help."

"Not my job," she reminded him. "Besides, you apparently have someone else for that." She didn't sound entirely pleased, but there wasn't any real bitterness to her tone. "You don't need a mommy. I know you—the king of giving advice. So take some of your own, and think about what makes you happy. Then try it out on this amazing new guy of yours."

"Fine," he grumbled. He blunted the edge in his voice. "Love you."

Ainsley laughed again, light and free, and he liked the sound of it. She sounded good in a way he didn't remember from their undergraduate days. "Love you too. Now shoo. You have some planning to do." She hung up.

Adam sat at the table, considering. The Internet was his friend; with any luck, there was a web site on How to Court the Man of Your Dreams. Maybe there was even one in Italian.

Chapter Eight

It was late afternoon before things slowed down enough in the health center for AJ to turn responsibilities over to the next shift. He was in the midst of throwing his books into his bag when Lauryn walked in. AJ's gut churned; he wasn't sure how friendly she would be after the mess he'd made with Donny. There was no reason to assume she was there to see him, though, so he zipped his bag and tried to slip out around her. She stopped him by stepping into his path.

"Hold it right there," she commanded, so he did.

"I'm off duty," he tried. "Carrie's here for another half hour if you need—"

Lauryn put up her hand. "I came to see you. Can we talk?"

AJ glanced into the break room. It was empty, so he nodded and led Lauryn behind the counter. She plunked her own bag down and sat at the table. AJ pulled a pitcher out of the fridge, retrieved two cups, and poured them both some of the filtered water. He slid into the chair across from Lauryn. Before he could say a word, she started talking.

"I'm sure you know this is about the other night," she said. "You meant well, but you overstepped. Donny and I talked about a lot of things before I agreed to a date with him."

"I know, and I'm sorry." AJ frowned. "Did he send you to talk to me?"

"No." Lauryn sighed. "You and I got along so well because we understood each other. We're cut from the same cloth. I've chosen to be upfront before I accept a date because I feel more comfortable. It's a personal choice, and I realize you didn't know it was one I would make. What you should have known is that I'm well aware of how many of my sisters have died in the last year, and I'm familiar with the risks I take by being public. You did not need to chaperone my date."

"I did know," AJ agreed. "I've also known Donny for more than ten years."

Lauryn tilted her head and studied him. "You weren't really trying to protect me, were you?"

"Not exactly," AJ admitted. "I thought you'd be perfect for Donny. Outside of the work you do, you like a lot of the same things he does. Plus, you're everything he likes in a woman—smart, athletic, and direct, not to mention being a fan of movies where things explode. I wanted him to see how amazing you are before he had the chance to turn you down for one aspect of you."

A smile lifted one corner of her mouth. "Well, I am pretty terrific. But you should have trusted both of us." She put her hand on his. "I think there's more to this than what you're telling me."

AJ rested his cheek on his fist. He pulled his hand away and toyed with the rim of his cup, trying to find the words. He couldn't tell her the truth any more than he'd been able to talk to the guys. What had happened to him was bad, but he didn't see it as being anything compared to the ongoing struggles the others had. He'd pitched himself into work, school and activism, which was how he'd met Lauryn. A piece of him wanted to control the situation before everyone found out all his own secrets—including her. If he kept everyone in their safe, separate corners, working on their problems and not his, not one of them would have the chance to pry the lid off the box. It was much easier to let them think he simply wasn't over a bad breakup.

At last AJ sat up straighter. "Donny hasn't been the most

understanding. He doesn't get the work I do. When will he get scared and try to protect you from yourself?"

"You'll have to let us be the judge of when someone has crossed a line." Lauryn sat back and folded her arms. "Anyone else and I'd have taken to my website to tell the world about the ass who thought it was his job to speak for me. Because of the work you've done—and how you inspired me when I transferred here—I'm not going to do that. Instead, I'm sitting here telling you to your face to step down."

"Okay," AJ said. "I'm sorry."

"I won't ask you to stay away, but give Donny and me some time. Maybe it will go smoothly, and we'll be one of those happy-ever-after couples. And maybe it won't because he snores too loud or he hates the way I dry my pantyhose over the bathtub or we can't agree on whose night it is to pick the movie. You'll have to let us work things out." She stood up and brushed off her skirt.

"I trust you," AJ said.

"Good." Lauryn smiled and leaned in to kiss his cheek. "Donny's right, you know. You're always trying to fix everything and make it perfect. Real life is too messy for that." Her eyes crinkled. "Try finger painting instead of such careful brush strokes."

It was only a metaphor, and there was no way Lauryn could have had any idea her words would have any other meaning, but they hit AJ so hard his head snapped up. His instinct was to fight back, but he would have confused her. Instead, AJ breathed through the panic like he'd done with Renee at the library and so many other times prior.

When he was calmer, he said, "Maybe I should."

Lauryn winked. "I'll bet the cute redhead would like to help you try."

AJ relaxed the rest of the way. Thoughts of seeing Adam again filled his head, and he grinned despite the tension. "I'll bet he would," AJ agreed.

He walked Lauryn out to the entrance and said goodbye to her. When she was gone, he turned to tell Carrie he was leaving. She was busy lecturing the pair of students who had been too involved in their own relationship drama to be of any use. Shaking his head, AJ retrieved his bag and made for the door. As he was about to open it, he was forced to take a step back.

Adam.

AJ's heart skipped several beats. Adam looked terrific—the same casual-on-purpose he usually sported, as though he were trying to look good but not too good. He had on a patterned deep blue short-sleeve button-down and a pair of skinny jeans, and his wild red hair was a work of art. As he entered, he tucked his sunglasses into his breast pocket, turning to face AJ. His grin was the one AJ would previously have described as full of himself but he now saw as mischievous and sexy. In his left hand, he had a colorful bouquet of flowers. AJ was on the brink of not being able to hold back a smitten gasp. He reined it in barely in time, but he was sure Adam caught his reaction.

"Hey, love," Adam said. He leaned in and gave AJ a peck on the cheek, simultaneously handing over the flowers.

AJ's mouth opened and closed, but no words came out. He'd forgotten how to move his tongue, and all his brain cells were devoted to keeping the whirling mass of emotions in check. It had been ages—or possibly never—since anyone had made him feel this way. No doubt about it, Adam was something else. And then it hit AJ in warm rush that shook him to the very center of his soul. He liked Adam. As in, stomach-flipping, hot-all-over, text-every-five-minutes *liked* him. A casual benefits relationship—with or without the friends part—was never going to be enough to satisfy either of them.

AJ froze, warring with himself. He wasn't sure at all he was ready for what came next. He'd never meant it to go this far, but now that it had, there was no way to stop it. AJ stepped back, still holding the flowers and trying to breathe. When he looked up again at Adam and saw his expression melt from eager and happy to confused and disappointed, AJ's heart turned into a slushy puddle. He let out all the tension in a long exhale. Forget the fact that he hadn't had a long-term relationship in over two years or that it wouldn't last for so many, many reasons. Enjoy it now, question his wisdom later, right?

He met Adam's gaze again then grasped his hand and dragged

him into the break room, pushing the door shut with his foot on the way in. A split second later, he had Adam's back to the wall and their mouths inches apart. His heart pounded, and he felt the puffs of air from Adam's rapid breathing against his cheek.

"Okay?" he asked.

"Yeah," Adam said, the word extending on a long, shaky exhale.

And then they were kissing, far past what they'd done outside Adam's apartment building. Adam rested his hands on AJ's hips, and AJ threaded the fingers of his free hand in Adam's wild hair. He'd longed to do that, and it set his skin on fire. They only came up for air when Adam groaned into AJ's mouth and AJ was suddenly reminded of where they were. He pulled back and looked at Adam's red face and swollen lips then chuckled a little before stepping away a couple of paces. He cleared his throat, and Adam grinned, his eyes twinkling.

"Well, that's a way to greet a guy," he remarked.

"*Mio tesoro*," AJ murmured, still a little out of breath. "*Grazie mille.*"

"I think I know what at least some of that meant, and you're welcome," Adam replied, reaching for AJ's hand.

AJ chuckled. "Very good. I might be rubbing off on you after all."

Adam's face lit up. "You mean it?"

"Oh, God!" AJ exclaimed. He laughed, relieved to be back on familiar ground. "You took that wrong. Or...well...fine. Maybe I should have phrased it differently." He huffed, but it was with amusement and not irritation. "Freudian slip?" he tried.

"I sure hope not." Adam tugged on AJ's hand. "Ready to work on the health fair?"

AJ glanced at the wall clock. "Don't you have work today?"

"Finished grading Dr. Weinstock's quizzes half an hour ago and told her I was taking lunch. I don't have much time, but I can help you out for a bit."

"And when will you actually eat lunch?" AJ raised an eyebrow at him.

Shrugging, Adam replied, "Later, *Mom*, at my desk. Data entry this afternoon, and then stupid shit like booking Dr. Weinstock's flight for some conference. I have no idea why she can't schedule it. It took her twenty minutes to explain to me where she's going, when, what airline, and what kind of flight she wants. It would have taken her five minutes to do it her damn self."

AJ laughed. "Wow. What does she think you're going to learn from that?"

"No clue. Anyway, what can I do here?"

"First let me put these in water." AJ let go of Adam's hand and crossed the room. "Coming?" he asked when Adam stayed where he was by the doorway.

"Not yet." Adam winked. "That's for later."

"Ass." AJ turned back around so Adam wouldn't see his smile. *Not yet,* he thought in agreement, *but maybe we can work up to it.*

He reached into a cupboard for a vase and tucked the flowers into it, then he filled it with lukewarm tap water and set it in the center of the table. Beckoning Adam to join him, he said, "If a guy gives me flowers, you bet your ass I'm going to put them out so everyone knows it."

Once again, the light danced in Adam's eyes. "Well, then," he remarked, but he seemed to have nothing else to add.

"Work?" AJ prompted.

"Right. Let's get to it."

AJ had wanted to see Adam again as soon as they could arrange it, but work and classes and his own personal rules about where he slept and with whom limited the options. So far, Adam hadn't pushed, despite his remarkable ability to turn nearly every exchange into something at least vaguely sexual. Instead, they managed to find each other in their spare moments. AJ's favorite so far had been the time Adam had pulled him around the corner into the shadow of the library and kissed him until he thought he might float straight up into the overhanging trees.

Every time, he was left breathless and trembling, and every time, once he was alone, he told himself he had to stop before the whole thing went any further. What they were doing didn't merely blur the lines, it crossed solidly from *nothing much* to *very definitely something.* AJ had a thousand reasons why it was a truly terrible idea, but being around Adam made him rethink his timeline on more than one occasion—especially when he woke up from shiver-inducing dreams about Adam's mouth on his lips...his neck...his dick. He was grateful he lived alone.

To circumvent more activities which would test his resolve, he suggested they meet up on Saturday to finish going over the detailed schedule for the health fair. He repeated their motto of work first, fun later over and over in an attempt to convince himself he absolutely under no circumstances wanted to skip directly to the fun part.

"Once we're finished," he said, "you'll be able to supply everything to the undergrads, including the layout in the student union."

Adam leaned in and pressed a chaste kiss to his lips. "I hope there's a reward in there somewhere." He winked.

"It has to be done," AJ replied without answering Adam. "Meet at the library again?"

Adam drew his brows together. "Why don't you come up to my apartment this time?" He dropped his hands and backed up.

AJ licked his lips. There was a world of trouble brewing in that idea. "Um..."

"Look," Adam said, "I'm not trying to pressure you. I'm the first to admit I'm not used to taking things quite so slowly, and all we've had so far is a couple of not-exactly-dates and some pretty fantastic lip action, especially that time behind the library. But it will be a lot quieter at my place, and we don't have to do anything you're not comfortable with, I swear." He pursed his lips and looked as though he wanted to say more, but he kept silent.

"What?" AJ asked, reading into Adam's expression.

"It's just..." Adam frowned. "Don't get mad, okay?"

"I'm not making any promises. Usually what follows is something I won't like." AJ crossed his arms.

"No, nothing like that, but you might think I'm rude." His chest expanded visibly as he inhaled a deep breath. "You keep avoiding the subject of taking this further than a few hot kisses between classes. Are you ace?" He quickly added, "Because it's fine if you are. I know lots of people who—"

"Asexual? No," AJ interrupted him with a snort and a wry smile. "You're used to going pretty fast, aren't you?"

Adam fidgeted. "Well, yeah. It's what most people want, isn't it?"

His answer both surprised AJ and didn't. He'd heard it for years himself: Greedy. Cheater. Open to anything. "Most people" meant "people like you," and the words were usually flung at him like they were his fault when he wouldn't cooperate with their plans for him. Adam surprised him by sounding as though he'd lived the stereotype long enough to get sick of it but didn't know how to stop.

"No," AJ said. "Not everyone. It's not what I want."

Adam cleared his throat. "You should know I sort of...usually..." His face turned red, and he shoved his hands in his pockets. "I'm a first-date kind of guy, you know? Or only date, as the case may be." He straightened his shoulders and dropped his hands to his sides in a defiant posture. "I'm not going to apologize that I like fucking."

AJ couldn't help it; despite the tight ball of confused emotions knotting his stomach, he laughed. "*Tesoro*, that's not something to apologize for, ever." He put his hand on Adam's arm. "I like sex. No, I love it when it's with the right person."

"Okay," Adam said slowly, breaking AJ out of his thoughts. "So...you're just cautious?"

AJ slumped. There had to be a way to tell Adam the truth without revealing everything. He wanted to, in a way, but other than Luke, his friends didn't know the full extent of what Michelle had done to him. The only thing they were aware of was how she'd broken his heart. He was pretty sure she'd broken a lot more than that, but he'd thought he was past it. The summer he'd spent with Piet's older brother and his then-girlfriend—now wife—had given him the time he needed to begin healing. The problem was, Garritt and Tiffany were the only other people who knew. He was sure someone like Adam wouldn't take him seriously if he ever found out. Regardless of where their relationship went, Adam never needed to know, any more than the other guys did.

He blew out a breath. Deciding it would be all right to give Adam something to go on, he continued, "I've always been this way, and my last relationship didn't work out because of it." That was putting it as delicately as he could. "Maybe that means we're not compatible, if you don't want to wait until I'm ready." Michelle's last words to him—that he was a failure at dating—charged their way to the front of his mind, and he struggled to conceal his disappointment that Adam might see it that way too.

A light flickered in Adam's eyes. "I want to try." He gave AJ a sheepish grin. "How hard can it be? I still have my hand, after all."

Snorting as the tension drained away, AJ slid his hand down Adam's arm to brush his fingers. "You do." The warmth of Adam's palm against AJ's as he squeezed back made AJ's pulse pound. Adam was willing to do that for him; maybe he'd read him entirely wrong right from the start. "All right. I'll agree to work at your apartment if you agree to another date."

"Can I still make sexual innuendo, and will you still teach me more dirty Italian?"

AJ guffawed. Leave it to Adam to turn anything into sex play, even if it was only verbal for the time being. On impulse, he leaned in and put his mouth to Adam's ear, poking out his tongue and licking the shell. "You'd better, and absolutely I will. Maybe I'll even tell you how to ask for favors *in italiano*. Fair?"

Adam broke out in a wide smile. "You're on," he said. "Where and when for our date?"

"Friday night. I usually go out with a couple of my friends—the gay ones this time. We can meet up with them for a bit and then do something else after. Luke doesn't like to stay late anyway, if he's even going to be there." AJ held back from saying anything else.

To his surprise, Adam chuckled. "You separate your gay and straight friends? Why am I not surprised?"

AJ huffed. "You've met Piet and Donny. Can you imagine if I tried to drag them to a gay bar?"

"Wasn't aware that was the only thing to do with your gay friends, and no, I honestly can't," Adam answered.

"Well, there you go. And we're probably not going to a bar anyway, but Donny in particular doesn't like to be around Luke." At least AJ now had insight as to why, though he didn't share the details with Adam.

"I got that impression," Adam remarked dryly. "So, what did you have in mind?"

AJ shrugged. "Don't know yet. I'll call Connor and ask then text you." He pulled Adam closer and reached up to kiss him again. "I promise, it'll be fun. You'll like Luke and Connor." He didn't add that Adam would probably not like Luke's boyfriend much, but if anyone could handle Greg's arrogance, it was Adam. Not that Greg was likely to give them the satisfaction of joining them on a night out, but it was always a possibility.

"Luke's the one who works in the restaurant, right?"

"Yes, that's him. He's very sweet once you know him."

"Okay." Adam pressed his lips to AJ's cheek. "Gotta run. Dr. Weinstock needs me back to go across campus and meet with someone in the math department. Why I can't use the phone for whatever conversation we're supposed to have is beyond me."

AJ laughed. "She really runs you ragged, doesn't she?"

Adam looked around then reached back and planted a hand on AJ's ass, causing him to jump. Grinning, Adam said, "Not too ragged to appreciate the finer things."

Swatting at him, AJ stepped away. "I'll text you, *tesoro*." He turned around and walked away.

"You'd better tell me what that means!" Adam called after him, but AJ didn't answer.

CHAPTER NINE

THE SOUND of his phone woke Adam, and he turned over and groaned, fumbling for it on the nightstand. He knew the ringtone, but he had no idea why Ainsley would be calling him so early on a Saturday. He dragged the phone half under the blanket and answered.

"Hello," he mumbled, intentionally making himself sound sleepier so she would get the hint about her timing.

"Morning to you too, sunshine," she said. "Did I disturb your sleep?"

"Yes," he groused. "You could have been interfering with other important morning things, you know."

"Like you've never interrupted me in the middle of getting myself off," she snapped.

"Only once! And you knew I was on my way, so I have no idea why your timing was so rotten." He sat up. "What couldn't wait until a more reasonable hour?"

"One, do you know what time it actually is? Two, I had to catch you before work because I have to be able to put in a request for the time off, and Meredith only told me about it over breakfast this morning."

"I don't care what time it is. It's early for me." He pulled his phone away from his ear and squinted at it then snarled. Ainsley was right.

"Late night with your new man?" she asked.

"Mm. Yeah." Adam smiled through a yawn. "He and one of his friends—Connor, I think—took me to this great little bookstore cafe for a live reading, and then we went to see some action movie another friend recommended with shit ton of explosions. Not really our thing, but at least the stars were hot, and we weren't watching the movie anyway."

"I'll bet not. Anyway, back to why I called. Want to do me a huge favor?"

Adam hummed. "Depends on what it is."

"House-sitting," Ainsley replied.

"In case you hadn't noticed, I'm three hours away from you. How exactly would that be possible? And why do you even need a house-sitter?"

"We need someone to watch the dog," she informed him.

"You have a dog?"

"Yeah. Hang on. I'll send you a picture."

A moment later, he had an image on his phone of a black and white dog with a goofy expression on its face. He laughed. "You have a pit bull?"

Ainsley made an annoyed sound. "Priscilla's an American Staffordshire, thank you very much." She sounded extra snooty when she said it, and Adam chuckled at how much of Meredith had transferred to her.

"Whatever. She's..." Adam searched for a word. "Very nice. Why do you need a sitter?"

"Meredith has a writing conference, and it's a good opportunity to meet specific contacts. She wants me to go with her."

"Doesn't solve the distance problem. I do have work and classes, you know. I can't make six hours' worth of commuting every day." Adam huffed.

"It's over Columbus Day weekend. I know you have it off because it's Canadian Thanksgiving, and I searched your college's calendar." There was a definite smile in her voice when she said,

"You can bring your guy with you, have a weekend away."

Ah, there was the real explanation for why they didn't simply kennel the dog. Somehow she was managing to meddle with out actually meddling. "And Meredith is okay with this?"

"Yep."

Adam scowled. That meant Ainsley had told Meredith about AJ, at least to the extent she herself knew about him. "How do you know he would want to?"

"Have you slept with him?"

"Ainsley!" he yelped.

"Oh, come on. You used to ask me that stuff all the time. Have we grown apart so much you can't tell me?"

Adam rolled onto his stomach. "Fine. No, we haven't, and if you must know, it's making me tense." He was trying, really he was, but everything about AJ got him hot all over.

"This guy must be something special," Ainsley remarked. "You never wait this long for sex."

It took a minute before Adam could answer. Ainsley deserved the truth. "He's worth it," he said and instantly yanked the phone away from his ear when she hollered his name.

After she'd calmed down, she said, "Then you absolutely have to invite him to come along with you. Spend a weekend away from everything and everyone, playing house and getting to know each other. It'll be fun. Please?"

"All right," he agreed. "I'll do it."

"Good. That means I can request the vacation hours. I'll let Meredith know, and we'll talk specifics later." She ended the call.

Adam flopped back onto his pillows and closed his eyes. He would ask AJ when he arrived to work on the health fair. A vision of himself with AJ, spending the weekend together, sprang up. There wasn't much more in that college town than in this one, but there were a few decent things to do. Besides, if all went well, they wouldn't be needing a lot in the way of entertainment. The thought brought a smile to Adam's face and a thrill down his spine, straight to his groin. He slid a hand down into his pajamas, hoping Ainsley didn't choose that moment to call him back with some detail she'd forgotten.

Adam had dozed off again briefly in the wake of his self-induced orgasm. It had taken him less than five minutes, and he hoped it was enough to get through an afternoon alone in his apartment with AJ. All he had to do was keep his mind occupied on anything other than all the fun they could have house-sitting for Ainsley and Meredith—provided their dog wasn't the nosy sort. He'd had a semi-regular girlfriend once who owned a cat with the worst timing in the history of everything.

Once he was out of bed, Adam spent the morning cleaning. He wasn't much of a slob, but he had the sense AJ was the type to notice if things weren't at least tidy. He tried to picture what AJ's apartment looked like, but the best he could do was conjure an image of a nearly empty space with a lot of modern art-style knickknacks. AJ didn't seem the sort, though. While he was pondering, the buzzer sounded. He let AJ in and pulled him into a quick but meaningful embrace. AJ smiled against his lips and pressed a bag into his hand.

Adam looked down. "What's this?"

"Lunch," AJ replied. "You'll probably want to reheat it."

Opening the bag, Adam discovered it was more food from the little Mexican kitchen where Luke worked. He removed containers and began heating them while setting the table, all the while ignoring the unreasonable pang of jealousy he developed any time AJ mentioned something related to Luke. AJ set up his laptop at Adam's desk then returned to help put out their meal. Once they were seated, AJ started right in on asking about Adam's ideas for the health fair schedule. Adam restrained himself from making a snide comment about how they could at least relax while they ate.

He lost the train of what AJ was saying, studying the man himself instead. AJ sounded so self-assured when he was talking business. He knew what he wanted and how to accomplish it. Adam couldn't fathom how anyone their age had their entire life planned out to the detail, right down to the trajectory of their career. He barely knew what electives he wanted to take. He hadn't processed much beyond getting into graduate school and earning another degree. The thought made him pause; he'd been avoiding thinking about his own future. He'd spent a year dicking around, not making any firm commitments, and now he wasn't even sure what he would be good at, outside of designing health fair flyers.

"So, what do you think?" AJ asked.

"Huh?" Adam blinked. "What do I think about what?"

AJ rolled his eyes. "Of the schedule. I talked to the different departments, and everyone is on board with having Q and A panels throughout the day."

"Yeah, sure, sounds good." When AJ made a you're-not-really-listening face, Adam added, "I trust you. If you have the list, I'll make it look good."

They rose from the table, and AJ reached for the dishes to help, but Adam waved him off. He suggested AJ bring up the files they needed so they could take a look. While he washed the dishes, he watched AJ out of the corner of his eye. AJ was concentrating on something and typing rapidly.

When Adam returned from the kitchen, he peered at the screen over AJ's shoulder. It didn't look related to the health fair. "Something for work?" Adam asked. He put his hands on AJ's shoulders.

"Sort of," AJ admitted. "Not my regular job, though. This is my side projects."

Adam read the first paragraph of the article AJ had open. "This looks like some kind of social justice stuff."

"It is," AJ confirmed. "I'm involved in a bunch of bisexual activist pages."

"Ah," Adam said. He'd never thought about what else AJ did in his spare time, but he supposed it made sense.

"Here," AJ said, pulling up a blog post dated from the previous day. "I've been messaging back and forth with this guy. He's a journalist who highlights our causes."

Adam bent toward the screen and scrolled through the article. He lingered over the writer's bio. "He's cute," he remarked.

"Is that all you can think of to say?" AJ demanded, glaring up at Adam. His skin was too dark to tell for sure, but Adam thought he might be blushing.

"I guess." Adam shrugged, grinning. "You think so too, don't you?"

AJ's mouth opened and closed a few times before he finally said, "No!" When Adam raised his eyebrows, AJ relented. "Okay, maybe a little."

"Ha! You have a celebrity crush on him."

"I do not." AJ huffed. "I admire him, that's all." His cheeks darkened again. "And he's hot."

Adam laughed. "Knew it." Waving a hand at the computer, he said, "I didn't know we had 'causes.' Why do you care so much about bisexual issues or whatever?"

"Why don't you?" AJ shot back.

"Because it doesn't matter. Why can't I just fuck who I want to fuck and the rest of the world can bite me if they hate it? Must everything be some kind of battle?"

AJ raised his eyebrows. "So, you've never had a woman you were dating ask if you were going to cheat on her? Or had a guy you liked accuse you of being too scared to come all the way out? Or had your straight friends tell you they're not interested in anything that sounds too gay or assume you had a 'gay phase' but you're over it? Thought you had a good thing going only to have your girlfriend ask if you were sure you could get hard for her?" Lines appeared on his forehead, and the look in his eyes was haunted. He shook himself a little and folded his arms across his chest, looking up at Adam.

Adam shrugged one shoulder. "I'm sure I have, but why should I bother with people like them?"

He thought about what AJ was saying. Since most of his dating experience consisted of casual encounters with people similarly uninterested in a long-term relationship, he'd never bothered making an announcement of his sexuality. He frowned, thinking about his last somewhat more serious relationship. He hadn't hidden his bisexuality, but he knew most people had assumed he was gay when they were together, and he hadn't bothered correcting them. It had never occurred to him to ask himself why—denying it had seemed like it might make being gay sound bad. What AJ said made him uncomfortable. AJ clearly hadn't allowed people to make assumptions, and he hadn't been as fortunate as Adam with how people had reacted. No wonder he kept his friends separate.

"I feel differently about it," AJ argued. "I get tired of splitting my time between my gay and straight friends and worrying about what they'll say if I bring it up. I'm tired of being invisible, erased by whoever I happen to be dating in the moment. It's hella awkward when I'm dating a woman and my friends suggest someplace she isn't necessarily welcome or we aren't welcome as a couple. I had a girlfriend get spit on at Pride once by an asshole who called her a 'breeder' and told her to go fuck her own kind. It's the same when I'm dating a guy, only I also have to keep a careful eye on who's around us if we want to kiss or hold hands. A former boyfriend and I once got jumped in the park walking home. My choices are to pretend and blend or get shit from all sides. Our lives are being swallowed up, and our statistics are being absorbed as generically 'gay, lesbian, biseuxal,' which doesn't help anyone because our communities have both common and unique interests." He clicked a few more times and showed Adam a graph. "This is us," he said. "The reality a lot of us live with. It's shit, and everyone knows it, but there are a limited number of us doing anything about it."

"So..." Adam frowned. "This is about visibility?"

"Were you not listening?" AJ sighed. "A little about visibility, yes. It's also about our lives and our health." AJ clicked a link within the page. "Here," he offered. "Look through and tell me our rates of suicide, violence, and poverty aren't at all a problem. Then tell me why our funding is abysmal."

Adam scrolled through, and he went from disbelief to shock. "I had no idea."

"Which is why we need to be seen and heard," AJ explained. "You didn't even know all this. Tell me something—can you even name three famous bisexual men?"

Adam opened his mouth a couple of times then closed it, pursing his lips. After a minute, he said, "Um...I can name a few bi women, I think."

"Uh huh," AJ replied. He typed something then hit enter and angled his laptop so Adam could see. "Here's a long list."

Adam scanned the list. "Whoa. I thought at least half of these guys were gay, and the other half...oh. I think I get it."

AJ nodded. "My point exactly. It's not like media is so

important. It's how we're not unicorns. When it's clear we exist, we get our statistics recognized, and we get funding for our specific needs. When that happens, we can provide resources and support the same way other groups do. That includes people like you who don't feel a need to specifically identify but still associate with our community. We can keep our kids from dying." He thumped his fist on the desk.

Somewhere along the way, Adam had become lost in watching the way AJ's eyes lit up with passion. As much planning of his life as he'd obviously done, Adam had never before seen AJ so excited. When AJ looked back up at him, breathing a little fast and with a fierce glint in his eye, Adam bent closer. He tilted AJ's chin and leaned in for a kiss.

"Mm. You're amazing, you know that? You are fucking sexy when you get all fired up about something," he remarked. Their proximity brought on a spike of desire.

AJ's laughter was shaky. "So are you."

"Am I?" Adam ducked his head. "I don't think I'm passionate about much." He laughed, but it was weak. "Sex, maybe."

"Oh, yes," AJ confirmed. "I believe it. But I've seen you when you get that spark. You have it when you're working on our project, you know. When you're in full-on professional mode."

AJ drew him closer and rested his cheek against Adam's hip. He brought his hand up to touch Adam's ass and nuzzled the space above his hip with his nose. Adam hummed with appreciation, but then he sighed and backed up before he responded too enthusiastically to what AJ was doing.

"Hey," he said, and AJ looked up. "Nice as that is, I promised you we could wait."

AJ closed his eyes briefly then looked up at Adam. "I know," he said, running his hands along Adam's thighs. He hooked his fingers in Adam's belt loops and pulled him nearer again. He said, "You've been very respectful, and I appreciate it. I'd like to show you." The last words came out with a slight tremble, and Adam heard the hitch in AJ's breathing.

"What did you have in mind?" Adam asked, though he had a good idea already.

AJ planted a kiss on Adam's thigh through his jeans then brought his hands to Adam's hips. He slid them around to the back and ran them over Adam's ass. He looked up. "Something like this, maybe. Finish what I started."

Adam sucked in a breath. "You don't have to."

"I know, and I wouldn't do it if I wasn't planning to enjoy it." He ran his nose along Adam's hipbone. "Is this okay?"

"God, yeah." Adam moaned.

AJ mouthed Adam's growing erection through his jeans, causing Adam to shudder. Something Ainsley had said to him pressed at his memory—how if he wanted more than a mutually-agreed-upon casual arrangement, he should seek one. They had never defined what they were doing, and this was more of a risk than if they'd simply jumped right to hooking up. But it felt good, and Adam hadn't had any company but his own hand since Renee. He dragged himself out of his own head and relaxed, placing one hand on AJ's shoulder to steady himself.

AJ unbuckled Adam's belt then tugged on the button and zipper until he had them open. At a snail's pace, he dragged them down until he freed Adam's semi from its prison; he wasn't wearing underwear, and AJ made a sound halfway between a groan and a growl.

"Yeah," Adam breathed at the vibrations against his skin.

"*Voglio succhiare il cazzo*," AJ murmured.

Adam twitched and peered down at AJ. He could guess what AJ meant, but he wanted to hear him say it. "What?"

"I want to suck your cock," AJ said.

Even though he'd known what it would be, the words still had an intense effect. "Oh, fuck."

"Condom?" AJ said, the air as he exhaled sending a shudder down Adam's spine.

Adam reached into the desk drawer and pulled out the condoms AJ had given him. He shuffled through until he found a flavored one and handed it to AJ, suddenly grateful for the random assortment. Swiftly, AJ rolled it on. As AJ descended his mouth onto Adam's cock, Adam wrapped a hand around his head. He pushed a little, his fingers threaded in AJ's hair. Panting, he rocked his hips and tipped his head back, his eyes closed. AJ slipped his hands around back to squeeze Adam's ass and control the pace and depth. He worked his mouth, sighing as though he'd been waiting all morning for this. Adam moaned at the feel of his thick cock sliding over the heat of AJ's tongue.

AJ slid one hand down in between Adam's cheeks, exploring until he reached his hole. He didn't breech it; instead, he rested his middle finger there and rubbed gently until Adam let out another string of profanity. Adam tightened and released the muscles in his ass as AJ continued touching him. AJ removed the hand that had been caressing Adam's ass cheek, and through the haze of arousal, Adam heard the faint slide of AJ's zipper. AJ shifted slightly, and the thought of AJ touching himself while sucking Adam had him ready to blow. His fingers in AJ's hair gripped harder and he braced himself on the desk with his other hand.

"Fuck…close…" Those were the only words Adam could manage as the pleasurable agony built.

Spurred on, AJ sucked deeper and more firmly. Adam rewarded him with several loud grunts as he filled the condom. AJ relaxed his jaw and continued more gently for a few minutes before he withdrew and ran his hand over his mouth. He looked up at Adam, his face flushed and sweaty as though he were the one who had just come.

Adam pulled AJ to his feet and kissed him deeply, running his tongue all around the inside of AJ's mouth and wishing he wasn't mostly tasting flavored latex. There was plenty of time for that in the future, though. He kissed a path from AJ's lips to his ear and nibbled on the shell then took AJ's earlobe in his mouth. AJ shivered and groaned.

"Your turn," Adam murmured. "Tell me what you want." He held AJ around the waist, supporting him as he slid his free hand down, touching AJ through his jeans.

"Yeah," AJ said, tilting his head back. He bit his lip, and it was sexy as hell.

Adam worked his hand into AJ's open fly, drawing a breathless whine from AJ's throat. He relished every sound AJ made as he inched closer to orgasm. "Like that?"

"Hell...faster...please..." AJ whimpered. "Fuck, I'm coming."

A desperate sound rose out of him, and a moment later, Adam's fingers were slick. He slowed his motions, working AJ through the last of his climax. When AJ's breathing settled to a more regular pace, Adam withdrew his hand.

AJ opened his eyes and looked down at himself. "Damn."

Grinning, Adam eyed him head to toe. "Do you need to clean up a little before we get back to work?"

"Yes, thanks." AJ shook his head and chuckled. "I think my concentration's shot, though."

"I'll tell you what," Adam offered. "How about we hang out for a bit first. Work can wait." He kissed AJ. "Bathroom's probably in the same place as in your apartment."

"Right," AJ replied before making his way down the hall.

Adam tidied up, tucked himself away, and flopped onto the couch. If the previous little while was any indication, waiting for a whole night with AJ could be well worth every second. Determining what, if any, meaning there was in it could wait for another day.

CHAPTER TEN

AJ WHISTLED while he restocked the shelves in the health center. One of the undergraduates was working a few hours that morning and kept looking sideways at him and sneering. It did nothing to dampen AJ's mood. It had been so long he'd almost forgotten how good sex felt.

He hadn't been planning on giving Adam an impromptu blow job while they were supposed to be working—not really, anyway. He certainly hadn't been planning what happened afterward, which was lying on Adam's ratty couch while Adam dozed off the post-sex haze and ending up half-undressed, kissing and jerking each other off. What had changed his mind was the way Adam had listened to him share something he cared deeply about and made him feel good about his work. Adam had offered him a kind of safety he hadn't felt in a long time, the freedom to show that side of himself.

They'd eventually accomplished some of what they were supposed to, but they hadn't completed the work. A glance at the clock reminded AJ he only had a short time before Adam would arrive to finish going over the plans. He'd texted first thing to say he had another idea for the health fair and wanted to run it by AJ. At least this time they couldn't be distracted, since they were in a far more public place.

Right on cue, Adam arrived, followed closely by Carrie. AJ looked Adam up and down, smiling but feeling a little warm when he remembered what Adam looked like with less clothing in the way. Carrie didn't miss a thing. She stepped behind the desk to dismiss the undergrad student and gave AJ a sly wink.

"I take it your date went well," she whispered.

"*Fantastico*," he murmured, and she giggled.

Adam raised his eyebrows at their secret exchange, but he didn't look upset—only amused. He came over and leaned casually on the desk, and AJ was glad he could hide a blush because Adam took on a look of smug satisfaction which was clearly for Carrie's benefit. She snickered as she pinned on her name badge.

"Go on, you two," she said. "Get some work done. That's not a euphemism!"

Laughing, Adam rounded the desk and pulled AJ into the break room. They sat down at the table, and AJ pulled out his laptop. He'd made a tentative schedule, and he wanted Adam to look it over before he emailed it to put it in a useful format for the health fair. Adam perused it, pursing his lips.

"This looks good," he said. "I did have one other idea, and I wanted to run it past you. Is the campus LGBT group doing anything?"

AJ shook his head. "This is for the academic disciplines, so none of the campus groups are really involved. A lot of the people running the booths are in various clubs, but this was meant to be used for credit in people's classes." He sighed. "Another way I would have liked to do things differently but was vetoed when they decided to make it interdisciplinary."

"You should go ahead and do it anyway," Adam said. "Or at least find some people in a related discipline. What about asking the Women's Studies department?"

"I could do that," AJ replied. "They don't have a booth, though they did supply us with some materials. Why?"

Adam shrugged. "I was thinking about some of what you said. A lot of the health stuff is really more directed at straight people." His cheeks reddened. "I, uh, looked a bunch of stuff up after you left the other day, with those charts you showed me. I guess I didn't really know a lot about it before, and I figure there must be other students who don't, either. Like, even the stuff about campus rape seems as if the information is mostly for straight women. I don't want to take away from that—it's obviously an issue. But why doesn't anyone talk about how it can happen to lesbian and bisexual women and to guys?"

AJ's throat tightened at Adam's words, and he had to swallow several times before he could respond. Instead of answering Adam directly, he said, "Didn't your undergrad college have an LGBT group?"

"Yeah, we did. I was president. But we didn't do a health fair or anything. We gave out penis pops at Pride one year."

AJ snorted. "Useful."

"Don't know about that, but it was fun." Adam grinned. "Speaking of, when is Pride around here? If it's near the health fair, we could combine some things."

"It's in the spring, and there are all kinds of campus activities then. There's even a student-led drag show, and some of the local performers run workshops to teach students how." AJ turned his laptop back around and pulled up the previous year's web page. "This is the health fair, so the emphasis is different. We need to concentrate on providing information. Let me guess—your group focused a lot of attention on gay and lesbian issues, right?"

"I suppose." Adam shrugged again. "I don't really know what you mean."

"Did your group talk about how bisexual people in different-sex relationships are sometimes barred from LGBT groups? Or about your college's policy on housing for trans students? Or how rape 'prevention'—" he choked slightly on the words "—affects asexual people?"

"Um...not really." Adam frowned.

"Those are important things. We don't need to point them out at the health fair, but you're right—we should do something to make sure it's inclusive. Why don't you contact the grad assistant in the Women's Studies department, and I'll talk to the LGBT group. Between us, we can come up with something good."

"Okay," Adam agreed. "Meanwhile, you send me the schedule, and I'll turn it into an event menu."

"Sure."

AJ typed up the email, and they were both silent while he took care of it. When he was finished, he looked up to find Adam scrutinizing him.

"What?" he asked.

Adam gave him a long look. "Are we going to talk about what we did?"

"Uh...why?"

It was a full minute before Adam answered. "Are you okay?"

"Sure." AJ's shoulders sagged with relief. He'd been afraid Adam was going to either tell him it didn't mean anything or demand more. He put his hand on top of Adam's. "I'm fine."

"Well, then, do you want to go out again?" There was a slight tremor in Adam's voice, as though he'd imagined AJ might say no.

"Definitely." AJ grinned.

"Friday?"

"That's my night with Connor and Luke," AJ reminded him.

"Oh, right." Adam sounded disappointed.

"Why don't you come with us again? We're going to Philippe's."

"What's that?"

"It's a coffee and dessert place," AJ said. "They have the most amazing stuff. Plus, it's fun. The servers all have a certain...aesthetic. You'll see." He leaned closer and said quietly, "Maybe we can do...something...afterward."

Adam swallowed audibly and his eyes darkened. "It's a date, then," he confirmed. "What time?"

"I'll pick you up at seven." AJ pulled away and rose from his chair.

"Perfect." Adam stood up and shouldered his bag. "I'll have the health fair menu prelim for you by then, too."

He leaned in and kissed AJ's cheek. It wasn't enough, so AJ put a hand on Adam's chin and turned his head gently so he could kiss his lips. They both sighed a little at the contact, then broke apart, laughing. Adam turned around and walked out, and AJ leaned against the door frame, watching him go and ignoring the goofy smile on Carrie's face.

The small college town was about thirty minutes from a larger city, and it was populated by a combination of people associated with the school and people whose families had been there for generations. The village was more or less the equivalent of "downtown," with the few restaurants and businesses situated along the river. Phillipe's was located the middle of a row of converted houses. At one end, a historic Victorian mansion had become a bed and breakfast. At the other end was the quaint local realtor's office.

AJ parked around the corner, and he and Adam met the others in the narrow lot. Connor had brought a date—a muscular, sandy-haired man with a lot of piercings. He didn't look familiar, and AJ raised his eyebrows at Connor. It wasn't like him to bring anyone with him, even when he was more or less seeing someone. Connor shrugged. Luke was there too, which surprised AJ. Knowing where they were headed, it shocked him that Greg had let Luke come alone.

Luke must have picked up on AJ's reaction because he leaned in. "He said he had to work late. He doesn't know I'm here, but I'll be back home in plenty of time."

"Ah, I see," AJ replied. He squeezed Luke's shoulder.

Inside, it was warm and dimly lit in the entryway. To the right, there was a small gift shop. From experience, AJ knew what was in there. It wasn't exactly an adult store, but there were items of a sensual nature available. Adam peered around AJ to have a look, but AJ put a hand on his arm.

"We'll check it out later. They have some good stuff." He winked, and he was pleased when Adam's cheeks grew pink.

On their way to the host's kiosk, they passed several servers. They were all dressed the same, men and women alike—tight-fitting black trousers and white sleeveless button-down shirts, open far enough to be moderately revealing. All of them wore light makeup, and all of them had an air of androgyny. Only their hair differed, though all of them were expertly styled. As the group approached the kiosk, a server with dark hair eyed AJ up and down, offering a half-smile. Out of the corner of his eye, AJ caught Adam trying to pretend he wasn't amused.

AJ turned to him. "You pay one price, and you get coffee and samples of the desserts they have available. You can get wine or beer for an extra cost. On the weekends, they have live chamber music." He glanced at the low stage. "Looks like a string quartet tonight." He collected money from them and paid their way in.

A host showed them to their table and handed them each a printed card. "Here's tonight's menu, including the available selection of coffees." The host flipped it over. "On this side is the wine and beer list. Someone will be with you shortly to take your orders."

After the host left, AJ began to relax. The evening was pleasant, complete with light flirting from their very attractive server. At this place, gender was of no consequence. Servers flirted openly with everyone at their tables, creating a sensually charged atmosphere. The desserts were decadent enough to earn a reaction even from Luke, who was typically reserved in his emotional output. As their server returned with another round of samples, Luke was putting the last bite of caramel apple pecan cheesecake in his mouth. He closed his eyes and gave a satisfied little hum.

The server laughed softly. "Bet it feels good to have your tongue around that."

Luke's eyes flew open, and his cheeks turned beet-red. "Um...uh..."

Adam nudged him. "It's okay. I get like that when I have something good in my mouth too."

Connor caught Luke's eye and grinned, which only served to make Luke sink down in his chair and Connor's date to raise his eyebrows. With a wink, the server deposited the new samples and whisked away their empty plates. Luke buried his head in his hands, and the others laughed.

It made the evening better, seeing Adam join in on the fun. AJ couldn't remember the last time he'd been out with someone who hadn't made a big deal over it. It made him curious, especially given the way Adam had proclaimed himself nearly an expert. He made a mental note to ask later on. Watching Adam flirt and hearing his suggestive comments from the outside of the exchange—as opposed to being the recipient—was an incredible turn-on, and AJ wanted to see where it would go.

When they were through eating, they made their way back downstairs. Adam ducked into the shop, and Connor followed with his date. Luke hung back, and AJ pulled him aside.

"You okay?"

"Yeah." Luke fiddled with his keys. "I can't stay. I have to make sure I'm back before Greg gets in, or he'll be pissed."

"Luke—" AJ started.

"Don't." Luke held up a hand. "Please? Let me do this my way. All's I need to do is make him happy for a little longer, and then it's done. Okay?"

"We won't be long," AJ said. "Are you sure?"

"Nah. It's not like I can bring something back. He'd know then."

"All right." AJ put his arms around Luke and kissed his cheek. "Call me if you need me, right?"

"You bet." Luke smiled at him before turning around and leaving the building.

AJ turned around to join the others in the shop, almost colliding with Adam in the process. He reached out to steady himself and looked up to see Adam peering over his shoulder with a frown, watching Luke's retreating back.

"What's going on?" Adam asked.

"He had to go home. Come on, let's find the others in the shop."

Adam followed him, but he glanced back over his shoulder a couple more times before they entered. They split up when Adam got distracted by one of the displays, and AJ meandered over to the shelf of massage oils. He'd always wanted to try them out. After a while, he went in search of the others. He spotted Connor and his date looking at the high-end lube, and Adam was browsing the selection of frilly undergarments. He held up a particularly skimpy pink, purple, and blue striped men's thong. When AJ was close enough, Adam leaned in and put his mouth against AJ's ear.

"God, you'd look hot in this," he murmured.

Laughing, AJ took it out of Adam's hand and hung it back up.

"How would you know?"

Adam craned his neck, peering around the shop. He pressed close again. "I think strings are sexy. Everything gets kind of emphasized because of the way they fit, but they still leave something to unwrap."

"Hm," AJ said, but he couldn't deny the thought of turning Adam on like that was exciting. It made him wonder again what Adam liked; it would be fun to figure it out.

With the tip of his finger, Adam touched AJ's cheek. "Besides, the bi pride colors suit you—the way you put everything you have into your work..." He brushed his lips against AJ's skin, and AJ smiled, turning his head for a proper kiss before separating to continue browsing.

In the end, Connor picked up a few items AJ didn't ask about, and AJ bought the massage oil he'd been looking at. He thought about what they were going to do next, and a thrill of anticipation ran through him. Inviting Adam to his place wasn't yet an option—he needed to be able to extract himself on his own terms—but if Adam was anywhere near as ready as he was, Adam wouldn't hesitate to invite him up later. They parted company with Connor and made their way to the parking lot.

The lot was nearly empty, and there was no one around. AJ wanted to offer Adam a promise, so he leaned against the car and tugged Adam closer. Adam grinned and bent down, pressing his lips to AJ's. He slipped his hand up underneath AJ's jacket, and his fingers were cool against AJ's warm skin. AJ parted his lips, inviting Adam inside. It was good; everything about kissing Adam felt as decadent as the desserts. AJ groaned softly into Adam's open mouth, and Adam answered with a shudder that sent heat racing down AJ's spine. Adam pressed forward with his hips, and they both inhaled sharply at the feel of each other's aroused state.

For several minutes, they continued to kiss and grind against each other. Panting, AJ tore his mouth away from Adam's. "Shit...we need to stop, or I'm going to lose it here in the parking lot."

"And that would be bad?" Adam's tone didn't quite make it to the teasing he'd probably been aiming for; he was far too breathless.

AJ's laugh came out with a slight whine. "Yes. I've been thinking about this all week, and I don't want it to get reduced to five minutes still fully clothed. Ready to go finish this somewhere else?"

Adam took a deep breath and stepped back. "Sounds like a plan."

AJ walked around to the other side of the car. Just as he unlocked the door, his phone vibrated. He pulled it out and looked at the message from Luke. He'd known their night out had been too good to be true. He sent up a silent prayer that this time wouldn't involve a visit to the after hours clinic, but he wasn't holding out much hope.

"Damn it," he muttered. There went his anticipated night of hot sex. He slammed his hand on the car in frustration.

"Everything okay?" Adam asked.

"No." AJ wanted to let loose with a string of vicious swears, all directed at Greg. "Look, I'm really sorry, but something's come up. I'm going to have to drop you off and go home." He sighed and tugged on his hair.

"Hey," Adam said. He rounded the car and pulled AJ into his arms. "Tell me."

AJ sagged against him. He wanted to; he wanted to pour everything out on Adam and have him say it would be okay—that they could figure it out together. Except he didn't want to violate Luke's trust, and he knew Adam would only tell him it wasn't his problem to solve. There was no way to explain why Luke was his responsibility.

"I can't," AJ said. "It's something with Luke, and I have to take care of him...it...myself."

Adam huffed. "I know you like saving the world, but are you sure this can't wait until tomorrow? It's not like someone died. You'd have told me that, right?"

"No one died."

"So is it really an emergency no one else can handle?" He slid his hand down to AJ's hip, letting his thumb work closer to AJ's no-longer-hard dick. "What about us?"

AJ shoved his hand away. "Is that all I am to you?" he snapped.

"I have to put everything else in my life aside so you can get me naked?"

"What the hell?" Adam backed off. "No. But you were awfully quick to put me off tonight."

"It's not that." AJ's eyes stung, angry with himself for failing both Luke and Adam in the same night. He reached up and touched Adam's cheek. "Please. It's not you. I have to take care of this. I'll make it up to you—I promise. Did you want to come out with us tomorrow?"

Adam didn't answer him right away. Finally he said, "I like your friends. I really do. But I want to date you, not them. I was hoping we could have some time alone."

AJ relaxed. "Yeah, me too. How about Sunday, then? I'm all yours, and I'll make sure nothing interrupts us. I'll even cook for you. Okay?"

With a sigh, Adam nodded. "Sunday, then."

AJ leaned up to kiss Adam, lighter this time. When they separated, Adam cupped AJ's cheek for a moment then dropped his hand and walked back around to climb into the passenger seat. With a heavy heart, AJ followed suit and drove them back to campus.

When AJ got back to his building, Luke was already out front, sitting on the ledge surrounding the raised garden bed. AJ took a deep breath, controlling the simmering rage at Greg for yet again causing an issue. He climbed out of the car and came to stand over Luke.

"What happened this time?" AJ was out of patience for asking in a roundabout way or pretending something didn't occur every other week. Luke would either answer directly or he wouldn't.

Luke looked up, squinting in the apartment's exterior lights. "I didn't make it home before Greg. He wanted to know where I'd been."

"He hit you?" AJ inspected Luke's face, but he saw nothing out of place. Didn't mean Greg hadn't done something else, though.

"Not tonight. Guess his meeting went okay 'cause he wasn't in too shitty a mood when I first got home. He'd bought some wine, and he said he'd hoped I'd be waiting for him so we could celebrate." Luke's expression darkened. "I know what he meant by that."

So did AJ. Greg wasn't particularly bothered with important details such as being sober enough to enjoy it. Or to consent, even. "Did he—"

"No," Luke said, stopping AJ before he could finish the sentence. "All's he did was ask where I went. He wouldn't believe me when I said I went out for a walk. Called me a liar. So I told him the truth, that I was out with you guys. He didn't like it and said if I couldn't even be home to hear about how great it went, I didn't deserve to stay with him. So can I crash here?"

"For how long?"

"I dunno. I mean, he's gonna let me go back soon as he's not so pissed at me."

AJ sighed. Campus rules allowed for weekend guests, but that was it. If anyone figured out he had someone who wasn't on student housing living there, he'd be in trouble. He could talk to Connor, but he already shared his larger campus apartment with two other people.

"You bring a bag?" he asked. He wouldn't have put it past Greg to kick Luke out with nothing but the clothes on his back.

"Yeah." Luke pointed behind himself.

Inside the apartment, AJ dropped his keys on the counter and looked around, scrubbing his face. Adam already didn't care for Luke, and it wasn't as though he could explain it all away with a simple, "Hey, Luke's boyfriend beats him, so cut him some slack." It wasn't his right to tell anyone about Luke's life. AJ would have to figure out how to explain everything to Adam. It also meant zero privacy while Luke was staying there. He huffed, realizing that meant either inviting himself to Adam's apartment or canceling their plans for Sunday.

Before AJ had a chance to work through what he was going to do, Luke said, "Aje?"

"Yeah?" AJ turned to face him.

Luke chewed his fingernail and studied AJ for a minute. "Did I mess up your plans?"

"Of course not!" AJ said quickly.

Too quickly, apparently. Luke eyed him. "I did, didn't I?"

AJ sighed. "I don't know."

Sitting down at the table and motioning for AJ to join him, Luke said, "You don't have to babysit me, you know. You could call him back."

"I know." AJ slid into the seat across from him. "I'm not sure I want to. Maybe this is a good thing, a sign I'm not ready yet. I thought I was, but maybe it's still too soon."

Luke raised his eyebrows. "Meaning you think it's more than a casual thing?"

"Yeah." AJ clasped his hands on top of the table, twiddling his thumbs and staring at a stain on the table. He'd thought he was ready, but as much as he'd been frustrated by having his night cut short, he'd jumped at the chance to end it. If he'd gone with Adam, there was still the matter of his no overnights rule, and he simply wasn't ready to make a drastic change to that one.

"Don't use me as an excuse," Luke said. "It's bad, but I'm not gonna to fall apart or run away or hell, go knocking on Greg's door at this hour."

"I'm not using you," AJ assured him, even though he wasn't certain he meant it.

"Okay," Luke replied. "But you'd still rather be here with me than with your new guy. How come?"

"Maybe I like your company," AJ tried with a smile, but it was obvious Luke wasn't buying it.

He tapped his finger on his teeth. "He means that much to you?" he asked. "Because I got the vibe from him that he would be totally fine with keeping it loose, you know?"

"I haven't felt like this since Michelle." There it was, out on the table in bold print.

"But that's a good thing!" Luke deflated a little. "Unless you think he's gonna be like her."

"God, no," AJ said, and that was one thing he felt certain of. "Adam can be sort of an ass, but he hasn't even pressed me on why we're not sleeping together. He's been pretty cool about it, actually."

AJ blew out a breath. "And I doubt he's the type to get me trashed and make me prove I can still get it up for him." He shuddered.

"So, then what is it?"

There was the real question, the one AJ had asked himself over and over since the party where he'd been too drunk to properly consent. He hadn't even been able to get hard, not that Michelle hadn't tried—in his sleep, no less—and she'd taken it as the sign she'd been looking for from the minute he came out to her. Up until Adam, AJ had never once questioned his identity. He'd spent a summer with Garritt and Tiffany, slowly healing, learning to enjoy touch again with them both. The feelings Adam brought to the surface, the long-lost need for something more than a sexual friendship, made him question whether Michelle had been right all along.

Except she wasn't. He might not be able to stay overnight yet, and he might still have people and places he preferred to avoid. She was wrong right from the start. Unlike Michelle, Adam had not once shown doubt about who AJ was or what he wanted. He'd read and listened and taken to heart what AJ had said the day they worked on the health fair in his apartment. And without question, he had believed AJ.

AJ sat up straighter and said, "He's not like her, is he?"

Luke gave him a puzzled look. "How would I know? Though she was really her own special kind of awful, so I imagine Adam's not like her much at all."

Sitting back, AJ smiled. "He's not like her," he repeated. He shook his head.

"Are you gonna call him?" Luke asked.

"Text, yeah, but I'm not going over. We have plans for Sunday anyway."

"You want me to make myself scarce?"

"No, that's all right. I'll ask if I can go to his place instead." AJ's shoulders sagged at the realization none of their conversation had resolved his other issues, such as the matter of sleeping in Adam's bed. "It makes it easier if I can just go home when our date is over."

Luke nodded. "I get it," he said. He stretched and yawned. "I think I could sleep a bit. Okay with you?"

"Of course. Give me a minute to get stuff ready."

There was only one bedroom, and he didn't have a spare mattress or a blow-up bed. Aside from his policy of never allowing anyone to sleep in his bed, AJ didn't want to share with Luke anyway. They were close but not that close. In days gone by, they'd been full of puppy love and the need to explore, but it had never gone anywhere. Both of them were content with a friendship minus benefits.

"I can sleep on the couch," Luke said. AJ had forgotten how easily Luke read other people's thoughts.

"No, you should take the bed. You've had a rough day."

"I'm fine," Luke assured him. "It wasn't so bad with Greg this time, and it's almost over."

Luke stood up and walked into the kitchen. He put his hands on AJ's shoulders, and his eyes searched AJ's face. Sometimes, AJ thought he seemed so fragile. Others, like tonight, he demonstrated how much he'd been able to survive. AJ wrapped his arms around Luke's waist and nodded.

"If you're sure."

"I love that you want to take care of me." Luke giggled a little, and it heartened AJ to see he wasn't crushed by Greg's reaction. "But you know what? I'm good. Remember, I'm gonna be okay. Out by Christmas, right?" He grinned.

"Yeah. I know." AJ pulled him into a fierce hug. "I love you. You know that, right?"

"I know." Luke stretched up and kissed him at the corner of his mouth. "I love you too."

"Come on," AJ said. "Let's get you settled in. We'll talk to Connor tomorrow and figure out what to do until Greg gets his head out of his ass this time. You want some tea while I get the extra blankets?"

"Yeah, okay."

AJ fixed the tea and left Luke in the kitchen. He pulled sheets and blankets out of the tiny linen closet in the hallway. Once he'd spread them on the couch, he returned to the kitchen. "All set," he told Luke.

Luke stood up and once again wrapped his arms around AJ.

"You're the best," he said, resting his cheek on AJ's shoulder. "Thanks."

AJ sighed and kissed his hair. "Hey, no problem."

"I mean it," Luke said, pulling back. "I promise, I'm gonna take care of you one of these days."

Instead of answering, AJ said, "For now, let's get some sleep."

He watched Luke burrow under the blankets on the couch then stood there for a long time, waiting until he was sure Luke had fallen asleep before shutting himself away in his own room.

CHAPTER ELEVEN

ADAM SPENT most of Saturday in the library, somewhere between "working hard" and "brooding over his sexual frustration." He could have worked in the silence of the nearly-empty Communications building—he had the key to the adjunct and graduate assistant office—but the hum of the main section of the library kept him distracted from his own thoughts. He had no idea what was going on with AJ, but whatever it was had them both on edge.

He'd texted with AJ the night before, to make sure he was okay. Something didn't feel right. Adam knew he could be a bit of an ass, but when he needed to, he'd always been there for his friends. Maybe AJ didn't know that yet, but Adam was determined to show him. How he was going to do so when AJ wouldn't tell him what was wrong was beyond him at the moment. Adam didn't like admitting how much it bothered him when AJ jumped to take off with Luke rather than him.

To keep his mind occupied, he was grading tests for Dr. Weinstock. Technically, he didn't need to do them until Monday—she'd left the weekly quizzes in his mailbox like she did every Friday, and he wasn't expected to finish them over the weekend. However, he didn't have much of his own work to do, and he needed something to keep himself occupied. While he was grading and keeping track of the most frequently missed questions, a shadow fell over his papers. He looked up.

"You're here early," Renee commented.

"Shut up," he muttered at her. "I'm trying to work."

"On a Saturday? And here I thought I was the workaholic." She plunked her books on the table and flung herself into the chair opposite him. "What's eating you?"

"Well, not AJ, that's for damn sure," Adam snapped.

"Uh..." Renee snickered. "That was more information than necessary."

"You asked."

"Not about your sex life," she countered. "Though now you've brought it up, tell me more."

Adam blew out a breath. "I'm sorry. It's just that I've never had a relationship move this slowly before. My last boyfriend–" He glowered at Renee when she raised her eyebrows. "What?" he demanded.

"Yeah, see, you told me about that. I don't think he was exactly a boyfriend. But do go on." She leaned forward, elbows on the table and her chin in her hands.

Sneering at her, Adam said, "Fine. He wasn't my boyfriend. But we had way more sex than I'm having with *my actual boyfriend* right now."

"Is that what AJ is?" Renee sounded surprised.

"I don't know," Adam admitted. "We didn't really define it. I thought I was okay with this, and mostly I am, but..."

"But you're horny and you want to get off with him?"

Adam swallowed. Renee wouldn't judge him if he said yes. The problem was, she was wrong. "No."

"Okay...I'm confused. First you say you're frustrated at the lack of sex. Now you're saying you're *not* frustrated?"

"I'm frustrated," Adam growled. "Just not for that reason." His shoulders slumped. "I want–wait. Can you promise not to make fun of me if I tell you?"

Renee sat up straighter. "This sounds serious. Cross my heart, I will not make fun of you."

"Good." Adam took a deep breath and let it out slowly as he contemplated the right words. "For once, it's not about scratching an itch, okay? AJ means a lot more to me than that. We were supposed to spend the night together after we went out on Friday, only he backed out because something's going on with him and his friend Luke that he won't tell me about." And there it was—Adam's real fear, the one he couldn't tell Renee: that AJ was holding him off because Adam wasn't good enough for him. *But Luke is*, the nagging voice prompted him.

Renee nodded. "You think he did it on purpose to avoid sleeping with you? Or is there something more going on between the two of them?"

"I don't know, nor do I have any idea why he would suggest going home with me and then change his mind the second his friend sent him a message."

"Maybe it's not about his friend. Maybe sex isn't as important to him as it is to you," she said. "Or maybe he's the kind of guy who needs more than one relationship, though I do think he should be honest if so. People with mismatched sex and romantic drives make it work all the time. He's obviously into you, so I can't imagine it's anything else. Have you talked to him at all about this?"

"And say what? I'm not even sure what the problem is."

"And tell him the truth. You and I have only known each other for a month, but I at least know a few things. You don't go without sex easily, but you also don't like to have big discussions about it. With me, I had to spell it out that all I wanted was to 'scratch an itch,' as you put it, and once I said it, we were fine. If this thing with AJ is more than casual, you have to figure out what your real needs are, and you have to be open to his."

Adam scrubbed his face and sat silently for several minutes. He didn't know how AJ would take such a conversation. Come to think of it, Adam wasn't sure how he did, either. Everything he'd done had been because he was in the mood and it seemed like a good idea at the time. It was why it had never worked out with Cody—they wanted different things, or maybe they wanted the same things but never at the same time. Adam hadn't been clear on it because he and Cody had never had an in-depth conversation about it. Instead, they'd screwed each other over repeatedly, both literally and figuratively, and then yelled at each other about nothing, often in public.

"Maybe you're right," Adam said at last. "I guess it can't hurt to try."

"Exactly! I mean, you and I, we never really followed up because it didn't seem necessary. We had fun, and then we moved on. If AJ's so important, you have to talk about longer-term stuff." Renee squeezed his hand. "Look. I don't really want to be the meddling friend here, so I'll leave it at that. I think deep down, you know exactly what you want and how to have it. Trust yourself, yes?"

There were other things Adam wanted to say to her, about how she'd been the one to do all the talking before they slept together, about how much more comfortable both she and AJ were with themselves, about how he only pretended to have a clue what he was doing. He didn't, though.

"Trust myself," he repeated. "Right."

If only he could make himself do exactly that.

On Sunday, AJ called Adam about their plans. "Hey, *tesoro*," he said. He sounded tired.

Adam hoped he wasn't calling to cancel. "So, what's the deal today? You mentioned wanting to cook something. What time should I come over?"

"Um." AJ fell silent for a minute. "About that..."

"Now what?" Adam didn't bother being polite. He gritted his teeth. Of course there was a problem.

"Can—can I come to yours instead?"

"Oh, for the love of—*why?*" Adam demanded. It wasn't as though it was a big deal, but it was a little weird that AJ didn't want him to come over.

"We won't have any privacy here." There was an obvious cringe in his words.

Adam relaxed. "Maintenance crew in again?"

"It's Sunday," AJ reminded him. "No, not that. It's just...don't get pissed, okay?"

"Not promising."

"Luke's here."

"What? Why?"

"He's going through a rough time. It's not something I can talk about without his permission. Anyway, unless you'd like to rethink your view on dating my friends instead of me, how about I make you something at your place?"

Adam swallowed the jealousy threatening to bubble over into his reply. AJ wanted to be alone with him, and he had to trust his gut. "Okay," he said.

"Great!" AJ sounded relieved. "I need to pack everything up and stop at the store for a couple things, but then I'll be over."

"Sounds good." Adam ended the call and sat staring at his phone for a long time before putting it away so he could clear up the worst of the mess in his apartment. He hoped there wouldn't be any interruptions this time.

A short time later, AJ showed up at Adam's apartment with his arms full of groceries. Adam's curiosity was piqued when AJ began laying items out on the counter. While AJ worked, Adam hovered, until AJ looked back over his shoulder. Adam shrank back, expecting to be chastised for being underfoot. Instead, AJ smiled.

"Want to help?" he asked.

"Are you sure you want me to?" Adam was capable of cooking for himself, but not anything fancy. Not like what AJ was doing.

"Of course. It's not that hard."

"Yet." Adam grinned, unable to resist putting his arm around AJ's waist. As he slid his hand further down, AJ stopped him.

"Dinner first," he said firmly. He turned partway around and leaned in for a kiss. "Come on."

"What are we making?" Adam asked as he backed off and rolled up his sleeves.

"Real Italian food," AJ informed him.

"I take it you don't mean spaghetti and meatballs."

"Nope." AJ laughed. "I had to call Nonna to get her recipes earlier, and she talked my ear off."

"Please tell me she kept it clean."

Grinning wickedly, AJ said, "Sure, mostly."

They turned to their work, and in no time they were busily chopping, steaming, and simmering things until the whole apartment smelled good. What AJ prepared was nothing like the food Adam had eaten even in upscale Italian restaurants. It felt elegant, too much for a simple dinner at home. And yet the recipes hardly used any ingredients, and they weren't challenging to put together. Even making dressing for the salad from scratch was a matter of a few handy ingredients right from Adam's cupboard. He lent a hand, but he marveled at the ease with which AJ moved around the kitchen. It made Adam feel a bit like a sous-chef.

When everything was done, they sat at Adam's table, dishes of food on the stove to leave room for the multiple plates. At the first bite of what AJ called *spaghetti alla puttanesca*, Adam couldn't contain the same pleasure he'd had at tasting the food from the tiny Mexican kitchen. He closed his eyes and savored it, eating more slowly so he could draw it out. He usually liked food the way he liked sex—taking everything as though it might be the last time he had it, racing to the finish. This, however, called for taking his time in a way he wasn't used to.

"God, AJ. If you fuck the way you cook, we may never leave my apartment."

AJ snickered, and Adam's eyes flew open. He realized he must have said it out loud, and his face heated. But AJ's eyes were alight with pleasure, his pupils blown and his lips parted. A rush of arousal unfurled in Adam's groin, and the muscles in his ass tightened involuntarily.

Leaning forward, AJ spoke low. "I think I can show you something equally sensual in bed, yes."

They cleared the table, and AJ brought out the coffee and dessert. They ported them to the living room and sat on Adam's couch, half-facing each other with their legs touching. AJ fed Adam bites of the tiramisu—which wasn't homemade but had come from the bakery on Main Street and was probably richest thing Adam had ever eaten. By the time they finished, he was stuffed, but in the best possible way. Much as he wanted to ravish AJ—or have AJ ravish him—he needed to digest a bit first. They sipped their coffee slowly, and Renee's suggestion for Adam to talk to AJ about a few things surfaced. He wasn't known for being delicate, but he wanted to get it right this time for AJ's sake.

He said, "The other night—you know, when we went out—I've never been to a place like that." He moved closer to AJ. "Our server was hot. Kept looking at you like they wanted to eat you."

AJ laughed. "Not that they weren't doing their share of ogling you. Or were you not aware?"

"Oh, I was aware." Adam's eyes narrowed. "You were enjoying it."

"Yeah," AJ admitted. "It was...intense, watching you flirt. Watching someone else hit on you."

Adam cleared his throat. "I've always had a pretty high sex drive. I mean, ever since I was old enough to figure out masturbating."

AJ tilted his head, studying Adam. "Okay," he said. "I can definitely see that about you."

"The last person I was involved with was mostly sex." He drew his knees up, as though the physical separation might shield him from having to say more of what was on his mind.

It didn't work. AJ's eyes were trained on him, and Adam had the impression AJ could read what was under the surface. He said, "It hasn't been easy, going slow, has it?"

Adam let out a breath. "No. I want to, but I feel sometimes like maybe I want this more than you do."

AJ put his hand on Adam's cheek. "*Mio tesoro*, no. I want you very much." His laughter was soft. "You often talk about all the things you've done, and I thought you were showing off, trying to impress me. I like you better this way—being honest."

"So if I ask you to be honest with me, you will?"

"I'll do my best."

Adam worked up all his courage to say, "What's holding you back with me? Is it inexperience?"

AJ didn't answer right away. He grasped Adam's hand in his own, and his fingers trembled against Adam's. "I've done a lot more than I talk about, some of which you might not like. It's not because I'm afraid or I don't know what I'm doing."

"Then what is it?"

For a while, AJ didn't say anything. He kept hold of Adam's hand, and he closed his eyes. "I haven't been serious with anyone in a long, long time." He opened his eyes again and focused on Adam. "My last relationship ended badly in a way it's not easy to talk about. I don't do hookups, so I've kept it to friends with benefits. It feels…big, taking on more than that."

Adam didn't know how to respond. He took his hand back, more confused than he had been before. "Is that what we are? Friends with benefits?"

"That was what I'd intended." He chuckled, startling Adam. "Before you kissed me."

"So you *did* feel something."

AJ rested his palm against Adam's cheek. "Yes."

"Are you—can we—" Adam struggled to find the right words, especially because AJ's warm hand made him feel lightheaded.

"Sh." AJ shifted, maneuvering so he was closer and forcing Adam to move his legs. "Tonight, let me show you how ready I am. I brought the massage oil I got at the shop when I was planning on using it the other night. Do you want to try it out?"

"Yeah."

Everything else Adam wanted to say or do or ask was forgotten with AJ's exciting suggestion. Adam ignored the warning in the back of his mind—that they shouldn't continue until they fully understood one another—because the voice sounded too much like both Renee and Ainsley scolding him. Instead, he pressed against AJ, and they shared an open-mouthed, sensual kiss. They took it slowly, AJ sliding his fingers up underneath Adam's shirt, and Adam's hand finding its way between them to rub AJ through his pants. AJ groaned and pulled back.

"If you keep doing that, we're not going to make it to the massage."

Adam gave a breathy laugh, but he backed off. "Can't have that. I want to see what you have in mind."

He stood up and pulled AJ with him. They retreated to the bedroom, where they slowly undressed, giving both of them time to cool down a little and draw out the anticipation. Adam lay down on the bed, sliding over to make room for AJ.

"Turn onto your stomach."

Obediently, Adam rolled over. AJ knelt behind him, and when he uncorked the bottle, Adam inhaled the warm, smoky, woody scent. It tingled his nose. Lightly at first and then with more pressure, AJ began to rub his back. He used long, firm strokes, and as he worked, Adam relaxed into the mattress, the sheets soft around him. He sighed in contentment, melting into it as AJ massaged more deeply.

The sensations were at once sensual and soothing, and Adam closed his eyes, focusing on every place AJ touched him. When AJ withdrew, Adam opened his eyes and turned his head to look. AJ leaned down and kissed him.

"Turn over and come here."

AJ sat back, propped upright against the pillows with his legs apart, and Adam settled between them. Wrapping his arms around Adam's chest, AJ lifted his legs to rest his calves on Adam's thighs, keeping them spread. Adam sucked in his breath and tilted his head back until it rested on AJ's shoulder. AJ kissed his neck.

Humming, AJ ran his hands up and down Adam's arms. "So beautiful, *mio tesoro*," he murmured. "*Ti desidero*."

Adam closed his eyes, wanting to fully experience the sensation of AJ's hands on his body. He felt AJ's fingertips wander down from his shoulders, finally reaching his nipples. AJ circled them with the pads of his index fingers, and then he began to roll them between his fingers and thumbs. Adam's breathing sped up, and he groaned; AJ squeezed more firmly. While AJ touched him, he moved his own hand from where it rested against AJ's hip to between his own legs. He wrapped it around his partially hard cock.

"No," AJ said. He stopped playing with Adam's nipple long enough to bat his hand away. "Let it get hard on its own, just from this."

"Oh, fuck," Adam muttered.

It didn't take long. AJ's pinching and rubbing sent sparks of desire straight to his dick, and he moaned, squirming against AJ. With his right hand, AJ reached down, and Adam was sure he was going to touch his now aching erection. He didn't, though. He ran his fingers over the smooth, completely bare skin around the base then cupped his balls. He rolled them gently between his fingers, and it took everything Adam had not to demand AJ jerk him right then and there. The man behind him knew what he was doing, and he'd promised it would be sensual.

AJ's mouth was right up next to Adam's ear, his breath tickling as he spoke. "Do you like this?" he asked. At Adam's nod, he continued. "I want to play with you," he murmured. "Do you want me to touch you here?" He slid his fingers underneath Adam's sac, pressing on his taint. "Like this?" He slid his hand down further, brushing against Adam's hole. "You want me to put it in, fuck you with my finger?" Adam whimpered, and AJ withdrew his hand. He put it up to Adam's lips. "Suck on it."

Adam wrapped his mouth around AJ's middle finger, slicking it. AJ pulled it out, trailing a long string of saliva with it. He lowered his hand once more, tucking it between them so he could get a better angle. For a moment, he rested it against Adam's pucker then pushed in, keeping his other hand on Adam's nipple. Adam grunted and gasped at the intrusion, but the initial jolt was replaced by intense pleasure as AJ began to move. He slid his other hand down until he reached Adam's balls.

"You want to come like this?" he asked. "Just riding my hand, with me palming your balls?" Adam couldn't answer; all he could do was pant. So AJ continued, "Or do you want me to touch your dick now?"

Swallowing, Adam finally managed to say, "Your hand—my cock—"

AJ obliged by wrapping his fingers around the hard shaft. He moved it slowly at first, gathering speed and pressure. Adam pushed down against his hand. He was so close, needing relief. He knew he was making noise, grunting and groaning as he ground down on AJ's finger and up again into his hand.

"That's it," AJ said. "Fuck yourself on my finger. Yeah." His voice was breathy, as though he too were right on the edge. "God, you feel so good."

That did it. The tingling pressure built to its peak, and Adam let go. He lifted his ass slightly and held still as he pulsed and pulsed over AJ's hand. He moved again as the waves of pleasure retreated.

AJ growled and let loose a string of profanity before the wet heat hit Adam's lower back. The sensation and the knowledge AJ had come just from touching him sent a shudder through Adam almost as intense as his orgasm. He moaned, wanting AJ to know exactly how he felt about what they'd done.

AJ shuddered and then relaxed again. For a long time, Adam lay against AJ's chest, his pulse still bounding. Gradually, the thudding faded, replaced by the boneless floating of post-orgasmic bliss. He'd never had a hand job to rival that one, so slow and sexy that it made time stand still. AJ nuzzled his neck, and a wash of emotion overcame Adam. He'd never opened himself like that to anyone, not even Cody—and they'd had sex in every position Adam could think of. Tonight, in AJ's arms, he felt safe, cared for.

"*Mio tesoro*," AJ whispered. "My treasure."

So that's what the word meant. That did it. Adam sniffled, and his eyes stung as a few tears gathered. He wiped them and moved to lie down next to AJ. "I—" he started, but he couldn't complete the sentence. He couldn't say, *I love you*. Not yet, anyway. "I'm sorry," he finished.

"Hey," AJ said, brushing his thumb over Adam's cheek. "It was good for me too."

Adam huffed a laugh and rolled onto his back. "You're a top," he said. Not accusing, merely observing.

"Yes," AJ agreed. He lay so his shoulder touched Adam's. "Always have been. Maybe we should have talked about that first, but I assumed after you said you wanted me to fuck you into the mattress. Are you okay with it?"

Wriggling a shoulder in an attempt to shrug, Adam said, "I'm vers, but I used to—never mind." He didn't want to talk about, or even think about, Cody anymore. It didn't matter what he used to do. AJ was gentle and generous, and Adam could get used to being doted on.

AJ's laughter was soft and breathy, and if Adam hadn't just come all over the place, he'd have been turned on again by the light, free sound. Given enough time, though, he might be persuaded. Before he could suggest making a night of it, AJ sat up and swung his feet over the side of the bed.

"Hey," Adam said. "What's up?"

AJ stood up and began putting himself back together. "I need to get home," he said.

Adam frowned, confused. "Wait...what? I assumed you would stay."

During the long pause, AJ seemed to fold in on himself. "I can't," he said quietly. "I don't want to leave Luke alone. Besides, we both need to work in the morning." He came over to the bed and leaned down for a kiss.

"Okay." Disappointed, Adam stood up as well. "Did you want to take any of the food home?"

"No, you keep it." AJ smiled. "*Buona notte, tesoro.*"

"Good night," Adam replied, making AJ's smile brighten.

Adam walked him to the door, closing it gently after him and leaning on it for a long time before finally dragging himself back to bed. He lay awake for a while, torn between wanting to text or call AJ and wanting to give him space. As he closed his eyes, he remembered the things he'd been supposed to say before they had sex and wondered if he would come to regret not asking. A vision of AJ with Luke rose to his mind, and he buried his head in the pillow to snuff it out. *Next time I'll say something*, he promised himself right before he slid into sleep.

Chapter Twelve

They were in Adam's apartment again, after work and classes. Adam had done the inviting this time. After dinner, they settled on the couch, and Adam pulled up an app to help them decide on a movie. They laughed at the suggestions for "independent lgbt drama" crossed with "action comedy." Eventually they picked something which fit neither category and reclined against each other.

AJ mostly ignored the movie, toying with Adam's hair and hovering somewhere between relaxed and pleasantly turned on. He thought about the last time they'd been together and what he was doing there now. It was as though Sunday had broken the barrier between them, and they were both letting down their guard. Adam hadn't pressured him in any way, showing incredible trust by offering his body for AJ to explore. Not only had it surprised him, it excited him.

He pushed on Adam's shoulder a little, causing him to tip his head to look up at AJ. Adam grinned, and AJ suddenly wanted to lick the wicked expression off his face.

"I want you," he said, low.

"I'm all yours," Adam replied.

Adam sat up and turned off the movie, dropping the remote onto the floor. AJ adjusted their position so he was half on top of him. He leaned in to kiss Adam, controlling the pressure to leave Adam wanting more. When Adam put a hand on the back of AJ's neck, AJ descended again. He kept up the same pattern, each kiss longer and deeper than the last until Adam was panting. AJ straddled his leg and moved slowly against his hip, pressing against Adam's hard length with his thigh while he devoured his mouth.

There was something so satisfying about seeing Adam writhing beneath him, hungry and needy. AJ's blood ran hot, and his heart thundered with his own urge to finish what they'd started. He sat back, waiting for Adam's move.

Adam took a couple of breaths and gazed up at AJ. "Did you want to continue this in bed?" His expression remained open, indicating it was a question not an assumption.

"Yes."

AJ climbed off and held out his hand to Adam to pull him to his feet. Anticipation drove them to rush down the short hallway to Adam's bedroom. He shoved open the door and tugged AJ inside. They cast their clothes off, and Adam snagged a towel from the closet. He threw it to AJ, who spread it out on the bed, and then he rummaged in a drawer until he came up with some lube and a handful of condoms. He pitched most of them onto the floor, but he held up two different ones.

For a moment, Adam seemed to hesitate before he said, "Would you like to fuck me?"

The question caught AJ a little off-guard for being so direct, but it also sent a thrill right through him. It had been so long, and he was ready. "Yeah, I would."

Adam grinned with dark humor as he held up a condom in each hand. "Lime green or glow-in-the-dark?"

"Oh, fuck the glow condoms. I won't feel a damn thing with one on," AJ said, but then he laughed. "Though, my God, if I didn't want you so bad I would suggest playing with them. Next time?"

A groaning whine rose out of Adam in place of a proper answer, and he dropped the glow condom. He flicked the other one at AJ, who caught it neatly. AJ spread his legs and put on a show of touching himself. Adam stalked to the bed, stroking himself on the way. He stood between AJ's legs then bent down to kiss him. AJ slid over on the bed to make room, and Adam climbed in. He moved to straddle AJ, but AJ stopped him. That was one position he would never do again. Instead, he rose onto his knees and waited for Adam to decide which way he wanted it.

Adam got on all fours with the towel under him. Behind him, AJ opened the lube and went to work opening him up, Adam's sighs and moans encouraging him. At last AJ rolled on the condom, no longer caring what kind it was, and pressed into him. AJ kept one hand on Adam's shoulder, the other tangled in Adam's hair, tugging lightly every so often. His thrusting wasn't frantic; it was controlled, measured, designed to wring as much pleasure from both of them as possible. Adam braced himself on one arm, his free hand rapidly pulling on his cock.

With a long, low growl, AJ came. He slowed his pace but didn't stop, using his now-breathless voice to coax Adam toward orgasm. "Come on," he said as Adam's whine rose in pitch. "That's it. Yeah. I know you want it."

Adam cried out and spurted over his hand and onto the towel, gasping and twitching. He collapsed, and AJ slipped free. Tipping sideways, AJ landed on the bed next to Adam, bouncing slightly as he hit the mattress. He threw an arm over his eyes, and for a long time, the only sound was their noisy breathing.

AJ rolled to the side and kissed Adam lightly then shifted to clean himself up. He stripped off the condom—mercifully not sporting an image of a deceased President—and pitched it into the trash. Meanwhile, Adam had already tidied up and grabbed a bag of chips he'd stashed next to the bed. AJ eyed them and laughed.

"What?" Adam asked. "That was fucking fantastic, and now I'm hungry."

AJ shook his head, still chuckling. "Most people fall asleep. You eat."

"Your point?" Adam countered. He held out the bag. "Want some?"

"Hell, yeah."

They lay there, unashamed of being naked or getting crumbs in the sheets. Adam popped a chip into AJ's mouth, and AJ licked the salt from his fingers. With a grin, Adam leaned over for a kiss then sucked AJ's lips. AJ tasted the grease and flavor on Adam's mouth, and he hummed with appreciation. Adam dropped a chip onto AJ's belly then nibbled it off him, tickling AJ's stomach with his mouth and causing him to snort with laughter. He pushed at Adam's head and made him sit up again. Adam took another chip and crunched thoughtfully for a moment, and AJ could tell there was something on his mind.

Eventually Adam said, "So, tell me what you meant the other night about how you thought I was showing off. What was that about?"

AJ rolled over on his stomach and propped his chin on his crossed arms. "You told me you'd done it all. Made it sound like you were some kind of expert on sex." AJ gave Adam a sideways glance. "Obviously you haven't done literally everything, but I'm curious just how kinky you are."

Adam gave a loud laugh and slid down. He shoved the chip bag onto the floor. "Not very," he said. "I'll try a lot of things once, but I'm all about finding positions that maximize feeling good. Mostly I just like to fuck—a lot, in every position I can manage. What about you?"

"I'm probably a lot more experienced than you think I am." AJ closed his eyes and turned so he was face down, avoiding Adam's gaze.

The hand on his back was warm. "Why don't you like talking about it?"

"Not everything I've done was enjoyable." *Or consensual*, he added silently.

"Oh." Adam was quiet for a moment then said, "So, tell me something kinky you've done that you did enjoy."

AJ snorted, amused and relieved Adam hadn't asked what part hadn't been so good. "I had a partner who used to like being tied up while I sucked on their toes."

"Interesting." Adam snickered.

"Not very," AJ admitted. "I only liked it because I was really into them at the time. Your turn."

"Um...okay. Piss play."

AJ sat up. "Really? That's hot. I was with a couple who enjoyed that. I would definitely do it again."

Adam had an odd look on his face. "A couple? You mean more than one of your partners?"

"Uh...no." AJ wished he'd chosen his words more carefully, but the idea Adam might want to try something at least slightly less vanilla—particularly something AJ liked—had appealed, and he'd forgotten himself.

"But you said...oh." Obviously the light bulb had gone on. "So you've..." He trailed off as though he didn't want to pry, but then he continued, "You've had a threesome?"

AJ shifted so he was stretched across Adam's chest. He licked his lips, thinking about what to tell Adam. There was one particular time he didn't want to talk about because it was too personal, but he thought he might be all right confessing the other. "I have, yes."

"Really?" Adam's mouth dropped open. "I don't usually ask because a lot of the time, people think it's kind of...I don't know. Rude or gross or a stereotype, I guess. They think I'm fishing. A shit ton of 'bisexual' dating profiles list they only want a bi woman for sex, so I try not to act like a dick about it. It's not like I do it all the time, but it's nice to be with someone who doesn't think I'm an awful person if it's something I'd enjoy."

"No, I don't think that. I haven't done it often, and never with two women."

Adam leaned in. "Tell me about it?"

"Why?"

"I want to know what you like."

AJ closed his eyes briefly, picturing it. "It was my friend's brother, Charlie. Because of Charlie's medical condition, he can't always do penetration. He wanted to ask someone else to fuck his boyfriend, Neil. I thought it was going to just be, you know, kind of...task-oriented, I guess, like they'd be really into each other and then when the moment came, I'd be expected to finish him off with ass sex. It wasn't like that at all—it was really sensual, and they got off on both of them making me feel good. For me, it was beyond sexy seeing how much they love each other. The whole thing was incredibly intense. We did it a few times, but I think they were interested in finding someone who would eventually be in a long-term relationship with them. They had hoped we would have that connection, but it didn't happen. None of us felt more than friendship. So we parted on good terms, but that was it."

"Wow." Adam ran his hand over AJ's.

Sharing something as private as the relationship he'd had with Neil and Charlie was overwhelming. He rarely discussed it with anyone for a number of reasons, including how he'd met Charlie and Neil in the first place. Adam hadn't judged, though. He hadn't called him greedy, but he hadn't suggested he was overly sentimental, either. He'd let AJ's story simply be what it was. The knot of insecurity in his chest loosened, and he brought himself into the moment. He heard Adam saying something, but it didn't quite register.

"Hm?" AJ asked.

"I said, would you ever do it again?"

"Oh. Probably, if I were with the right person." AJ shrugged. "What about you?"

"I don't know," Adam replied. "When I've done it, it was casual, you know? We were in the same place at the same time, and it was what we wanted. What you're describing sounds okay, but I'm not sure about getting with a couple."

"You realize there's nothing wrong with what you did either, right? It's not like it's better because it's what I wanted." AJ ran his hands over Adam's chest, wanting to assure him there wasn't any judgment on his part either.

Adam raised himself on his elbows. "Is that what you're looking for now?"

"What do you mean?" AJ sat fully upright.

"Someone to be in a relationship with you and your boyfriend."

"What?" AJ backed away, confused and hurt by what Adam was suggesting. He'd thought Adam sounded accepting of what AJ had done, but now he wasn't so sure. "I thought *you* were my boyfriend, and I'm not trying to add a third."

Adam scowled. "I meant Luke."

"What about Luke? I already told you he's a friend. If he were anything else, why would I be here with you?"

"There's way more going on between you than you're telling me, what with him staying at your place." Adam shoved AJ and got up to root around in their discarded clothes. He pulled on his underwear and began cleaning the room, making every gesture look angry. "I don't want both of you."

AJ drew his knees up, wary of what had brought on the sudden change in Adam's demeanor. He wasn't sure how much to tell Adam or whether it would make a difference. It was Luke's business to explain about Greg, but everything else belonged to AJ too. He sighed.

"Luke is my best friend," he tried.

"Uh huh." Adam continued tossing things into drawers, his back to AJ.

"He was my first."

That got Adam's attention. He turned around, holding a t-shirt. "First boyfriend? First gay sex?"

AJ rolled his eyes. "I'm bisexual, not gay, so no, it wasn't 'gay sex.' He was my first any kind of sex. I mean, I'd felt my girlfriend up through her clothes, but that's as far as it went. She dumped me when she found out I was bi. Luke and I made love in my bedroom, right after my sixteenth birthday. It was...nice."

"Congratulations. Why are you telling me this?" Adam began hanging things in the closet, most of which looked like they'd lived on his floor for months. AJ took it as a good sign he hadn't left the room, though.

"Because you need to know that it didn't go anywhere. We were kids, and when I said it was nice, I meant it—the sex was all right but not earth-shattering. It wasn't some grand love story for the ages or anything. It was two somewhat awkward boys who wanted to explore. That's all."

"But you love him?"

"Yeah," AJ said. "He's one of my closest friends. He knows things about me—really big things—no one else does, and I know things about him." He stood up and crossed the room, taking a hanger out of Adam's hand. "But I'm with you now for a reason, and I hope we can get to that place too."

AJ tossed the hanger onto the floor and stepped in front of Adam. He took Adam's face in his hands and tugged him closer to give him a closed-mouth kiss. It wasn't meant to be more than a reassurance, but Adam had other ideas. He softened in AJ's embrace, and the kiss bloomed into something hotter, more fierce. For a long time they stood in front of Adam's open closet, tasting, teasing, and brushing fingers over sensitive skin. AJ felt Adam's cock thickening against his still-naked hip, and he tugged on Adam's briefs. Adam yanked them off and kicked them aside.

They found their way back to the bed, grinding against each other, writhing and gasping as they both closed in on release. Remembering how emotional Adam had been the other night, AJ poured everything into it he could to make Adam understand how wanted he was—how there wasn't anyone else he would rather be with. Beneath him, Adam let go with an almost pained cry, and he dragged AJ with him into a desperate climax. AJ shuddered, panting, still lying on top of Adam.

AJ held on even after their breathing had slowed, covering as much of Adam's body as he could with his own. Adam had to know AJ didn't want anyone else, not even—or maybe especially—Luke. Not the way he wanted Adam, as a lover, a partner. AJ would do anything to convince him.

"Come away with me for the weekend," Adam was saying, his voice sleepy.

Anything but that.

AJ sat up, his heart pounding for a different reason than before. His throat closed, and he forced back bile. It was too soon; he couldn't even sleep in Adam's apartment. Luke was a good cover for it, but he wouldn't have been able to yet anyway. Speaking of which, what would he do about Luke? He didn't feel right leaving him for an extended time. Not when Luke was going through so much and Greg was still an unknown factor. He'd already had to field six calls from Greg demanding to know where Luke was after Luke turned off his phone and wouldn't take Greg's calls.

"Say that again?" AJ asked.

"I want to go away with you this weekend. Here's the thing. My best friend is living about three hours south of here with her..." He paused, seemingly searching for a word. "...Partner. Meredith has some kind of conference to go to, and Ainsley wants to go with her so they can have a weekend at a fancy hotel in a semi-tropical location. She asked me to house-sit and watch their dog."

AJ furrowed his brow. "I don't think—"

Adam stopped him by putting a hand up. "It's totally fine. Ainsley said I should invite you. It's over Columbus Day, so no classes or work, and I thought maybe..." He puffed out his cheeks. "I thought you could come with me, and we could, you know, have an extended time alone." He spit the last words out in a rush, as though he were embarrassed to say them.

"Oh," AJ said. His jaw tightened. "I don't think that's a good idea."

Adam put his hand on top of AJ's and curled his fingers around it. AJ trembled, but he didn't pull away. "I don't understand," Adam said. "Why don't you want to go with me? It's not like we have any obligations. I'm not leaving until after work on Friday."

"That's not it," AJ said.

"Then what?" Adam's face had turned stony.

Now AJ took his hand back. "It's not the missed work—it's the trip. I'm sorry."

Adam sighed and scrubbed his face. "Yeah, me too," he said. It came out with a bite. "What big plans do you have instead?"

"Nothing specific. I just can't," AJ said.

Adam pushed so they were no longer connected and pulled himself to sitting. "Are we back to this again? Why the hell not? It isn't like we're not already fucking and you need to keep your precious virginity or whatever."

That had gone downhill quickly. "Will you listen to yourself?" AJ flew out of bed and began throwing his clothes on. "Here I thought we were sharing something meaningful, but clearly all I am to you is a fuck." He shook with both rage and anxiety, wishing he'd known better before letting down his guard.

Warm hands touched his shoulders, stilling his motion. Adam said quietly, "Hey. I'm sorry." He kissed AJ's neck. "You're more than a fuck, okay?"

"I want to believe you..."

"Then do. Please?" Adam kissed him again.

AJ turned around. "I can't even sleep here, let alone stay with you at someone else's house. It's too soon—I can't take off with you for a weekend yet." He clenched his fist, realizing too late he'd said more than he should have, creating more questions than he'd answered.

"What do you mean, you can't sleep here?" Adam's brows knit together.

"It's nothing. Forget it." AJ backed up, waiting for Adam to press for more.

Adam regarded him, and for the moment, he was neither the arrogant ass nor the insecure boy. "Is this about the big things you keep secret?"

"Some, yeah." AJ dropped his head to Adam's shoulder, soothed by Adam's arms encircling him. "I need time. I'm not ready."

"I hope you are eventually," Adam said. He let AJ go and began getting dressed again. "I'm disappointed, but I'm trying to understand."

"I know." AJ offered him a half-smile and a solution. "Phone sex? We can do video chat."

Adam laughed. "All right. For now, did you want to stay for a bit, maybe finish the movie?" There was a lot in those words, and they both knew what Adam meant. AJ wouldn't have to spend the whole night.

He took Adam's hand, considering. "Sure."

They stepped into the other room, and AJ plopped down on the couch to turn the movie back on. Adam pulled a couple hard ciders from the fridge and handed one to AJ after popping the tops. They settled next to each other, knees touching but nothing else. AJ relaxed into the cushions, glad to simply be in Adam's company. For the moment, it was enough, even if he knew he was closing in on having to tell Adam the truth. He turned his attention to the movie, ready to lose himself in critiquing the film for its stunning lack of diversity.

In the morning, AJ woke to a note from Luke saying Greg had

taken the day off and wanted to spend it together so they could work things out. It didn't sit well with AJ, especially given that Luke had been avoiding him for days. But Luke had written a P.S. reminding AJ it was only temporary. AJ wasn't clear on whether Luke had said it merely to appease him or because he was serious this time. Stress clawed at him, remembering every one of the previous times Luke had said the same thing. The only thing keeping AJ from going after him was the knowledge Luke had taken steps he hadn't before. He gave Luke the benefit of the doubt and headed in for work.

AJ slipped out between his health center duties and his afternoon classes to have lunch with Adam. They stayed on campus, since Adam had to pack for his weekend away. For the time being, their disagreement was shelved. It was going to be a long weekend apart, but at least AJ had the other guys to keep him company—not to mention the prospect of hot phone sex. It had been ages since he'd done that, and it made him shiver a little to think about.

Afterward, AJ walked Adam back to his apartment. The weather hadn't quite turned yet, and the tree-lined campus was warm from the sun filtering through the branches. AJ threaded his fingers with Adam's, and the answering press of Adam's hand sent a thrill through him. It had been too long since he'd enjoyed this. They stopped in front of Adam's building.

"Sure you won't come with me? You'd have time to pack." Adam brushed AJ's temple with his lips, enticing.

AJ closed his eyes, enjoying the light hum of pleasure at Adam's touch. "Next time," he promised.

"Okay."

Adam's sigh was full of dashed hope, and it gave AJ a hollow feeling in his chest. Part of him knew Adam was right—the time away would have given them a chance to get to know each other without the distractions of work and classes and life in general. It made AJ wish he were capable of letting go of his cautious nature. He held firm, though, and instead of giving in and agreeing to take the weekend away, he pulled Adam into a long, simmering kiss. They took their time, making their goodbye last. When Adam stepped away at last, he had a tiny, sad smile. He brushed his knuckles over AJ's cheek.

"See you Tuesday night when I get back?"

"Absolutely." AJ grinned slyly. "And I can call you."

Adam chuckled. "Right."

One last quick kiss, and he disappeared into the building. AJ waited for the outer door to thump closed before turning around and walking slowly back across campus. He needed to pick up his books and head to his last two classes before the long weekend.

A text message came through just as AJ shut the door to his apartment. He glanced at the number, saw it was from Adam, and set the phone on the table while he threw books and supplies into his bag. Adam was probably letting AJ know he was on his way and his ETA. He wouldn't be available to respond while he was driving anyway, so AJ didn't worry about texting him back immediately. By the time he arrived at his destination, AJ would be through with classes, and they could talk longer then.

Once he had everything together, AJ read Adam's text before leaving the apartment. He sighed; Adam had begged him one more time to change his mind. AJ sent a quick note back as the buzzer for his apartment sounded. Leaving his phone on the kitchen counter, he answered it to hear Luke's voice, hollow and quavering as though he was on the verge of tears.

"AJ? Please, I need help."

"Hang on, Lukey. I'll be down in a sec."

As he opened the door, he heard the distinct ping of another message. Ignoring it for the moment, AJ dashed down the steps and opened the door. Not seeing Luke right away, he looked around.

"Lukey?" he asked.

Luke stepped closer, out of the shadow of the building, and AJ sucked air into his lungs when he saw him. Luke's face was a mass of rapidly discoloring bruises, his lip split and his nose swollen. He held a wad of tissues under it. There was a long cut down one arm where his shirt sleeve was torn. Dark red spots bloomed all along Luke's neck, just visible around his collar and the right size and shape for fingerprints. He wasn't crying, but his eyes were red and puffy, and he took whimpering breaths as though he was trying not to burst into tears.

AJ moved forward and put his hands on either side of Luke's face, turning it so he could see the damage. Luke shivered, and AJ wrapped his arms around Luke's slender body, holding him close for a long time while Luke worked to control his breathing. He ran his hand over Luke's hair soothingly.

"Sh, it's okay, Lukey," he whispered in Luke's ear. "Come on. Let me get you inside, and I'll call Connor."

AJ turned and slid an arm around Luke's shoulders, guiding him into the building with Luke limping and leaning heavily on AJ. They moved slowly, and Luke gasped when he tried to put his foot on the first step up to AJ's apartment. AJ shifted to support Luke around his waist. They made their way upstairs, and AJ let them into the apartment to deposit Luke on the couch. The first thing he did was pull ice out of the freezer and put it into a baggie.

"Here." He handed it to Luke, who put it on his face. "I'm calling Connor."

"What about your classes?" Luke mumbled from beneath the ice pack.

"Screw my classes," AJ said as he hit Connor's number.

While they waited for Connor to trek across campus, Luke sat staring at nothing. He didn't move a muscle, facing straight ahead with the ice against his nose and his eyes fixed on the square window in front of him. He didn't even bother brushing away the tears that had started to flow silently. It wasn't until Connor arrived that he showed any sign of awareness. At the sound of the door, he slowly rotated to face it.

"Lukey?" Connor rushed over to the couch. "Shit. What happened?"

Luke shook his head, and then the flood opened. Connor pulled him into his lap, and Luke sobbed against Connor's shoulder for a full fifteen minutes before his choking gasps subsided. AJ sat next to them, rubbing Luke's back in gentle circles. When Luke finally took a deep, shuddering breath and sat up again, AJ handed him a tissue. Luke wiped his face, brushing against the mess of bruises and cuts on his face. He cried out, and AJ stood up to search for the first aid kit. They'd done this what felt like a thousand times before, but it had never been so bad.

While Connor tended the injuries, Luke talked, hesitant and stopping to take shaky breaths every so often. "He tried—he was going to kill me," Luke said.

"What?" Connor's face contorted with rage.

"He found out," Luke whimpered.

"That you were leaving," AJ said. He didn't need to phrase it as a question; he knew.

Luke turned to look at AJ. "He took the money. Every last penny." Fresh tears formed, and Luke closed his eyes.

"Oh, fuck," Connor said. "Oh, Lukey."

"I don't care what the campus rules are," AJ said. "You're not going back home. Stay here with me as long as you need, and we'll figure it out."

"You can't hide me forever," Luke said, sniffling.

"It's not forever. We're going to find a way to keep you safe, and for now, this is what we'll have to do. I'll talk to Adam later and tell him everything—I'm sure he or his friend Renee would help, and Carrie knows people too." AJ put his hand on the back of Luke's neck. "You're not alone. We'll help you."

Luke shook his head. "It's over," he said. "I'll never get out of there. He won't even let me go back to work now." He made a small, frightened noise. "He'll find me."

Connor shook his head. "We're gonna keep you safe, Lukey." He set the first aid kit aside and tugged until Luke rested against his shoulder. Connor held him, running his fingers through Luke's hair. "How did you get away?"

"I don't know." Luke's answer was muffled by Connor's shirt. "It's a blur. He had a knife, and I tried to get it from him. He said I was dead. And then he started hitting me, saying I had to tell him where I got the money. Said I owed it to him for letting me live there." Luke shivered and twisted in Connor's arms. "Somehow I got past him, and I was almost to the door. He grabbed me and cut my arm. All I remember is that I shoved him as hard as I could, and then I ran. The last thing I heard him say was, 'You're dead.'" He sniffled, but he didn't cry.

"Sh. Oh, baby. It's okay. You're really brave," Connor whispered, placing a gentle kiss into Luke's hair. He peered up at AJ and mouthed, *Police?*

Luke pulled away. "I saw that," he said. "No. No cops. No hospital. I'll figure it out, I promise. Just...please?"

Exchanging a glance, Connor and AJ both nodded. They couldn't push Luke right away, but they would try again in the morning. It wasn't their decision, and they couldn't force him. Maybe some sleep would give him the chance to clear his head. AJ backed off, taking the first aid kit to put it away.

When he returned, he saw Connor stretched out with Luke tucked up into his side. Connor was running his fingers through Luke's hair and whispering to him. AJ watched them for a moment, and then he realized what he was seeing. He couldn't imagine why he hadn't noticed before. It was too soon, but when everything was over, he hoped they worked it out. Connor would be good for Luke. Relaxing a little and knowing Luke was in good hands, AJ retreated to the kitchen to text Adam again. With any luck, Adam would get back to him as soon as he arrived. Now that he knew it was all right to tell him everything, he was sure Adam would be willing to help them figure it out.

When AJ picked up his phone to send the message, his heart leapt. The last text from Adam said only, *I love you.*

CHAPTER THIRTEEN

AINSLEY HAD texted detailed instructions to Adam about his stay in her house. He conveniently didn't mention he would be going alone, though he suspected she knew when he didn't give her a real answer about leaving out towels and other supplies for two and requesting he wash the linens before leaving. He snorted at the last one; he figured he could manage not to get anything on her pristine sheets—at least, not the way she'd implied.

After setting everything on his bed, he made one last attempt via text, asking AJ to change his mind. Adam wasn't looking forward to explaining to Ainsley why he'd arrived by himself. Foolishly, he'd imagined he could convince AJ to change his mind, so he hadn't bothered explaining anything to Ainsley. It was fifty-fifty whether she would feel sorry for him or tell him to get over himself. He was surprised to find he would prefer the latter.

As he threw clothes into his bag, he thought about it. Disappointed though he remained, even he had to admit their weekend apart wouldn't necessarily be a bad thing. And that was what worried him—when had he become sentimental enough to think the anticipation might be as good as the real thing? Realization dawned on him, and he had to sit down on the edge of his bed to keep from dropping over in shock. AJ was much, much more to him than someone he could have in his bed. And if that was true...then what? He couldn't have said for sure, but he knew he was on the edge of something.

His hands shook, not from nerves but from excitement. He no longer cared that they were spending the next four days separated from each other. Coming home would be that much sweeter, and as AJ had pointed out, they were only a phone-sex call away. There was no possible way he could wait until his return to tell AJ how he felt, though. He wanted to tell AJ in person he didn't care anymore about going alone because they had as much time as they wanted when he returned. Rising from the bed, he snagged his duffel on the way out of his bedroom. A quick glance at the clock and he knew if he hurried, he could catch AJ before he left his apartment for class.

Nearly giddy, Adam drove to AJ's building, parked out front and got out of the car, his whole body on overdrive. As he approached the building, he spotted AJ's friend Luke walking up the path. He tripped on his way but caught himself. Was he under the influence of something? It might explain a few things AJ had said about Luke dealing with something. Adam stopped where he was, caught between a twinge of jealousy and the rational part of his mind which reminded him he was intruding.

Luke pressed the buzzer, which surprised Adam because he'd thought Luke was staying there. Adam texted AJ in the meantime, hoping they might still steal a few minutes together, even if Luke was there. A few minutes later, AJ appeared at the door. He said something to Luke, but Adam was too far away to hear. Then, to Adam's surprise, AJ put his palms on Luke's cheeks and leaned in. The two of them shifted positions so AJ had Luke folded into his arms. They embraced for several moments, and then AJ wrapped an arm around Luke's waist and led him into the apartment and up the stairs. Adam's grip on his phone loosened, and he almost dropped it into the dirt. He stared at the place where AJ and Luke had been not a minute before.

His heart thundered, and he told himself what he'd seen couldn't have been what it looked like. He did not just see the man he was head-over-heels for taking another man—the very one AJ had assured him wasn't more than a friend—up to his apartment after a decidedly more-than-friendly greeting; it had to be something else. Except his less reasonable side was already taking over, making him sweat and horrible, mind-wrenching anxiety race through him. It was Cody all over again, like the time he'd gone to see Cody and found him in roughly the same position. Or the time he'd called Cody about a date they'd planned and heard another man's laughter in the background, which Cody shushed by calling him "babe." Or the once when he'd tried to surprise Cody for his birthday and discovered someone else had beaten him to it, interrupting them mid-blow job. Every single time, Adam promised himself it was the end, only it wasn't. He'd gone back again and again for more of the same, more feeding each other lies and more rough makeup sex and more promises they couldn't keep. They'd done the same tango over and over until they ended it for good with a crushing and publicly humiliating fight.

For a long time, Adam didn't move, frozen in place by disbelief warring with anger. Then, shaking all over, he retreated to his car and got in. He tossed his phone into the cup holder, ignoring it when it vibrated noisily against the plastic. No wonder AJ had been putting him off. Of course he wouldn't have wanted to go away for the weekend, since he would be free to do as he liked while Adam was gone. And of course he couldn't ask Adam—the person he'd been seeing—to come up to his apartment. He would have had to explain too many things that had nothing to do with privacy. Adam thumped on the steering wheel and pulled away as fast as he could, seething. If AJ wanted to stall their relationship because he was cheating, fine by Adam. Two could play at that game. He'd been willing to take things slower, to forgo other hookups, for AJ's sake. Not anymore.

He could spend a weekend looking for whatever he needed to forget about whatever might have been with AJ, but he was sure it would take a lifetime to fill the hollow place in his chest.

Adam spent the entire three-hour drive trying any method to distract himself from his own thoughts. Not only was he angry with

AJ, he was embarrassed, too. He'd allowed himself to believe AJ was telling the truth when he said there was nothing going on between him and Luke. He should have listened to his gut, especially after AJ had admitted their relationship had once been more than friends. It was another stark reminder of everything Adam lacked.

He didn't stop for anything on the way, wanting to get there as soon as possible. Not that he was going to tell Ainsley what had happened and risk her judgment that he'd gotten himself involved in yet another doomed relationship. At least she was a friendly face, though. God knew he could use something to take the edge off his careening emotions.

Because he'd driven straight there without a break, by the time Adam reached Ainsley and Meredith's house, he had to piss so bad he thought he'd be lucky to make it. Add one more thing to his list of ways he could be embarrassed that day. He rang the bell, praying it would be Ainsley and not Meredith who answered.

He was in luck. Ainsley threw open the door. "Ada...!"

"Not now," he muttered. "I need the bathroom really, really bad."

"Geez," Ainsley said, and it was obvious she was trying not to laugh. "This way."

He ignored the enthusiastic greeting from the dog and shoved past to the bathroom, not even bothering to latch the door. He should have, though. Just as he'd gotten himself out and was relaxing into his well-earned pee, his pocket vibrated. He reached around to feel for his phone at the same time the dog shoved the door open and came to stand next to him. He looked down in time to see the dog put out her wet nose right up to his crotch. The simultaneous myriad sensory experiences made him jump and miss the bowl. He let out a loud, frustrated yell.

The dog gave him a reproachful glance and backed out of his personal space. Meanwhile, Ainsley poked her head in and giggled. "Everything okay?"

"Yes! Would you get out? Argh! Oh, my God." Adam ignored another text as Ainsley shut the door, closing it all the way this time.

He finished then tidied himself and the bathroom. At last he washed his hands and emerged from the room to find the dog sitting right outside the door, looking up at him as though he had offended her deeply. He glared at her.

"You are evil," he remarked then softened and rubbed her ears. He was certain she was laughing at him.

"So," Ainsley said, peering cautiously around the corner. "You're here." She frowned. "Alone."

"It's a long, stupid story."

Adam brushed past her on the way to the living room, where he plunked himself down. The dog hopped up next to him and laid her head on his leg. Remembering the texts, he pulled out his phone and promptly wished he'd gone on ignoring them. All three were from AJ.

I'm sorry, tesoro. I haven't changed my mind, but call me later & we can have some fun. That one had been sent not long after he'd asked AJ again to change his mind.

Sorry to bother you. You're probably driving. Please call me. I love you too, tesoro.

Adam? Call me. Please. It's important.

Adam snarled, his anger increasing after each subsequent message. He had no interest in talking to or messaging or seeing AJ for the foreseeable future. He had a lot of nerve, saying he 'loved" Adam after what he'd done. AJ had claimed Adam was treating him as another warm body, and yet he'd done the same thing. Worse, maybe, because he'd led Adam to believe it really did mean more—while Adam hadn't done the same until AJ pressed. AJ wouldn't spend the night with him or bring him home, and yet there he was, taking Luke up for whatever they were going to be doing.

"Adam?"

The gentle voice behind him brought him out of his thoughts, and he looked up at Ainsley. He growled, and the dog barked at him.

"Sorry. Just some texts I don't want to deal with," he said.

Ainsley sat down. "Something's wrong," she said. "You came alone, and you're upset."

He scrubbed his face, trying to work out what to tell her. He opened his mouth to speak, but Meredith chose that moment to walk in.

"Hello, Adam," she said, setting down her suitcase by the door.

Ainsley looked up, and her smile was soft. Adam studied her for a moment, wondering what he was seeing. There was something ever so slightly off, and it occurred to him her own trip might mean more to her than she was letting on. It disappointed him to think they weren't close enough anymore for Ainsley to confide in him the way she would have once. Maybe she thought Adam didn't need her now that he had AJ. Thinking about AJ sent a fresh wave of anger through Adam, and he curled his hand into a fist. Meredith raised an eyebrow, and he realized he was scowling. He relaxed enough to greet her.

"Hello," he replied.

"I thought Ainsley said you were bringing your boyfriend," Meredith remarked.

"He's not my boyfriend."

"What?" Ainsley turned to him. "When did that happen?"

Adam leaned back against the couch and blew out his breath. The dog huffed and adjusted too, so he laid his hand on her back. "Right before I left. I caught him with another guy."

"Oh, Adam." Ainsley scootched closer and put her arms around him. "I'm sorry."

"Yeah, well, history repeats itself, right? I obviously didn't learn from my previous mistakes."

Ainsley made a noise some where between a snort and a harrumph. "That would require you to have *actually had a relationship*, which as I've said before, you did not."

"It doesn't matter. I clearly have a type, and I might as well give up."

"I really am sorry," Ainsley said. "I guess I hoped this time would be different."

Adam shook his head. "Me too, but it wasn't, and now I'm here alone with a whole weekend to think about what went wrong."

Ainsley squeezed him one last time and let go. "You're not alone. You have Priscilla to keep you company." She patted the dog's head.

"She looks like she's gonna sleep the whole time."

"She might."

Meredith beckoned with her head, and Ainsley stood up. She retreated to the bedroom and returned with her suitcase. Adam stood and stretched then followed Ainsley to the kitchen with Priscilla hot on his heels. She'd developed a weird affinity for him already, and he wasn't sure what to make of that. He half-listened while Ainsley went over everything related to the dog and the house then handed over the key. Slipping it into his pocket, he trailed after her back to the front door.

Ainsley leaned up to kiss his cheek. "Be good," she said. "And don't dwell too much on what happened. If he wasn't the one, then someone else is."

He held onto Priscilla while Meredith and Ainsley left the house. He heard the car doors slam and then the sound of the engine turning over, signaling the start of his long weekend. Alone. Priscilla made a wuffling sound, and he looked down.

"Well," he said, "might as well take you for a walk, eh?"

She barked and wagged her tail then put her paws up on him. He laughed, shoving her off, and went to find her leash.

The hours after Ainsley and Meredith left were long and dull. Adam was in full-on bored mode by the time he'd had dinner and taken Priscilla out for another pee, which turned into treeing three squirrels and barking at a cat sitting under a Beware of Dog sign. She was good company, but she was too mellow to be interesting. He had coursework he could complete, but it seemed like a waste of a Friday night. All of that only served to remind him he also didn't have a phone-sex date to look forward to because no way in hell was he calling AJ for any reason.

He debated for a while what to do. It wasn't too late, he'd already let the dog out, and there was fun to be had, even in this town. It all depended on what he was in the mood for. He rose from the couch, and Priscilla gave him a reproachful look but made no move to follow him. Ainsley had said she didn't need to be crated while he was out as long as he didn't leave his things where she could root through them. He set her squeaky bone on the couch next to her just in case, and she half-heartedly nudged at it. He waited a heartbeat before deciding she was fine. Grabbing his keys, he headed out the door into the night.

In town, there was a good pool hall, Sticks and Stones. Unlike going to one of the clubs, there was no pressure to do anything but pay up and play. This particular spot offered more than the usual beer on tap and vending machines—they had a fully stocked bar and deliciously greasy appetizers. Open until two, it might be enough distraction to make Adam's night less painful. He drove straight there, ignoring the other options he passed along the way.

It didn't take long to become absorbed in a game with several other patrons. Clearly, many of the locals spent a lot of time in there, and they provided tough competition. A number of rounds—both pool and beer—later, Adam was relaxed and happy. That was, until he looked up at the sound of the bell over the door and nearly lost it when the last person he expected walked in.

Cody looked as good as he ever had. Better, maybe, Adam thought as he watched Cody saunter in the door. He was with several other people, none of whom looked familiar. Adam could have smacked himself. Of course Cody would be there. Sticks and Stones was a regular feature when they'd been...whatever they were. A good night consisted of friends, pool, beer, and several rounds of mind-blowing sex. Even now, especially seeing how Cody was no less magnetic than he had been, Adam was responding like he had muscle memory. His nerves lit up like Christmas, right along with a hot streak of anger at Cody for everything he'd put Adam through.

At that exact moment, Cody looked over, and their eyes met. A slow, predatory smile spread across Cody's face, and even from that distance, Adam saw his eyes darken. There wasn't any chance of escape now. Clearly their explosive history didn't matter much to Cody, who was likely there to do exactly what he'd done for the entire history of their relationship. He never could resist the chance to play games of multiple sorts.

As though the whole world had gone into slow-mo, Adam stood there with his cue poised, watching Cody's approach. It was like watching a car accident in the making, but there wasn't any way to stop it. Cody came in for a landing right at Adam's table, and the few people who he'd been playing with shifted away.

"Hey." Cody's tone was casual, but there wasn't anything laid back about his posture or his intent.

Adam swallowed. "How have you been?"

"Not bad." Cody tilted his head and smiled again, charming. "Grad school treating you well?"

"Sure."

"Want to play a round?"

The double meaning wasn't lost on Adam, and the pull was irresistible. He had a sudden and insatiable need to prove he had moved on and Cody couldn't get to him anymore. Except the mere fact that Adam was thinking about it meant he hadn't done such a good job of it. He stood with his hand tight around the stick, his other fist clenching and releasing as he debated. This time, he had no intention of getting pulled into Cody's vortex. A game of pool and nothing else.

As he was about to respond, his pocket vibrated. Adam's eyes flicked to the clock on the wall, the time displayed reminding him what he was supposed to be doing instead. He ignored the incoming call, and his phone went still. He licked his lips; time to make Cody sweat and remind him of what he gave up.

Adam met his gaze directly, gave him a lusty grin, and replied, "You know it."

It was late when Adam woke the next morning. He padded down the hall, stopping by the open door to the guest room. Cody was sprawled on his stomach, snoring softly. Adam watched his back rise and fall steadily for several minutes swallowing back the feelings evoked by the sight of Cody's ass, partially visible above where the covers had slid down. He held his breath as he tiptoed past on the way to the bathroom. All remained quiet; even the dog was nowhere to be seen.

He breathed a sigh of relief and slipped inside the bathroom to shower, needing something to clear his head. The hot water eased the tension in his neck, and he closed his eyes, hands braced on the wall, letting it hit him. He wanted to wash away the entire previous night, but no amount of scrubbing would erase the wrongness of it all. He should have known better than to think he and Cody wouldn't fall back on old habits the minute they were within circling distance.

Except they hadn't. They'd gone outside after their games, hot and riled up from the tension and the competition. There, in the shadows behind the pool hall, Cody had kissed him with familiar toe-curling lust, and Adam had foolishly invited him home. A few beers, shutting the damn dog away, and a half-watched something-or-other on late night television later, Cody had his tongue in Adam's mouth and his hands all over his body—willing, warm, and *right there*. And yet Adam couldn't do it. All he could think about was AJ. So he'd told Cody the beer was too much for him, and he'd set Cody up in the guest room in favor of going to bed alone. All night, Adam had felt cold, even under the blankets. His stomach had been in knots, and it had taken an eternity to fall asleep.

Now he knew why. His entire relationship with Cody had been emotionless, nothing more than the physical and a Porn Level 8 number of *yeah, baby, fuck me harder*'s every time they were in bed together. Each and every one of his non-relationships had been the same way, to varying degrees of enjoyment, but none were anything more. There was no one to stroke his back and urge him to come as though his pleasure was the most important thing in the world. No one to call him *tesoro* or whisper dirty Italian phrases in his ear. No one to—

To cheat on him with someone else. Except that part was all too familiar, and all the reasons Adam had tumbled back into it with Cody rushed into his mind. He slammed his hand against the tiles with a rough growl.

The knock on the door startled him. "Yeah?" he called.

"Ad, you okay in there?"

"I'm fine. Sorry if I woke you." He grabbed the soap and started washing properly.

"If you're sure." Cody actually sounded concerned, which would have to be a first for him.

Eventually, Adam shut off the water and got out. He wrapped the towel around himself and stalked back to the bedroom to find Cody sitting on the edge of the bed, hands folded in his lap. In the light of day, he didn't have the same sexual energy he'd had at the pool hall the night before. He was sleep-rumpled, his face a mess from not having washed off whatever he'd put on his eyes and his hair sticking up at odd angles. The tousled look was more stomach-turning than appealing, and Adam wondered again what had possessed him to do something so monumentally foolish.

"Look," Cody said. He peered up at Adam and continued. "I know I'm not really the type to care all that deeply, but I've known you a long time. You're different, and I can tell something's bothering you."

It hit Adam how much more mature Cody sounded than he had the night before. He still did as he pleased, but maybe he was no longer interested in doing it in ways that left others crushed into pieces. He might not have given Adam a romantic night, but it obviously nagged him in a way it wouldn't have before that he might have done something wrong. For a moment, Adam simply stood there, wondering who Cody had become. It occurred to him he'd never even asked pertinent questions, like what Cody did for a living or what he liked to do besides pool and beer. They'd simply gone right back to the only thing they'd ever been good at together. Adam deflated, wondering if Cody had grown up and left him behind.

"It's nothing to do with you," Adam assured him. "Not directly, anyway."

"Good. I was worried for a moment that you were still wanting to turn this into more than what it was and that's why you said no last night."

And there it was—Cody being self-centered. That was more like it. "No. I told you, I'd had too much to drink. I'm only here for the weekend anyway, so I wasn't looking for more than a hookup." Adam pulled on a pair of sweatpants, carefully keeping his distance from Cody.

"It's for the best, you know." He stood up and moved so he was in Adam's path. "I realized a lot of things after the last time we split, especially in the last year. I'm sorry I hurt you before, but I'm not remotely ready to make a happy nest with someone else." He shrugged. "Maybe I never will be. But I can at least make better choices about how I handle that."

Unlike the choices Adam had been making of late. He put his

hands on Cody's arms and ran them up and down. "Sounds like you've got it all figured out."

He sighed and let go. There wasn't any more to be said about it. He wouldn't ask Cody to spend the rest of the weekend with him and try again. Pizza, movies, and Priscilla would be companions enough, and when he got back to school, he could work on the rest. Maybe what happened with AJ was his wakeup call, his motivation for finally deciding what he really ought to do with his life.

"Breakfast?" Cody asked.

With a strained laugh, Adam shoved him playfully. "Sure, as long as you're cooking."

CHAPTER FOURTEEN

AJ TRIED to call and message Adam several more times with no response. They'd been meant to talk on the phone, but Adam hadn't answered. AJ texted Adam again in the morning before he got out of bed, with similar results. By that point, AJ was more alarmed than confused. His mind raced between possible scenarios, everything from Adam's car in a ditch somewhere to someone attacking him. He contemplated calling Renee, except he didn't know her phone number. Adam had given him the phone number and address where he was staying, but no one answered that phone, either.

Meanwhile, they had to figure out what to do with Luke's situation. Connor had stayed the night after a fruitless attempt to get Luke to go to after hours or the emergency department. AJ had gotten up to check on Luke a few times. At first, he and Connor were talking quietly, but the last time, Luke had fallen asleep in Connor's arms. They were still asleep when AJ fumbled his way to the kitchen to check his messages again. There was still no word from Adam.

AJ was torn between finding out what had happened to him and making sure Luke was safe. He began putting things out for breakfast while he debated his options. Adam had given him the address, just in case, but AJ had already made it clear he wouldn't be going. He considered making the three-hour drive in hopes it was something as simple as Adam's phone dying or no cell phone service.

"Hey, Connor?" AJ called as he stepped into the living room.

"Yeah?" Connor shifted, sliding out from underneath Luke and leaving him still asleep. He stood up and came around the back of the couch to AJ.

"Have you and Luke got things under control here? There's something I need to do today, and I may be back late." He cleared his throat. "Or not at all."

Connor's eyebrows shot up. "Like what?"

"I'm driving down to where Adam is supposed to be staying."

"You can't just call him?" Connor frowned.

AJ shook his head. "I tried that, but he's not answering his phone."

"Why not?"

"I have no idea. The last time I saw him, we said goodbye for the weekend and confirmed plans to talk last night. He didn't call, and he didn't answer my calls or my texts. He's not online, or I would have found him that way, and he's not answering the house phone where he's staying. I don't know what's going on." AJ tried not to sound as panicked as he felt, the worry over what might have happened gripping him.

He swallowed, knowing it was more than that. He didn't think there was anything Adam could do, but he needed to draw on Adam's strength, and he needed some distance while he figured out what to do about Luke. All he could think of was wrapping himself around Adam and holding on until he was clear-headed enough to know what to do. But Adam had disappeared, and AJ couldn't bring himself to voice his fears out loud. He begged Connor silently to make the connection.

Connor's posture relaxed and he put his hand on AJ's shoulder. "Do you think something happened?"

AJ shook his head. "I don't know."

"It may not do any good to go looking, you know."

"I have to try," AJ said.

"All right. If you're sure."

"I'm sure. If it makes you feel better, I'll call you when I get there, okay?"

"Okay." Connor nodded. He leaned in for a one-armed hug. "I'll take care of Lukey."

"You will?" a sleepy voice asked from the couch. A moment later, Luke's head popped up. AJ winced when he saw Luke's face.

Connor's cheeks reddened. "Yeah, I will." His smile was crooked.

"I'm driving down to see Adam," AJ explained to Luke. "So Connor's going to stay with you. I still think you should get those injuries checked out, though."

Luke shook his head then groaned. "I'll be fine. Just need a few days to heal up." His mouth turned down. "What would they do for me, anyway? None of it was bad enough for stitches, I didn't get a concussion, and no one's ever going to believe what happened."

"They would this time!" Connor insisted. "Your face is all mashed in."

Drawing himself up, Luke looked into Connor's eyes. "I tried once, you know," he said. "The last time he punched me, he broke my nose. Knocked me into the wall so hard the pictures fell off, and the people in the next apartment called the police. Because we were being too loud, not 'cause Greg hit me. Not like they ever helped me before. 'Boys will be boys,' the cops told the neighbors. And I heard one of them mutter as they were leaving that it was 'just a fag fight.' They don't give a shit about people like me. They're more likely to help beat me up than to arrest Greg." His eyes softened. "You and I both know it's true."

Connor's shoulder slumped. "You're right. I wish you weren't."

"Me too," Luke whispered.

Connor returned to the couch, sitting down and drawing Luke close to wrap him in a tight hug. He looked over the top of Luke's head and nodded at AJ. Leaning over to pat Luke's shoulder on his way past, AJ retreated to the bedroom to gather a few things for his trip, just in case. He swallowed his nerves and shouldered his bag. With one last wave of acknowledgment to the others, he headed out of the apartment, leaving the two of them to themselves.

The drive was long but uneventful, though the whole time AJ kept a lookout for Adam's car along the side of the road. Every so often, he repeated the words, "He's okay" to himself. It took just under three hours to get there, and the house wasn't hard to find. Relief coursed through him when he saw Adam's car in the driveway, along with another vehicle he assumed belonged to the owners. It was quickly replaced with confusion as to why Adam hadn't returned any of his calls or texts. He got out and hurried up the path, anxious to see Adam and be reassured everything would be all right.

He knocked on the door, but there was no answer, only a few barks from within. For a long time, he stood there, debating on whether he should try the door and simply walk right inside. As he was about to knock again, he heard a few muffled thumps and eventually a faint, "Coming!" A moment later, Adam opened the door. He was bare-chested, wearing only a pair of loose sweatpants. Even though AJ had seen Adam naked before, his mouth still went dry at the sight of Adam's chest and the way his pants hung so low he was hardly covered.

He was about to launch himself at Adam when Adam's face went from shock to scowling in the length of time it took AJ to say, "Hey." AJ frowned. Something didn't feel right.

"What are you doing here?" Adam demanded.

AJ stepped back. "I—I came to talk to you," he said. "I got worried. You weren't answering your phone."

"Yeah, well, there was a reason for that," Adam snarled.

His vicious tone hurt. AJ shrank back. "I don't understand. Did something happen?"

"Don't even play that game with me," Adam snapped.

"You're not making sense. Why are you so angry? Maybe we can—"

"Maybe we can nothing. You bet your ass I'm angry."

Before Adam could say more, someone else stepped around the corner from the other room, also shirtless and rubbing his hair with a towel. "Hey, Ad, who's this?"

The stranger was good-looking, in a bit of a too-much kind of way. He smiled at AJ and went to step around Adam. With a snarl, Adam put out a hand to stop him. "It's no one important."

AJ's mouth dropped open. "You—you—" he stammered.

"I what? Hooked up? It's not like you weren't doing the same thing, only the difference is, you told me you weren't. I made no such promise."

"What?" Now AJ was lost. He had no idea what Adam was talking about, only that he'd made it clear what the other man was doing there. Blood pounded in AJ's ears, and he couldn't think of a single response to Adam's accusation.

"You heard me. You couldn't even wait until I was out of town to bring him up to your apartment. You won't let me in, but the minute I leave, your twink friend shows up to play around. Now it makes sense that you didn't want to come with me this weekend. You needed me out of the way so you could bring him in. You lied to me when you said there was nothing going on between you. Have fun fucking your new toy." Adam slammed the door on him, and AJ's pleading for him to open it so they could talk made no difference.

AJ stood on the porch, and he heard the sounds of talking from inside the house. He wondered whether they were discussing him or negotiating more rounds of sex. He didn't care which it was. It wasn't his fault Adam had cheated, nor should he be blamed for the nasty things Adam had said about Luke, but the confusion was entirely his doing. If he'd been *normal*, the kind of guy who could spend the night or take a weekend away or hell, even be honest about what was happening in his life, he might have prevented the whole thing.

And then it hit him. He was doing the same thing Luke did—rationalizing, justifying, taking the blame. Adam had already cheated on him once, barely five minutes into their relationship. He couldn't be trusted, and AJ was right to have been wary. He regretted everything from their first date onward.

Until he remembered the way Adam had bantered with him, brought him flowers, and made him feel almost safe. The way his lips felt against AJ's and the taste of his skin. The way he'd asked about AJ's sexuality instead of simply pressuring him. The way he'd writhed under AJ's fingers as he worked the massage oil, and the way he came undone at AJ's sensual touch. Those weren't the marks of someone who couldn't keep his hands to himself, but AJ had no other explanation for any of it.

Defeated, he backed away from the door and turned toward his car, breaking into a sprint and throwing himself inside. He slammed the door just before he let loose, yelling in rage and pain as he banged his hands on the steering wheel.

AJ was prepared not to speak to anyone when he returned, not wanting to admit yet what had happened. He would tell them there was nothing Adam could do to help them, but beyond that, everything else was his to deal with when and if he chose to do so. He climbed the stairs to his apartment and entered, expecting to talk to Connor and Luke about what they were going to do next. Instead, he walked into a roomful of people.

Luke was curled up on one end of the couch, talking Lauryn's ear off, and Connor was in the kitchen with Donny, Piet, and Dara. AJ's first thought was how strange it was for all of them to be in the same place at the same time. His next thought was to be irate that they'd all made themselves at home in his apartment while he was away. With all of them conversing at once, it was loud, and it was more than AJ could take at the moment. He shut the door but made no move to advance into the room, instead standing just inside it and fuming.

When he'd had enough, he yelled, "Hey!" The room fell silent.

"Hey, AJ," Piet said. He was clearly attempting a casual tone, but something in his voice implied he was on high alert.

AJ glowered at them all, not sure who he wanted to snarl at first. He settled on everyone. "What the absolute fucking hell are you all doing in my apartment?"

No one moved. Six sets of eyes were trained on him, and a muscle in Donny's jaw twitched. He cleared his throat and stepped around the others to approach AJ, stopping a few feet away.

"You remember what I told you about Jax," he said.

"Of course," AJ replied tersely. "That wasn't my question, and what does Jax have to do with why you're holding a town meeting here?"

"We were waiting for you," Piet put in. "You weren't answering your phone, and we were trying to decide what to do."

AJ deflated. He'd taken longer than he'd planned to return, and he'd ignored any calls and texts. Once he reached the car, he'd been too upset to drive far, so he'd spent several hours at a used bookstore with a cafe, drowning his misery in decadent, frothy beverages and new-to-him novels. He'd cut himself off when the trashy bisexual space cowboy romance only made him feel worse because the main character was a redhead with a dirty mouth—in more ways than one.

"I'm sorry," he said, scrubbing the side of his face with a shaking hand.

Connor went to him. "You were there because Adam didn't return your calls, and then you didn't return ours. We didn't know what to think. Are you all right?"

AJ wanted to tell him no, he was not all right and might not ever be. Instead he said, "Yeah."

"You're not," Luke said from the couch. He still looked awful—as though AJ had thought a single day might heal his face—but he was more relaxed than he had been. "What happened?"

"A lying, cheating, asshole happened," AJ snapped.

On cue, Lauryn and Dara stepped over to wrap their arms around him. AJ wasn't going to fall apart, not yet, but he couldn't deny their warmth felt good. He sighed and melted into their embrace. When they let him go, everyone appeared to have silently agreed not to press him for more details he wasn't going to give anyway.

He repeated his question more politely. "Would one of you please tell me why, other than waiting for me, you're all here?"

Donny returned to the kitchen and brushed his hand over Piet's shoulder gently. "I have to get Jax out or at least do something," he said. "He—they—called me last night. So much shit is going on, AJ." Donny leaned back against the counter and ran his hand over his hair. "My sister—Nisha—is pregnant, and my parents are busy dealing with it, but not so busy they can't blame Jax. It's bad."

AJ frowned. "They're blaming Jax?"

"Yeah." Donny rubbed his eyes. "Like she was so wrecked over finding Jax trying on her dresses that she went out and got herself pregnant." Donny clicked his tongue. "Forget that it wasn't Nisha's clothes. She took Jax shopping for his own, and she was already pregnant but hadn't told anyone."

"Nisha's twenty, not a child. Why are they so upset?"

Donny shrugged one shoulder. "They're good Catholics. These things matter to them. Also, her boyfriend's an atheist, and they're both happy about the baby—not scared, upset, and begging God's forgiveness. I think my parents feel like they've failed in their Christian duty to raise us all right."

"My parents are good Catholics too," AJ mused. "So am I, for that matter." He let out a long sigh. "Is there anything I can do?" At least he would have something to keep his mind off Adam.

"Yeah," Donny said. "I gotta go back, and I have to get some stuff ready so Jax can stay with me and Piet and Dara long-term. I mean, it's not like our parents are gonna chase us down or anything, but when I tried talking to them about it, they said if I took him away, I could stay gone too." He slumped, a look of utter defeat on his face. "I have to try again, for all of us."

"What do you need from me?" AJ asked

Donny's expression turned pleading. "I don't know. Come with me?"

AJ looked between his friends, his gaze coming to rest on Luke before turning his attention back to Donny. "What about Piet or Dara?"

"They don't know the stuff you do," Donny said. "You get all that stuff with Jax. Plus, Piet's not feeling so great, and Dara works all the time. I don't wanna bring Jax back here until—" He cut himself off and glanced at Piet. "Sorry."

Piet shrugged. "I probably should've said something." He looked to AJ. "I didn't want to put it on you to worry for me because I have to go for more tests in case the cancer is back."

AJ took in Piet's pinched features, pale skin, and hunched posture. He sighed; he couldn't be too upset that Piet had hidden it from him how he was sick again. After all, AJ hadn't breathed a word about large portions of his own life. Still, it disappointed him to find out about Piet's health like this.

"I'm still not understanding," AJ said. "I think there's something you're not telling me."

Donny stepped closer and leaned in. "You're good at this stuff, Aje. I'm hoping if you come with me, Jax'll talk to you 'cause you get it, you know?"

AJ frowned, torn. "I already have Luke staying here." At Donny's sorrowful expression, he relented. An idea occurred to him which might solve multiple problems, and he went from his own stress to take-charge mode in a heartbeat. "Take Luke with you," he said.

Donny glanced between them. "Why?"

"Because he knows from the inside about being kicked out of his parents' house." AJ stepped around them into the kitchen and retrieved a pen and pad of paper from the drawer. He jotted down a few notes. "Bring Jax here. It's the shelter where my dad works. Kelly will be there even if no one else is. You can't miss him—he's a homeless guy who volunteers at the shelter in exchange for food and clothes and stuff. He knows as much about it all as my dad does. Luke can stay with Jax while you talk to your parents."

Donny accepted the paper. "Okay, but then what?"

"Ask my mom for help with the legal stuff. You should be fine taking Jax out for a while, but you're going to need help if you want to be their legal guardian. She'll get you started." AJ looked at Luke. "She might have something for you, too. Are you able to get away for the rest of the weekend?"

Luke nodded. "I went to work today, and Señora Guzman told me to take some time. Are you sure it's okay for me to go with Donny?"

"Positive. You need some time away too, and I'm sure my parents will be glad to see you. I'll check in with you in a few days and see how it's going." AJ tilted his chin at the door. "Donny, go get your stuff and come back here. Luke and I can get his bag packed."

The group dispersed. Piet and Dara bid everyone else

goodnight, and Dara offered Lauryn a ride across campus to her dorm, so she followed them out. Donny crossed to AJ and nodded.

"Thank you," he said before he slipped out as well.

Once the door was shut, the apartment felt still and silent, even with Luke still there. Luke returned to the living room and pulled out his duffel. AJ followed him, and together they collected his things from around the living room. Luke ducked into the bathroom to retrieve the few supplies AJ had given him the night before when he crashed there. He came back and plunked down on the couch.

"Guess it's just us now," AJ said. "You want anything?"

"You have any hot cocoa?"

"Probably." AJ chuckled. "Not a beer or something?"

"Nah." Luke half-smiled, and AJ cringed at how much it must have hurt.

AJ rummaged around in his cupboard until he produced a canister. He worked silently, the energy draining out of him and his earlier frustration and anguish returning now that the apartment was quiet again. He set the steaming mug of cocoa on the table, and Luke padded into the kitchen to sit at the table. AJ worked on tidying the counters. Out of the corner of his eye, he caught Luke watching him while he blew on his drink. AJ pretended not to notice. If he sat down, if he gave Luke his attention, he wouldn't be able to hold in everything the day had brought.

Unfortunately for him, Luke wasn't letting him off the hook so easily. "Are you all right?" he asked.

AJ kept his back to Luke, continuing to wipe the same spot on the counter. "No worse than I was."

"Tell me," Luke said.

"I caught him with someone else." AJ finally turned around. "It's an endless loop, isn't it? If they're not accusing me of cheating, then this." He frowned. "Or really, it was both. He thinks—never mind." AJ didn't want to burden Luke with something he couldn't have prevented.

"AJ," Luke said, and if AJ hadn't been so upset, the slight scolding tone would have been funny. "What does he think? Because I can guess, but maybe you need to say it."

AJ took a long, slow breath. "He thinks I wouldn't go with him this weekend because you and I were going behind his back."

"Why would he think that? Unless..." Luke's brow furrowed. "You didn't tell him the truth about why you wouldn't go, did you?"

"No." AJ gritted his teeth and said, "It wouldn't have mattered. He wouldn't listen to me when I tried to tell him he was wrong about us, and he didn't waste any time finding someone else to hook up with. I don't know what I was thinking, getting involved with someone like him."

"What does that even mean, 'someone like him'? What's he like?"

AJ pulled out the chair and sat down, staring at Luke's mug while he considered how to answer. What was Adam like? Full of himself, overtly sexual, the type of guy to wing it through life. A salesman who could draw a person in with a single glance or a well-placed word. An ache developed in AJ's stomach. Adam was also funny, smart, and top-notch at his work. Sex-positive and enthusiastic but attentive to consent and in tune with the needs of his partners. Nothing added up when it came to Adam's behavior that morning.

"He's possibly the best and worst thing that's happened to me since Michelle," AJ admitted.

Luke didn't say another word, reaching across the table to press his hand on top of AJ's. He stood up from the table just as the buzzer sounded. AJ rose as well, rounding the table to give Luke a long hug.

"Take care," Luke said, picking up his duffel.

"You too. I'll call in a couple of days, unless I hear from you or my parents before then."

Once Luke was out the door, AJ readied himself for bed even though it was still early. The commotion in his apartment had temporarily taken his mind off Adam, but as he lay in his bedroom staring at the ceiling, it all rushed back to him. A lonely ache settled in his chest, and he closed his eyes against the pain. He prayed for sleep, hoping things would look better in the morning.

AJ threw himself into work after the break with extra vigor. His head was too full of tangled thoughts—Luke, back from the trip and holed up again in AJ's apartment; Jax, temporarily in AJ's parents' care while Donny worked on things from his end; and whatever was going on with Piet that he wasn't sharing. Whenever AJ wasn't dwelling on any of those, his mind snapped to Adam, half-naked in his friend's house with another man. AJ fought off the swell of conflicting emotions while he restocked pamphlets in the caddy by the door.

He hadn't been at it long when a hand rested lightly on his back. He turned around and met Carrie's eyes, full of concern. He shook his head and tried to turn back around, but she stopped him.

"Do you want to talk about it?" she asked.

"No."

"Okay," Carrie replied. She put her arms around him gently. "I'm here, if you need me. God knows you've listened to my worries long enough."

AJ smiled in spite of himself. Carrie might have enjoyed needling him now and again, but one thing AJ liked was how she never pressed him on anything. No meant no, and she simply accepted it. "Thanks," he told her. "I think I'll go see if I got a reply from Lauryn about whether the LGBT club wants to do something specific at the health fair."

Carried nodded. "I'm guessing they do. Meant to tell you when you got here, but Lauryn left you a message. She didn't say what it was about, though."

"Good to know."

AJ retreated into the break room and closed the door. He needed to shut out the distractions of the people in and out up front because they were only serving to set his teeth on edge. If he wasn't careful, he might snap at someone and cause more problems in his already overcrowded headspace. He pulled out his phone and hit Lauryn's number.

"Hello?" she said.

"Hey, Lauryn. It's AJ. Carrie said you called, and I wanted to check in anyway about the LGBT club and the health fair."

"Um," Lauryn said. There was a long pause. "Yeah, that's what I wanted to talk to you about."

AJ's stomach twisted. Something didn't feel right, but he pressed on. "Let me know what you have in mind, and we'll make it happen."

"We don't have anything in mind." Lauryn sounded tense.

"Okay." AJ was puzzled, but he realized he hadn't given them a lot of time, and he wasn't sure they'd met yet. "Well, we can figure it out, but I'll need to know in the next week or so."

"I don't think you're understanding me," Lauryn said. "We don't want to be involved."

"Oh." AJ sat back, disappointed but committed to keeping the peace. "That's no prob—"

Lauryn cut him off. "We're planning a protest of the health fair."

AJ sat up straighter. "When were you planning on telling me this?"

"It's why I called," she said. "I was appointed to let you know because we're friends and you were involved when you were an undergrad. They're trusting you not to make more of this than it is because it's meant to be a peaceful protest."

"Would you mind telling me why?"

"All those reasons why you called me in the first place. The health center doesn't care about the needs of what they think is a small percentage of the student body. It's not only the fair—it's all the time. They provide the bare minimum when it comes to educational materials, and we constantly have to adapt things to suit what we need. Have you ever tried getting anyone in the Dean's office to listen when there's a serious problem? So yeah, we could get involved in this one event and do something, but we want to see bigger changes all the time."

At first, AJ had a jolt because he knew exactly what Lauryn meant—it was why he'd never told anyone about Michelle. Annoyance overtook him, though, knowing how hard he'd worked to arrive at a point where at least one student resource was making the effort. He ground his teeth in frustration. "I go out of my way to make a difference for our LGBT students," he snarled. "You should know that."

Lauryn sighed. "I know you do, and Carrie tries too. But did you stop to think it's because both of you have an interest in it?"

"Carrie's straight."

"Yes, but she has connections with certain other communities, and she's a great ally. When you two graduate, unless they find someone else to do as good a job, we lose what you've built."

"I can't believe that would happen." AJ didn't like to think Kira, the director, would simply ignore a significant number of students simply because she no longer had employees taking care of their needs.

"I'm sorry, AJ," Lauryn said, her voice softer. "I did try to persuade the others to do this differently, but they feel the only way is to do it during a high-profile event." She was quiet for a minute. "You could consider joining us."

"No," AJ said. "This is part of my job. I was trying to do the right thing, but it obviously wasn't good enough."

"AJ—" he heard her say, but he hung up. He tossed his phone onto the table in frustration. A moment later, it vibrated, rumbling against the tabletop. AJ jumped then picked it up.

"Hello?"

"AJ?" asked a soft voice. "It's Dara."

Confused, AJ answered, "Yes, it's me. What's up?" His heart raced; he was sure he knew why Dara was calling, but he needed to hear her say it.

"It's Piet," she said. "He's at the hospital. He didn't want me to say anything until after he was there because he knew you guys would panic."

"Panic about what?" AJ demanded.

"He's having surgery again. The cancer is back. It's nothing to worry about!" she said hastily. "They'll just go in and get it out. Because it came back so quickly, they're looking at whether it's going to be ongoing rather than a one-time thing. They think it might need to be treated like a chronic illness."

"Is that even possible?"

"Yes, with his type. The doctor said chronic thyroid cancer isn't that uncommon, and he can learn to live with it. All it means is radiation or chemo on a rotating basis and more frequent checks." He heard the unspoken conclusion to her explanation, which was that he could as easily die from it if it ever spread. Neither of them had the heart to say it.

"When will he be out?"

"I'm not sure exactly. They didn't seem to think it would take long. If you like, I'll call you so you can visit him later."

"Okay."

They ended the call, and AJ sat with the phone in his hand, staring at the wall. Surely Piet hadn't really believed AJ wouldn't worry about him if he kept it a secret until the last possible minute. Hiding it only made AJ feel worse, as though he couldn't be trusted to be there for his friends. One more thing for him to have weighing on him, and he couldn't even escape it by going to see Adam and wasting their night in mindless movies and sex. AJ leaned forward and put his head in his hands, wishing he could make it all magically disappear.

He let himself feel overwhelmed for all of sixty seconds, and then he sat up, scrubbing his face. If AJ was anything, it was good at dealing with a problem. Or twenty problems, as the case might be. He'd spent too much time already doubting his own confidence and skill, but his friends never had. At the moment, the very least he could do was arrange people to bring food to Piet and Dara so they wouldn't have to cook while he recovered. AJ squared his shoulders, cracked his knuckles, and set to work.

Chapter Fifteen

TWO WEEKS. Two weeks without a single peep from AJ, not even about the health fair. Adam hadn't needed to be involved after he set things up with the Women's Studies department and handed over the publicity to the undergrads, but Adam had expected something other than the cold silence. An apology, maybe, or some explanation for what the hell was going on, both in his head and between them.

It had been confusing, seeing AJ at the door. Adam didn't regret letting AJ see Cody, but AJ's reaction bothered and puzzled him. He'd seemed shocked and upset, which Adam thought at first was a bit much. He'd let AJ believe what he wanted about why Cody was there, mostly to get at him for his own actions. AJ was the one who lied in the first place, so he shouldn't have been surprised or hurt—at least not to Adam's way of thinking. Except for the small detail of how the whole thing didn't add up at all.

Not that Adam had bothered to call AJ, either. There was no reason to. They were over. Maybe it had been too much, too fast. That was always Adam's problem, jumping into things on impulse. Now everything made sense—AJ's reluctance, the delay in turning their relationship physical, and all the hiding, hedging, and avoiding

AJ did. Everything had been lies and covers for being the same kind of manipulative user Adam regularly fell for. He made a secret vow to stick to women from then on, and not the kind who only wanted a no-strings arrangement. Women at least made it clear where he stood with them.

With a renewed sense of purpose—at least in regard to matters of the heart—Adam showed up for work, ready to see what miserable tasks Dr. Weinstock had in store for him. He booted up the ancient beast of a computer and checked his email, her preferred method of communicating the day's plan. The first order of business was to meet with her as soon as he was able, so he grabbed a notebook and pen and strode down the hall to the departmental office.

Having no patience for explaining himself and waiting for approval, he ignored the undergrad staffing the desk and went straight to Dr. Weinstock's office, earning a huff and a sneer from the student. Adam bit back a snotty response as he knocked on Dr. Weinstock's door.

"Come in!" she called.

He entered and shut the door then dropped into the chair across the desk from her. She peered at him over the top of her glasses, pushed her roller chair away from the desk, and spun on the seat to face the file cabinet. She began leafing through until she produced a set of papers. She turned around and pulled herself closer to the desk then plopped the papers in front of Adam.

"Have you given any thought as to what you're going to do next semester?" she asked.

Adam fidgeted. It wasn't quite pre-registration, and he hadn't even looked through the course catalog. "Not really," he acknowledged.

"I figured as much. You're smart, but you're not committed to any one thing. That's good and bad." She chuckled. "I loved what you did for the health fair, and I think you might consider something in the realm of public relations. What you did wasn't so much good graphics or even good marketing. It was the way you connected people from different departments, made arrangements, and had an eye for exactly what was needed to bring more people into the planning stage. Have you considered earning your certificate of non-profit or taking some classes in grant writing?"

"Uh...no." Adam's stomach churned; AJ was working on his non-profit certification.

"Hm. Well, you should. Next semester, add Non-Profit Management and Grant Writing to your course schedule and see what you think. They're useful even if you choose another path." She handed him the papers. "These are the course syllabi from last year. Look them over, and if they suit you, we'll add them in when you come for your pre-registration advisement."

"Sure, okay," Adam said. He blinked, not certain what he had agreed to or whether he thought Dr. Weinstock knew him well enough yet to determine what was best for his future.

Dr. Weinstock raised her eyebrows. "You can go," she said. "I've sent you your to-do list."

"Right," Adam replied.

He rose from the chair and retreated from the office, looking back at Dr. Weinstock as he did so. She was already absorbed in another task, head down and reading something she'd spread out on her desk. Adam shook his head and pulled the door shut after him. He walked out of the department, hurrying past the undergrad so he wouldn't be tempted to do something juvenile like kick her seat on the way.

Once back inside the adjunct office, he plunked down in his chair and began reading through the papers Dr. Weinstock had given him. Both classes looked interesting, and he thought about what she'd said. As he considered whether or not to follow through, he recalled again that this was AJ's territory. Something about it nagged at him, but he couldn't call to mind what AJ had said that niggled. Something about all the study he was doing and had done, and the way he'd talked about it. Clinical, dispassionate, and like it was something he was doing out of obligation rather than desire. As Adam sat staring at the paper, their conversation echoed.

"Oh, my undergrad? Social Work, with a double minor in Health Sci and...Psychology. I'm finishing up my certificate of non-profit management as well as getting my MPH."

"Geez. Would you like fries with that?"

"My father is on the board of a non-profit. That's where I'm headed

when I'm done here—go back home, work for them. It's all lined up."

"What kind of work?"

"It's a network of homeless shelters, each with a different focus. Dad mostly manages work at the youth shelter, but I'm not sure where I'll be placed."

"And that's what you want to do?"

"Sure. I mean, it's a guaranteed job, right? Not everyone can say the same after six years of school."

"Sounds like you've got it all figured out."

"I suppose I do. Better than flying by the seat of my pants."

Adam frowned; he didn't want to think about AJ anymore. He had no reason to be concerned about AJ's future after what had happened. And yet, something didn't feel right, as though he was forgetting or had lost a key piece of information. He had a bad feeling AJ wasn't as together as he'd wanted Adam to believe, and whatever was between him and Luke was part of it. AJ had said Luke knew things about him he kept hidden from everyone else. Nothing Adam had seen of AJ before catching him with Luke indicated he was the sort of person who looked for an opportunity and seized it on a whim. Something happened to leave him planning for a future he didn't want, and it was connected with his recent behavior. Adam didn't feel any less angry with AJ over hurting him, but now he wanted more than anything to find out why he'd done it.

He pulled out his phone and held it in his hand for a long time before texting a note to AJ. *Can we talk?*

Adam never heard back from AJ. He hadn't bothered sending any more texts after the first one because he saw no point. If AJ didn't want to talk to him, then so be it. Adam wasn't sure whether he genuinely hoped AJ and Luke were happy or if he only told himself that because some part of him wished it had all turned out differently.

In the interest of "interdepartmental cooperation," all the campus groups participating in the activities held a meeting to plan the setup. They were going to use the East Gymnasium for the fair, the larger of the two arenas and the best space for a big event.

Although Adam's department wasn't involved on the day of the fair, he and Renee offered to help. Dr. Weinstock approved it as part of his work for the day, so they took off for the athletics building as soon as they were both ready.

When they showed up, there were already a good number of students sitting in one of the upper level classrooms. Adam spotted AJ's friend Connor. He looked up when the door opened, and their eyes met. Connor's expression darkened, and with a sneer he turned back around. Adam sighed and faced Renee.

"I'm going to go talk to that guy," he said, pointing to Connor.

"Why?" Renee asked. "He doesn't look like he wants to talk to you." She elbowed him. "He's AJ's friend, right? Is that what this is about? Because from the sound of it, you and AJ were both being major dicks."

Leave it to Renee to be blunt. Adam glared at her, tempted to be immature and tell her AJ started it. "I want to know why he did it. Since he won't tell me, maybe his friends will."

Renee rolled her eyes. "Right. You can't just leave it alone and figure you're better off without each other."

Adam wished he hadn't told Renee anything about what had happened. He still wasn't exactly sure himself, and he had mixed feelings about trying to piece it together. He knew it was a terrible idea to try to fix things, given his less than stellar history of holding on too long when it was clear he needed to let go. Telling himself his need to understand was for the purpose of not repeating the same mistakes, he brushed past Renee and approached Connor's table.

Connor looked up at Adam. He huffed and turned away again, but Adam leaned down. "Wait."

"What are you doing here?" Connor asked. "It's not like we need you to cheat on another department to help us."

Adam sighed. "Maybe you think I deserved that," he said. "But you obviously don't know the whole story."

Standing up to get in his face, Connor scowled. "What 'whole story'?" He leaned in closer. "You didn't return AJ's phone calls or texts because you were too busy fucking someone else. You're a real piece of work." He made to move out of Adam's path, and Adam was sure he heard him mutter, "Asshole."

Adam grabbed his shoulder. "Please," he said. "Just listen. First of all, that's not what happened. Second, something's wrong, and I want to understand."

When Connor faced him again, he looked like he was ready to punch Adam. "I have absolutely no idea what you're talking about."

"I caught AJ with Luke before I went out of town," Adam said quietly. "And I can't figure out why he was cheating on me."

"Oh, that's just fantastic. You screw someone else at your friend's house and then try to blame AJ for it? Fuck you."

"Jesus H. Christ!" Adam barked. "I already said that's not what happened." He drew in a deep breath and tried to calm down. "I was going to hook up with my ex, yeah. By the time I figured out I would rather not, we'd had a bit to drink, and I didn't think he should drive home. I let AJ think we had sex because I saw him with Luke."

Connor glared at Adam. "He wasn't cheating on you with Luke."

"But I saw them!" Adam exclaimed. "I saw them kissing the afternoon I left, and then I watched Luke go to his apartment. AJ put his arms around him and they went upstairs."

"You really should ask questions before you assume shit," Connor said. "I gave AJ the benefit of the doubt when he started hanging out with you, but I think his first impression was right. You're kind of a dick." He curled his lip in disgust. "And you're not all that bright."

Adam scowled. "So enlighten me. What was really going on?"

Connor looked over his shoulder then motioned to Adam to follow him. They stepped outside the classroom and ducked around the corner into the alcove by the bathrooms. Connor was silent for a while then said, "Lukey's boyfriend hits him." He said it like he was discussing the weather or what he'd eaten for lunch—matter-of-fact, with no emotional investment, though his eyes told a different story.

"Oh, shit." Adam closed his eyes. AJ had mentioned trying to protect a friend, but he'd never said who.

"Well, yeah," Connor agreed. "He'd come over because Greg

had beaten him so bad he thought his nose was broken again, but he wouldn't go to the hospital."

"Again?" Adam stared.

"This has been going on for years." Worry lines creased Connor's brow.

"Why doesn't he just leave, then?" Adam asked.

Connor's mouth fell open. "You are so clueless. Are you for real? You obviously have zero experience dealing with someone like Greg. Or like Luke, for that matter."

Adam growled. "Fine. Let's pretend you need to educate me."

"It's not as easy as you seem to think. There are literally hundreds of reasons someone might stay. This time, Greg stole Lukey's money—everything he'd put away to start over. When Luke found out, he tried to go anyway, like he has a million and one other times. He thought Greg was going to kill him and then off himself, and he nearly did. You'd have to ask Luke for the rest of the story, but I doubt he'd tell you. Aside from that, he has his own other reasons." Connor shook his head. "It's bad. We've tried to get him out so many times, but he always goes back. He thinks he's protecting us, too."

"Why the hell don't you call the police on this guys' ass?" Adam wanted to know.

"You don't think that's been done?" Connor snapped. "They don't do a damn thing for us. No one takes it seriously as a domestic when it's a pair of gay boys going at it. He told us the neighbors called once, and one of the cops called them faggots. Wouldn't even file a report, even though they're technically supposed to. Lukey can't get any help from the shelters because they all tell him the women won't feel safe with a man there. Never mind how Lukey feels when he's shut up in that apartment with Greg raging and pounding the shit out of him." Connor's speech left him breathing hard, his nostrils flaring and his eyes red and shimmering with unshed tears.

Adam tilted his head as he studied Connor. There was more in his body language than only a need to take care of a friend. "You love him."

Connor looked away for a minute, brushing his thumb under

his eyes, then returned his gaze to Adam. "Of course. He's my friend."

"No, it's more than that." Adam recognized a distinct difference between how Connor reacted to Luke and how AJ did. He wanted to kick himself; he'd missed the signs before because of his own unchecked insecurity, but now it was clear as day.

Running a hand through his thick, brown hair, Connor replied. "Yeah. Have for a long time. He'd never go for someone like me, though, and definitely not now. He doesn't need a new boyfriend. He needs to be able to make it on his own first." He *"hm"ed* in the back of his throat. "But when he's ready, if he ever is, I'm here."

Adam nodded. "I need to talk to AJ."

Connor's demeanor changed back to angry. "You need to stay the hell away from him. You mistook what he did and then let him think you were the one cheating. You have no excuse for not finding out the truth first."

"I know," Adam said. "I freaked, all right? I was with someone who did nothing but string me along and cheat on me because he said what we were doing wasn't serious. It wasn't the first time, either. I thought AJ was the same way."

"He's absolutely not like that." Connor crossed his arms. "You wanna know how we met?"

"Is it relevant to my situation?"

Connor opened his mouth to speak, but nothing came out. After a minute, he smacked Adam in the shoulder, hard. "Yes, you ass."

"Fine."

"I kissed him. I was pretty sure he was gay and his girlfriend was a cover. Turned out I was wrong, and he was pissed as hell. She didn't like it much either, though, and she was convinced he was cheating on her because she saw the whole sorry episode. It's like this weird Bisexual Twilight Zone or something where literally every person he's been with was convinced he was going to leave them."

"Even Luke?" Adam asked quietly. At Connor's surprised expression, he added, "Yeah, I know about the two of them."

Connor huffed. "Yes, even Luke. He used to say he thought he 'might be bi' before he figured out he was gay, and he assumed AJ was the same. He thought being together was how AJ was confirming it, like it was for Luke. When AJ told him nothing had changed for him, it freaked Luke out. He assumed it meant AJ would get tired of him or miss being with girls."

Adam frowned. "I don't see why he has to make a big advertisement out of it. I never bothered."

"Because he doesn't want to hide who he is," Connor replied. "Why should he have to? I don't. Luke doesn't. AJ's other friends don't."

"They're straight, though."

"What does that have to do with anything? It's important for all of us to be ourselves and not have to pretend depending on who we're with." He was silent for a moment then said, "AJ acts different when he's with Luke and me than with Donny and Piet. I've never been able to figure out why he keeps us all in separate spaces. None of us care—we love him no matter what and no matter who he's with."

Adam drew his lower lip between his teeth, considering what Connor had said. "He told me about him and Luke. They're close, and I thought maybe he was hiding still being together." He closed his eyes briefly. "No, that's not it. He...he said Luke knows big things about him, but he didn't want to tell me. In my head, I made it bigger than it was."

"He doesn't deserve to have everyone always watching their backs like he's going to chase after every single person on the planet." Connor's shoulders slumped. "He thinks I don't get it because I live in some kind of gay utopia or whatever where we, like, never experience that shit. But I do get it. My parents are totally straight, and they both spent their entire marriage having affairs. I lied to them for a long time about my sexuality, and even when I was out, I didn't make the best choices. I caught my first boyfriend with his hands in another boy's pants. I know what cheating looks like, and I know what the inside of the goddamn closet looks like." Connor took a deep breath. "AJ needs someone safe, and we all thought—hoped—it might be you."

"But I proved all of you wrong, didn't I?" Adam leaned back against the wall, raking his hand through his hair. What he'd done was bigger than a single night; he'd obliterated any chance to recover what he'd lost.

"You did," Connor agreed. He was quiet for a minute. "He thinks none of us know what really happened with his last girlfriend, and if he hasn't told you, it's not my place. If he'd been honest, with us and with you, we wouldn't be having this conversation. The thing is, though, you made a choice too. You have a lot of ground to make up."

"I know. Isn't there anything I can do?"

"Tell him what you told me, and hope for the best," Connor said.

"Right," Adam replied. "Provided he'll listen."

Connor shrugged. "I'm sure you'll figure out how to get his attention. Meanwhile, I'm going back inside to work on the health fair."

He stepped around Adam and stalked off, leaving Adam to wonder what it would take to get AJ to notice him for the second time.

Chapter Sixteen

AJ WENT through his days without really experiencing them. He visited Piet and said appropriately sympathetic things to Dara. He suspected both of them were aware his mind was miles away, but neither of them complained. Piet was doing as well as could be expected.

Donny had gone back to work as soon as he returned from trying to reason with his parents and then getting help for Jax. There was a lot more to that story, but rather than asking, AJ put together meal schedules and took trips to the apartment to make sure Donny, Piet, and Dara were set up for a couple of weeks at least. He had no idea what they were all going to do long-term, but he made sure they knew they could count on his help.

In the meantime, he alternated phone calls to his mother between finding legal help for Jax and looking for resources for Luke. Connor had been more than happy to get involved as well, which in and of itself presented a new worry for AJ. They were teetering on the edge of something that could hurt them both. AJ considered it for the best that Luke continued to stay at his apartment because Connor's roommates didn't want another guest. However, AJ was no closer to a solution for Luke to recover his losses, and he was tired of Greg's incessant hang-up calls and middle-of-the-night long text rants demanding to know where the hell Luke was. Luke had begged him not to call the police until he'd sorted things out himself, so AJ gritted his teeth and took it.

As yet, nothing had been resolved with the health fair, either. Donny said he didn't know anything and wasn't getting in the middle when AJ tried to pull information from him about Lauryn. She had been silent as well, not answering any of AJ's messages. He didn't want to burden Carrie or Kira with the problem either. Instead, he continued trying to get hold of Lauryn in a way that wouldn't result in problems for both of them.

He'd had exactly one text from Adam, which he refused to answer and deleted. Whatever it was Adam thought he was going to accomplish, AJ wanted no part of it. As far as he was concerned, they were over. It was just as well; AJ had never been any good at maintaining relationships anyway, and now he had one less thing to worry about when he went back north after graduation.

After work, he returned to his apartment. Luke wasn't there, and for half a minute, AJ couldn't be bothered to care where he'd gone. He hadn't had a single moment alone for over two weeks, and he was tired. Sleep was a precious commodity, and he hadn't been doing much of it. When he saw the note on the table, however, he pitched his bag into the corner and rushed to pick it up, worried something new had happened. It only took reading the first line for him to be torn between rolling his eyes and fighting alarm.

Hey AJ–

Gone to the store with Connor. We'll bring you stuff for dinner. Adam stopped by and left something for you. No idea what it is.

Love you,

Luke

AJ looked around and spotted the box on the other end of the table. He left his worry about Luke and Connor running into trouble while they were out and picked it up. When he opened the box, he couldn't decide whether to laugh or throw it. There was a small bag of gummi bears nestled in red tissue paper with a note in Adam's scrawling script: *Life without you is unBEARable.* Underneath everything else was another note.

AJ,

You didn't answer my text. I'm hoping this works better. We need to talk sometime. I was an ass. Forgive me?

Love,

Adam

AJ snarled. Luke actually let Adam in the apartment? With this ridiculous gift? He couldn't possibly have been thinking. The guys were all clear on what had happened and why AJ had a list of rules: No talking to Adam; no talking about Adam to AJ; no making AJ talk about Adam. Apparently, he would have to add "no letting Adam into the apartment to drop off horribly cheesy gifts and apologies that in no way make up for what he's done."

Crumpling the note, AJ tossed it aside and began rooting around in the cupboards for something to cook. If he'd learned anything from his Nonna, angry cooking produced some fantastic results. Luke and Connor might be bringing him dinner, but he could make something for dessert that would put whatever it was to shame. Not only that, he could drown his feelings in decadent sweetness while trying to convince the other guys he was just fine, thank you very much.

Except he wasn't, and he knew it. When he discovered he didn't even have the right ingredients—hello, not shopping for ten days straight—he picked up the box of butter he'd set out on the table and hurled it at the refrigerator. At that exact moment, the apartment door opened and Connor walked in, followed closely by Luke.

"AJ?" Luke asked, his voice quiet and brittle.

AJ turned to face him, and all the rage drained away. He was scaring Luke, who had already been through enough trauma. "I—" he started.

"Hey," Connor said, crossing the room in a few long strides. "Hey, come here."

He folded AJ into a tight embrace, and a moment later, AJ felt Luke's warmth against his back. AJ sank into them, closing his eyes and allowing his breathing to slow down. When he felt all right again, he let go of Connor. Luke and Connor backed away.

"Are you going to tell us what crime the butter committed?"

Connor asked.

"No," AJ replied.

"Fair enough. Then are you going to help us get dinner ready?"

AJ laughed, still a little shaky. "Yeah, fine. What did you buy?"

"Real food," Luke said. "You do realize we can't live on canned tomato soup forever, right? God. I would never survive the apocalypse."

This time AJ's laughter was stronger. "Wimp," he said. "Anyway, I would call Carrie if that ever happened. She can build stuff out of anything."

Luke shoved him playfully then kissed his cheek. Out of the corner of his eye, AJ saw Connor raise an eyebrow, but he didn't seem upset—especially when Luke delivered one to him as well. They set to work on preparing dinner, and for the first time in a while, AJ thought maybe he might be okay after all.

In the morning, AJ was drying his hair when the apartment buzzer sounded. With a huff, he answered. "Yeah?"

"Aje, it's Donny."

Frowning, AJ replied, "Aren't you supposed to be at work?"

"Yes. I'm on my way there, but I have something for you. I wanted to talk to you anyway."

AJ let him up and met him at the door. Donny had a small bag in his hand, and he held it out like it was an item of vital importance. Suppressing a laugh, AJ accepted it and said, "I'm getting ready to go to the health center. What's in the bag?"

"Dunno. Ran into Adam on my way here. He gave it to me."

"Oh, God. What now?" AJ muttered. Louder, he said, "Uh, okay. So, what's going on?"

Donny looked worn out, and AJ wondered if something new had happened. He stood in the doorway, watching AJ for a long time. "Jax called me last night. I don't know the first thing about this," he said. "I thought if I got him—them—out of there, it would be all right."

"You can't fix it overnight," AJ reminded him.

"I thought I could," Donny said. "I got pissed at you for messing in my life, but you take care of all of us. I can't even manage this one thing."

AJ winced. He hadn't taken care of them—not really—in a long time. "It'll work out," he told Donny, but it sounded hollow even to himself. "And anyway, it's not your job to solve everything." He wasn't sure if he was talking to Donny or himself anymore.

"I guess so." Donny made to leave but turned back around. "I know I haven't done much for you—"

AJ cut him off. "Don't worry about it. I'll be fine. Take care of Jax, and keep me posted, okay?"

Donny nodded and left the apartment. AJ shut the door behind him and turned around to see Luke eying him. He glanced down at his hand and realized he still had the bag from Adam. Sighing, he stepped into the kitchen, set the bag on the table, and started pulling things out for breakfast. He didn't usually bother cooking, but with Luke standing there, he thought he might as well.

"You don't have to go to any trouble. I can grab something on my way to work."

"It's no big deal."

AJ cracked a few eggs and whisked them vigorously, hoping to distract himself from wondering what Adam could possibly have given him. Something more annoying than the gummi bears, no doubt, although AJ had to admit those had been pretty good. He and Luke had shared them while watching Netflix and most definitely *not* chilling, no matter what Adam had thought.

"What's that?" Luke asked.

"Eggs?" AJ tried, even though he knew what Luke meant.

Luke huffed, clearly not put off by AJ's non-response. "On the table."

"No idea. It's from Adam."

"Aren't you gonna open it?"

"Nope."

"Well, can I look, then?"

AJ set down the bowl of eggs and the whisk and faced Luke. "Why?"

"'Cause I'm curious." Luke shrugged.

"Yeah, whatever. Knock yourself out." AJ waved a hand at him. He didn't want what Adam had given him anyway.

He started cooking, and he heard the rustle of paper behind him. A moment later, he heard quiet giggling.

"Oh, my God." Luke didn't bother covering his laughter. "You have got to look at this."

AJ's curiosity was piqued. "Oh?"

"Yeah...wow. Adam knows you really well, apparently."

"What? Why do you say that?" AJ turned off the stove and came to stand beside Luke.

Luke handed over a stack of color-coded laminated index cards, hole-punched and held together with rings. "Check these out. Pretty interesting."

After the title card—which read simply *Flash Cards*—was a note suggesting the cards could be used in an "educational or recreational setting." AJ flipped through, and the heat in his cheeks increased with every one as the double meaning of the title became clear. It was a flip-book of sex positions and intimate acts, along with instructions for use as a game, a classroom discussion starter, or a bedroom resource. The color-coding had to do with type of activity, and the cards were inclusive of gender and sexual identity. AJ didn't read them word for word, but he skimmed enough to get the gist.

He finally looked up at Luke. "I don't think these are necessarily appropriate for the health fair."

"Why not? Though, I'm pretty sure that's not what Adam intended anyway," Luke countered. "Not gonna lie, some of those are damn hot. Why isn't he your boyfriend anymore?"

AJ growled. "You know exactly why not."

"See, this doesn't strike me as the kind of thing a guy who cheats on his boyfriend does." Luke picked up the cards again before AJ could stop him. "I mean, he went out of his way to find something so perfect for you and which you could use for work—not something he thought seemed nice enough to back up his sorry." He cleared his throat. "And I would know."

AJ touched Luke's hand, but then he pursed his lips. "Maybe. I'm not sure I'm ready to forgive him."

"You don't have to, but maybe you could at least find out what he wants."

"Of all people, you should understand why I can't."

Luke's expression darkened. "No, of all people I understand better than the others." He softened. "I know you're doing the best you can, but I see how you are. You're avoiding again, just like you did with Michelle. Adam's not Michelle—you said it yourself, ages ago. She never would have cared enough to do something like this."

"I'll think about it."

AJ returned to the stove to retrieve the pan of eggs and bacon. They were quiet for a few minutes while AJ put food on the table. While they ate, AJ eyed the index cards next to him. Adam had gone to a lot of trouble, but AJ still wasn't sure what to do. He added it to his growing list of things crowding his brain. Every one of his mental boxes was crammed full, and sooner or later, he would need to figure out how to unpack them all. Until then, he would keep the lid tightly sealed on every single one.

When AJ walked into the health center, Carrie was waiting for him, along with Adam's friend Renee. AJ almost groaned, but he caught himself at the last minute and remembered his manners. He bit back any commentary and approached Carrie. He handed her the sex position note cards.

"Got any use for this?" he asked.

"Oh, man!" Carrie exclaimed as she flipped through. "This is terrific." She turned it over to the back. "There's a web site, and it looks like they have other decks—kinks and such. I'm going to have a look later."

Relieved at having found something to do with the cards—keeping them would have reminded him of what he wouldn't be getting to try out with Adam—AJ put the rest of his things down and hung his coat on the hook behind the counter.

"So, have our friends the undergrads gotten over their breakup snit yet?"

Carrie snickered. "No idea. They're not in yet." She set a stack of papers on the counter. "These are for the health fair. We need to copy and collate them to hand out at the door."

Looking at the elegant design and layout of the pages caused AJ a deep sense of disappointment. It wasn't Carrie who should be looking over the final copy with him. "Okay. After that, we can start boxing supplies we'll need."

"You two sound like you've got it all under control," Renee put in. "Before you get started, AJ, can I talk to you?" She nodded at Carrie. "In private?"

AJ didn't bother concealing his sigh this time. "All right. Carrie, can you give us a sec? I'll be right in to help you."

Carrie nodded and disappeared into the conference room, and AJ wondered how much Renee had talked to her before he arrived. As soon as she had left, AJ turned to Renee. He backed up a little, still put off by her perfume. He breathed slowly until he could tolerate it. She didn't appear to have noticed anything. Reaching for a package on the desk, she grabbed it and held it out to AJ.

"From Adam," she said. "I don't usually like to get in the middle of things. In fact, I told him that exact thing this morning, but I was headed here anyway. You two are adults, and you need to handle it like adults."

"I am," AJ informed her. "Part of being an adult is getting to decide who I have in my life. I don't need cheating boyfriends."

"I know," she said. "But you're missing about six key details there. I'm only telling you this because you won't talk to him. He thought you were the one cheating on him. And that's everything I'm going to tell you because, like I said, it's not my place. It's up to you whether you want to listen to him or accept his attempts at apology."

"I'm not sure I can." He frowned, not sure whether the revelation of Adam's motives made him more angry or less. It explained things, but he was tired of the same song on repeat with everyone he dated. Was there something about him specifically that screamed *cheater*? He wasn't sure whether it said more about him or the people he went out with.

"That's fair," Renee said. She studied him. "Please believe me when I say you two are peas in a pod, in a way. He's not angry at you for wanting nothing to do with him—he's angry with himself for ruining what he thought was the best thing to happen for him in a long time. Maybe...maybe think about it a little and talk to him so if you do end it permanently, at least you both walk away with dignity." She put her hand on AJ's arm, and he flinched. Surprise registered on her face, and she backed off. "I think you both deserve better closure than you've gotten."

AJ watched her turn around and walk out before he looked at the package in his hand. It was a series of boxes, each one labeled with a different one of the five senses, stacked and tied with a ribbon. Intrigued, AJ untied the ribbon. Before he opened the first box, Carrie walked back out of the conference room. Her eyebrows went up.

"From Adam?" she asked.

"Yeah." AJ was too hot all of a sudden, and he removed his hands from the boxes. "I don't know what's in them."

"Are you going to open them?"

"Not here," he said.

"Aw, come on. It's kind of cute that he's begging you."

"Or it's creepy and intrusive."

Carrie sighed. "I'll give you a few minutes to look while I count pamphlets for the health fair. After that, I expect you in there to help me." She turned around and stalked into the back.

AJ stared at the boxes for another minute or so and then opened the top one, labeled *Annusare*. To smell. AJ frowned, not quite understanding. A little bar of soap the same brand as the massage oil he'd used lay inside the tissue paper underneath a note which read, *I've fouled things up, and I'd like to come clean.* AJ lifted it to his nose, inhaling the fragrance.

The second box was labeled *Ascoltare*, to hear. Adam had printed the link to a playlist from a web site. At the bottom of the note, he'd written, *I know you don't want to listen to me, and I don't blame you, so maybe you'll give this a chance instead.*

The third box, labeled *Assagiare*, to taste, contained several anise hard candies. The note on top read, *That little bakery where you bought the tiramisu also sells Italian candy. You have quite the mouth on you, so I thought you'd like to put it to another use.* AJ's cheeks flamed thinking about all the things Adam knew about his mouth and what it could do—and all the things he knew in return.

When AJ opened the fourth box, *Toccare*—to touch—he wasn't surprised to see more of the massage oil. What did surprise him was what Adam's note said. *I don't expect you to save this for me. Enjoy it in your own time with whoever you like.*

Finally, he was down to the last box—*Vedere*, to see. Slowly, AJ removed the lid and peered inside. He had to fan himself with the note before he could read it. With shaking fingers, he withdrew the tiny scrap—that was the only word for it—of material. The note was longer this time, and AJ stood there reading it over and over. *I can't even tell you how sorry I am. It took everything in me to buy this for you, knowing I'd probably never see you in it. It hurts to think someday, you'll wear it for someone else and maybe won't even give me a second thought. In the end, though, I did it because it represents everything wrong with what I did. So wear your bisexual flag with pride, and know you mean a lot to me even if our time together was short.*

AJ packed everything back into the boxes and retied the ribbon. He drew his wrist across his eyes and composed himself just as the undergraduate employees walked in. They were holding hands again, and AJ restrained himself from rolling his eyes. One of them pointed at the boxes and snickered. AJ glared, and both students clammed up and went straight to work. AJ picked the boxes up and toted them into the other room.

"Hey," he said, hoping his voice didn't sound as shaky to Carrie as it did to his own ears.

Carrie looked up and smiled. "Good timing," she said. "I could use a hand."

"Sure." He set the boxes on the counter by the sink and sat down across from her. "We'll just have to periodically go monitor the freshmen. They're back to being a couple."

"Fun, fun," Carrie replied. She shoved two stacks of papers across the table. "Here. We need to make packets of these."

AJ glanced one last time at the stack of boxes he'd set aside then put all thoughts of Adam out of his mind and concentrated on collating information packets. He could decide later how and when he wanted to address the gifts.

Chapter Seventeen

Adam was up with the sun on the morning of the health fair. He'd ordered something for AJ from a specialty shop in the village, and he'd picked it up the night before. It sat in his living room, waiting for Adam to cart it over to the East Gymnasium. He'd debated whether or not he should wait for AJ and hand deliver it but decided against doing so. The two of them wouldn't be making use of it, and it had been painful enough buying him the thong to wear for a future lover. Instead, Adam would take it to the health center's table to make an attractive and fun centerpiece students could help themselves to. He reasoned it might suit AJ better to share it anyway.

He showered and dressed quickly then picked up the large basket. It had been expensive, but he thought it was fitting, given how he and AJ had met. The basket contained two dozen condom roses, twenty condom lollipops—each with a different cartoon character sticker—and an assortment of loose condoms in different colors and varieties. The rest of the basket was filled with bulk hard candy and gum. Adam had specially ordered it, and it was a thing of beauty. If nothing else, the students who wandered by the table would likely be talking about it for months afterward.

After peering into the large paper bag containing the basket and reassuring himself it was all still intact and ready to go, Adam picked it up and set off for the East Gymnasium. His palms were sweaty, slipping on the steering wheel so he had to keep wiping them on his jeans. He almost couldn't process the thought of seeing AJ face to face again. It was a big risk; AJ might talk to him, or he might not. Renee had said she asked AJ to consider it, but she hadn't given any indication of which way AJ might be leaning on the matter.

When Adam pulled up in the parking lot, he frowned. There was a crowd gathered outside the building, waiting to go in. Apparently, the advertising put out by his department had done its job, though this was considerably more than he'd expected to be there before the doors even opened to the student body, especially on such a chilly morning. He climbed out of his car and grabbed the bag from the back seat then made his way to the door.

His confusion increased when he saw the signs. He couldn't fathom why anyone was staging a protest against the health fair, unless it was one of the campus religious groups. They sometimes showed up to LGBTQ events and picketed. He supposed it was possible they had issues with some of the health center's content, but he hadn't known there were so many of them. After a closer look, Adam was even more surprised. There were a few religious types, but the rest all seemed to be from the campus LGBTQ group. Adam scanned the crowd and finally spotted a familiar face. He excused himself and wiggled through the mass of people.

"Hey, Lauryn!" he called.

She looked up, saw him, and came over. "Adam," she acknowledged him.

"What's going on?" he asked.

"We're protesting this event," she said.

"Yeah, I see that. Why?"

Lauryn took a moment before responding. "The health center isn't always good about meeting our needs, and neither are other people on campus who should be keeping us safe." She put up a hand at Adam's attempted interruption. "I know AJ is doing the best he can. This isn't about him. When he's not there anymore, they will go right back to thinking they can ignore us because we're a small group. It's a lot more effective to protest at an event like this than to keep pushing over and over for what we will never get."

"Are they even going to let me inside?" he asked, glancing back at the group.

"Of course. This is a peaceful demonstration, not a riot." Lauryn handed him a flyer.

He looked down at it then up at Lauryn again. "I understand," he told her.

Lauryn put her hand on his arm. "AJ didn't," she said. "I think he's angry with me."

"That makes two of us," Adam said. "Only what I did was my own fault."

Lauryn nodded. "Come talk to me later if you want to," she said.

Adam acknowledged her and turned away again. He made his way between the protesters until he reached the building and entered. Inside the gym, all the tables were set up in exactly the fashion he and AJ had discussed. The committees had done a fantastic job, and everything looked good. Students and a few faculty members were putting the finishing touches on a few of the booths, and the music department representatives were tuning their instruments for the demonstration. Adam bypassed all of them and headed straight for the health center's booth.

AJ was in the midst of setting out multicolored information packets. He turned when Adam cleared his throat. Their eyes met, and for a moment, Adam was sure AJ would say something. He didn't, though, going right back to his task. Adam deflated a little.

"I brought you something," he said. He pulled the basket out of the paper bag and set it on the table. "Party favors."

The papers in AJ's hand rustled as he set them down. He reached out and ran his finger over one of the condom roses, and a hint of a smile played on his lips. It faded though, and his eyes were dark and sad when he turned around again.

"Later," he said. "We'll talk later. Okay?" He put out his hand, hesitated, then rested it on Adam's forearm briefly before turning around again.

It was the best Adam could have hoped for. He tried not to take it personally; it was a busy day for AJ. At least they were able to exchange a few words, and that would have to be enough until the event was over and they could sit down to talk things through properly. Adam nodded in agreement and went to see where he could help out. When he was far enough away from AJ's table, he took a deep breath and let it out slowly. It was going to be one hell of a day.

By noon, it was clear the fair was a success. It was open to all students and their guests, so a number of community members had also been in and out. The protest outside had thus far been as peaceful as Lauryn promised, with several attendees stopping to ask questions. Adam was pleased to see students enjoying the condom basket he'd left at the health center table, even if it did give him a slight pang over not being able to share the humor with AJ.

Over the course of the morning, Adam had gone from station to station, pitching in as needed. He'd also listened to the music department's demonstration and caught a few minutes of several different panel discussions in the surrounding classrooms. Currently, he was stationed at the Nursing booth where he'd been enlisted to hand out nutrition information while the undergraduates did blood pressure screenings and the graduate students assisted the nurse practitioner in administering flu shots.

The crowds thinned somewhat during the lunch hour, so Adam contemplated telling Connor he was going to take a break as well. He stretched, and he happened to look over at the health center table. AJ was talking to Luke, and the two of them were laughing about something. Adam turned away, about to say something to Connor regarding food in order to take his mind off the ache in his chest.

Before he opened his mouth, Connor came up beside him. "Want to go eat?" he asked.

"Are you asking me on a date?" Adam teased.

Connor rolled his eyes. "You are so full of it. Come on, let's go." He shoved Adam playfully.

They grabbed their jackets, stepped out from behind the table, and started toward the door, still jostling each other and talking about the morning's activities. Connor spotted Luke, and he paused.

"Go ahead and ask," Adam said. He figured AJ might avoid them, but he understood why Connor would want Luke there.

Connor nodded, and they changed direction, heading for AJ's booth. They made it halfway when Lauryn rushed past, headed in the same direction. Surprised, Adam stopped and turned toward them. He couldn't hear what she said, but a moment later, she had a frowning AJ in tow, pulling on his coat as they headed on their way outside. AJ called to the others to stay behind. Puzzled and curious, Adam started walking after them, wondering what had AJ so upset.

"Hey, wait," Connor said. "AJ said to stay here. Let him handle it."

"Nah, you catch up," Adam told him. "I'm gonna find out what's going on."

Connor drew his brows together, but he turned back to Luke and motioned to him to follow as well. They moved more quickly to the door, where Adam peered through the glass, confused by what he saw. Stepping outside, he blinked in the sun but quickly directed his attention to AJ. He was at the front of the group of student protesters, facing the religious crowd. That side seemed to have grown exponentially since early in the morning. On closer inspection, Adam saw it was a combination of several groups—in addition to the morality police, there were a bunch of guys from at least one of the college fraternities and an assortment of other people who were either bandwagoning for fun or who actually agreed with the other groups.

AJ was mid-argument with a couple of the frat boys. "Both groups were doing fine before you all showed up," he spat.

"We're just helping out," one of the guys in front answered. "This side looked lonely against all the queers."

Adam was surprised at how calm AJ remained when he said, "You're free to come or go as you like, but you're in the way of people who want to get into the building. None of the others are harassing anyone, but you're out here making a scene and grabbing people as they go by. Find something better to do."

"Why would you care?" another one of the guys spat. "Are you one of them?" He nodded at Lauryn and the others behind AJ.

"Does it matter?" AJ asked.

"Of course it does," the guy answered, and three people behind him fake-coughed a few slurs at AJ.

Adam went to step up next to AJ, but before he could, someone emerged from behind the line of frat boys and grabbed one of the signs Lauryn's group had. Two others turned around and did the same thing to the religious students, calling them freaks. Adam couldn't tell whether they'd been planted there or if they were simply opportunists looking to get the crowd worked up even further.

It turned into a blur of shouting and people shoving each other, escalating quickly from where it had started. Adam lost track of AJ when too many people shoved in between them. He caught sight of Connor through the glass entry doors, on his phone, and Adam hoped he was calling security. He searched frantically for AJ, trying to make his way around the outside of the crowd without getting dragged into the fight.

He made it all the way to the edge so he could hold off or escort anyone trying to get through, but he stopped short at the sight of a stocky, muscular man bearing an angry expression. The man caught hold of him and held on despite Adam's wriggling to free himself.

"I'm looking for someone," the man snarled.

"Okay," Adam said, trying to stay calm. "I'll do my best. Who do you need?"

"My fucking boyfriend, for starters."

Adam wanted to bark at him how that wasn't helpful, but he didn't want this guy to snap him in two. Campus security was on the way to break up the burgeoning riot, so they'd deal with the intruder as well.

He said, "Can you describe him?"

The man grunted, but he didn't answer right away. His eyes flicked to a point somewhere behind Adam, and he let go his grasp on Adam's shoulder. Adam rubbed the spot and turned to follow the man's gaze. He spotted AJ, whose eyes were wide and mouth open. AJ wormed his way closer.

"What are you doing here?" he asked.

"I know you know where he is, you asshole!" the man shouted at AJ.

"We should talk about this somewhere else." AJ's posture was open, and his voice remained calm. Adam heard a slight tremor in it.

"No!" the man insisted. "You can't keep me from him. I have a right to see him!"

"And he has the right to decide whether he wants to see you."

"This is all your fault!"

The man advanced, forcing AJ backward. They drifted around behind the crowd of protesters, closer to the building. Whoever the guy was, he had it in for AJ and the alleged boyfriend he was looking for. The light bulb went on, and Adam searched behind him for Connor and Luke, hoping they were still inside the building. While Adam's brain raced to catch up to what was happening, the man lunged at AJ, hauling off and punching him. AJ reeled back, and the man came at him again. Several of the protesters surrounded him.

Adam sprang into action, racing up to grab the man from behind. The man roared and tried to get Adam off him. Adam clung on, hoping to hold him off until someone else gave them a hand, but the man was far stronger. He reached around and grabbed at Adam, pulling until he had hold of him then flinging him into the building. Adam's head snapped back, cracking against the bricks. His ears rang, and his vision blurred. While he tried to clear his head, the door opened and Adam was vaguely aware of Connor and Luke stepping out. Through a haze, Adam saw Luke's face twist in fear, his fair skin turning even paler. He shrank back against the doors.

"Luke?" the man said. "They wouldn't let me see you."

For a moment, Luke stood there, his arms around himself. "I don't want to talk to you." He jutted his chin out, but he was trembling.

The other man made to stalk toward Luke, but AJ broke free from the protesters and stood in front of him. The man growled and lurched forward again, and Adam regained enough awareness to do something. He rolled closer and reached out, catching the man's leg and yanking as hard as he could. The man went down, and Adam pushed himself up to get closer to AJ and Luke. His head throbbed, and he reached up to feel it, his hand coming away bloody.

Without any other warning, right from his position on his stomach, the man reached underneath himself and pulled out a folding knife, flicking the blade out. Several people screamed. He rose up on his knees and crawled toward AJ.

"Move the fuck out of my way," the man said.

With the last ounce of willpower against his raging headache and muddled thoughts, Adam hauled himself up and leapt at AJ, knocking him over and landing on top of him just as the other man lurched forward with the knife. A burst of hot pain rocked Adam, burning through his leg and spreading out in sharp contrast to the cold air around him. As if in a dream, he felt several more searing slashes followed by the sounds of someone yelling, a siren, and several heavy thuds. Those were the last things he remembered as a fresh wave of dizziness descended on him. He vaguely registered throwing up and hoping he hadn't hit AJ before darkness closed in.

The harsh lights made Adam blink several times. He groaned and tried to shift, but he couldn't move properly. It took a few minutes for him to remember why, but when he did, he gasped and tried to sit up. Pain radiated from his head and down his neck and up from his leg, and he flopped back against the pillow behind him.

"Hey," a quiet voice said by his ear.

This time, instead of trying to move, Adam turned his head. A flood of emotions rushed at him, and he almost tried to get up again. "AJ!" The exertion made his head pound, and he gasped against a wave of low-level nausea. He moaned and pressed back against the pillows.

AJ smiled. "I'm here."

Adam swallowed thickly several times to clear the pasty feeling in his mouth. "You're okay," he managed to say.

"I'm fine, and so is everyone else, except for Greg."

Adam frowned. "Who the hell is Greg?"

"Luke's ex-boyfriend. He's the one who stabbed you." AJ paused. "He freaked when he saw he'd done it, and he took off. Last I knew, he'd crashed his car trying to get away from the police."

"Yeah, I had to give a statement, but they didn't tell me what happened to him. Why was he after you?" Adam asked.

"He wasn't until I wouldn't let him get to Luke."

Adam vaguely remembered that part. "Is Luke okay?" It felt strange to be asking after someone he'd been so needlessly jealous of.

"I don't know," AJ replied. He closed his eyes briefly. "He's upset. He thinks the whole thing is his fault."

Adam didn't know how to explain that he felt the same way. Would anything have been different if he hadn't made so many assumptions? He realized it was an unreasonable train of thought, and he derailed it at the station before he said something ridiculous.

Instead, he told AJ, "It's not Luke's fault at all."

"You and I and everyone else knows that. It's going to take time to convince Luke."

There was a knock on the door, and they both looked up in time to hear Luke say, "Convince me of what?"

"That it's not your fault," Adam said.

Connor peered over Luke's shoulder. "Good luck," he said to Adam. "He won't believe the rest of us."

Luke came to stand by the bed. "I'm sorry," he whispered.

Adam patted the bed next to him, and Luke sat down. When he was close enough, Adam put out his arms. "Okay?" he asked.

Luke nodded, and Adam pulled him down and held him for a long time. Luke sniffled into his chest. It was awkward, but Adam didn't make a move to push him away. He understood now, and he wanted AJ to know he was all right with everything. Eventually, Luke sat up and rubbed his nose. Adam handed him a tissue from the over-bed table.

"Not your fault," he said, looking Luke in the eye.

"Are—are you gonna be okay?" Luke asked.

Everything was still a little jumbled from the concussion, but Adam mostly had a grasp on it. "Yeah. I'll be sore for a while, but they said they were able to repair most of it with the surgery. Crutches for a few weeks, physiotherapy for a few months. Lots of scars." He shrugged one shoulder as best he could. "Might not ever be quite the same, but it won't ruin my life."

"Okay." Luke nodded. His cheeks reddened again. "I finally filed a restraining order, you know."

Adam gave him a lopsided smile. "Good."

"That's what we all said," AJ agreed. "Adam, you could probably file a civil suit, especially because of all the medical bills and the possibility of permanent damage."

"I don't know." Adam frowned. "I don't think I could afford a lawyer."

"You might not have to. My mom's a lawyer," AJ informed him. "She has connections in a lot of places because of her charity work."

"Yeah? Huh. I'll consider it."

The rest of the morning was a blur of people rotating through Adam's room to visit him. He was tired and sore but touched by the cards and gifts. Through it all, AJ stayed right next to him, and that might have been the best gift of all. Adam drew on his quiet strength as he told his version of events to everyone who hadn't been there. At last they filtered out again, and Adam was alone with AJ.

"You literally took a hit for me," AJ said. "You really are unbelievable."

Adam managed a weak grin. "Does this mean I'm forgiven?"

AJ didn't speak for a moment, and as the silence stretched, Adam felt like a rock had dropped into his stomach. He closed his eyes and swallowed heavily. Of course AJ wasn't ready to pick up where they'd left off before he'd been so foolish. The sound of AJ clearing his throat caused Adam to open his eyes again.

"We still need to talk like I promised you," AJ said.

"Okay." It was all Adam could expect for the time being.

"So, what are you going to do when they let you out? Are you going back home?" AJ asked.

Adam looked away. "I don't know what I'll do. I'm not going back home, though." He grimaced as he shifted a little, both from the pain and the reason he wasn't clear on his next steps. "It was a huge fight with my parents. They left this morning because I told them I wasn't going with them."

"What? Why not?"

"Because they're treating me like a baby, and they want me to quit school. I'm old enough to make my own decisions, and I want to handle this on my own terms instead of theirs." He shook his head. "I think they're part of the problem, even though they don't mean to be. I guess it was time I told them I'm ready to grow the fuck up." Adam snorted, but he smiled a little, and AJ squeezed his hand.

"You can't stay alone when they let you out of here," AJ said. He chewed his lip and looked like he was thinking hard about what he wanted to say next. "You could stay with me."

"I don't want you to baby me either." Adam shook his head.

"That's not what I'd be doing," AJ argued. "I'm not going to keep you from making your own choices. I'm here to help you while you recover."

"If that's what you want," Adam said. He looked away again. "You let your friends in, but you never let me go to your apartment." It meant something, and Adam focused on what he could see out the hospital window. He returned his attention to AJ. "Is that what we are? Friends?"

AJ squeezed his hand again. "I'm not ready to make a final decision on it yet. Let's see how it goes, okay?"

There weren't a whole lot of available options, so Adam answered, "Okay. Are you sure about this?"

"I'm not too sure about anything right now." AJ ran his hand through Adam's hair. "Get some rest, and as soon as they discharge you, we'll get you settled."

Adam nestled down in the bed and closed his eyes. Vaguely, he was aware of the brush of AJ's lips on his forehead and his retreating footsteps before he drifted into a dreamless slumber.

After five days, Adam was cleared to go home with bandages, crutches, and a brace to stabilize his leg. AJ brought him to his apartment, and once they were inside the entryway, Adam looked up at the long flight of stairs with a resigned sigh. All the accessible apartments were on the first floor, with a separate entrance at the rear of the building. Theoretically, Adam wouldn't have needed one before. He knew he probably qualified now, and would for some time, but he hadn't had time to figure it out and speak with anyone from student housing. Wishing he had, he turned to AJ.

"I—" he began.

"I've got you," AJ said.

He wrapped his arm around Adam's waist, bracing himself between Adam and the wall. Together, they navigated the steps until they reached AJ's floor. AJ let go, and Adam used his crutches down the hall to AJ's apartment.

Inside, AJ flipped on the lights and helped Adam maneuver to his couch. He disappeared back down the stairs to retrieve Adam's bag, leaving Adam to sit looking around the apartment. What he saw took his breath away.

AJ was mostly tidy; there were a few things out here and there and some dishes in the sink, but either he'd cleaned up for Adam's sake or he was naturally organized. Adam was betting it was the latter. Like Adam's apartment, there were a few pieces of college-issue furniture—a desk and chair, a kitchen table, and a two-seat couch. There was probably a bed in the other room, and Adam wondered if AJ had replaced it with his own like Adam had done.

In addition to the provided furniture, AJ had added a few things such as another chair and a longer couch in the living room. The standard-issue desk chair sat in a corner by a bookshelf, and AJ had put a swivel chair at the desk. He had a coffee table with a few books. Adam glanced at them briefly, not terribly surprised to see mostly titles related to AJ's personal interests and activism. He was curious about the art history text, but he was distracted by something else.

The entire apartment was filled with artwork. There were paintings on the walls and ceramics and sculptures on the shelves. All of it was stunning, and clearly none of the paintings were prints—they were all originals. Adam wondered where AJ had acquired them and how much they had cost. Was this what he hadn't wanted Adam to see? Adam couldn't understand why, whether it was because AJ didn't want him to know he had money or because AJ was afraid Adam would think he was a snob for his choice in decor.

Before he had a chance to sort through it, the door opened and AJ walked in. He stepped into the living room with Adam's bag in hand. Adam peered up at him, trying to work out how to ask AJ about what was puzzling him.

"What?" AJ asked, frowning.

Clearly something of Adam's confusion showed on his face. "Surprised at how you've decorated, that's all. Where did you get your artwork?"

AJ dropped the bag, and it landed with a thud on the floor. He stood there, clenching and releasing his hands. At last he said quietly, "It's mine."

"Yeah, I didn't think you stole it. I meant—"

"No," AJ said. "It's mine as in I painted it."

"Wow," was all Adam could think to say. His eyes drifted to an abstract painting of what might have been a dragon hanging directly above the computer desk. "It's amazing. I had no idea you were an artist."

"You wouldn't have, no," AJ agreed. "I don't paint anymore."

"Why the hell not?" Adam wanted to know. "These are stunning."

"Because that was part of my life before." AJ shrugged.

It may have been true, for all Adam knew, but if it were only in the past, why had he kept them on the walls? Adam wanted to pry, but he was too tired to figure out which questions to ask to get AJ talking about his artwork. As if to prove it, he yawned.

AJ laughed softly, and the tension was broken. "Let's get you to bed."

He helped Adam off the couch and down the hall to his bedroom. Adam only had presence of mind to notice AJ had indeed replaced the uncomfortable college bed with his own, which was big enough for them to share. He almost invited AJ to stay, but by the time he was stretched out on the mattress, he could hardly keep his eyes open. Further thoughts and questions would have to wait for another day.

CHAPTER EIGHTEEN

AJ SHARED his apartment with Adam for the rest of his initial recovery. They didn't talk again about AJ's artwork or why he'd stopped doing it, a fact for which AJ was grateful. The pain meds made Adam too sleepy for much of any kind of coherent conversation, and the concussion had made him slightly fuzzy. AJ had only asked once about whether Adam needed any class assignments brought to him, and all Adam had said was that Dr. Weinstock considered getting stabbed to be an adequate excuse for missing work and class. Anything he couldn't finish before the end of the semester could wait until break.

He'd tapered his meds and now only rarely needed anything, though AJ suspected it was mostly a matter of refusing to use them rather than truly not being in pain. He claimed he wanted to be clear-headed while he worked on his end-of-semester projects and the tasks he could do from the apartment for Dr. Weinstock. He'd emailed for class notes and guidelines for the papers he had to write, spending his time on them while AJ was at work or class.

Nights were bad, though, and not only because of the pain. More than once, AJ had helped Adam settle down after waking in a cold sweat, shaking all over. The previous night had been one such, and AJ had almost stayed, even after Adam had gone back to sleep. He hadn't been able to quiet his brain, so he'd gone back to the other room and gone online to take care of some of his other projects. He'd fallen asleep at his desk.

When AJ woke, the apartment was still dark and quiet. He stretched, stiff-necked and aching all over from the awkward position and with his bladder screaming at him that he needed to pee. On his way to the bathroom, he peeked into his bedroom to see Adam's lithe frame stretched out, the covers pushed down to his waist and one foot sticking out. One arm was raised above his head, bent at the elbow, and the other rested at his side. His chest rose and fell rhythmically. AJ wished he could stand there staring until Adam woke; he was beautiful in his sleep.

Instead, he pulled the door shut and crossed the hall to the bathroom. After he'd peed and washed his face, he returned to the other room to fix a cup of coffee and check his messages. He was excited to see someone had found temporary housing for Luke with a family who would charge him a minimal amount of rent in exchange for helping around the house. Luke wouldn't be able to recover his financial losses yet, but at least he didn't have to worry about saving up again for security deposit and first month's rent. A fundraiser AJ had started for him and shared with his multiple online groups had generated enough to cover his textbooks for his first semester of school. It didn't solve everything, but it was a good first step.

AJ was halfway through the long list of replies he needed to send when he heard the bedroom door open. He rolled his eyes when Adam didn't bother shutting the bathroom door, clearly not the slightest bit self-conscious about the sound of his morning piss echoing through the tiny apartment. Recalling the number of times AJ had helped him in the bathroom for the first few days after the hospital, he realized there was no real reason to make it a secret act.

The water ran, and after a few minutes, AJ heard Adam brushing his teeth. He returned to his messages, losing track for a few minutes. The sound of an impressive fart brought him out of his musing, and he stifled a laugh. When Adam emerged, AJ was torn between pretending he knew nothing and getting it out of the way. Before he could decide, he was distracted by a new message. Hastily, he typed a reply. When he looked up again, Adam was right behind him.

"Come back to bed with me," Adam said.

"I was going to stay up," AJ said. "It's almost morning."

"Please?" Adam asked. "I'd like the company."

"Another nightmare?" AJ asked, keeping his voice low.

"No, but I'd rather not be alone."

AJ nodded and rose from his chair. He didn't need to sleep; he could stay with Adam and keep him company until he was able to rest again. He followed Adam to the bedroom, watching him limp down the hall. Adam no longer needed the crutches for short distances, but it would be a long time before he was back to his full strength. If ever.

Adam lay down on the bed on his good side, facing the wall, and AJ curled up behind him. It might not have been his best idea; they still hadn't talked about anything that had happened between Adam's trip and the health fair. But he felt Adam's whole body relax, and his own tension drained away. AJ couldn't help sliding into the strange space between asleep and awake, where he was vaguely aware of his surroundings but not quite taking them in.

"I'm so sorry," came Adam's muffled voice. "For everything."

AJ opened his eyes, the sleepy haze fading. He let go of Adam and rolled onto his back; a moment later, the sheets rustled, and Adam followed suit. In the semi-dark, AJ felt Adam's fingers slide against his own.

"Talk to me," AJ said. "I want to understand."

"I don't know if what I did counts for real as cheating on you, but you should know I didn't have sex with the guy you saw at Ainsley's house."

AJ frowned. "Not sure I understand. You seemed pretty clear on it."

"No, I let you think that because I was sure you were messing around with Luke behind my back." Adam sighed. "I made everything with him so huge in my head." He shifted and turned his face toward AJ. "I didn't know why someone like you was paying any attention to someone like me. I still don't."

Confused, AJ touched his shoulder. "Why?"

Adam's eyes drifted closed. "That first day we met, I thought you were gorgeous but so far out of my league. I fake it a lot, but you have real confidence. It's sexy as hell, but I don't know if I can keep up."

AJ propped himself up. "Wait...you think you're not good enough for me?"

"Nowhere even close."

The words settled into AJ's brain, and he turned them over. He reflected on all the times he'd refused to explain himself, pushing Adam away while trying to hold onto him. Too afraid to ruin what they had, but even more afraid of being honest. It was his turn to close his eyes.

"Because I made you feel that way."

"No!" Adam exclaimed, startling AJ into opening his eyes again. "No," Adam repeated more quietly. "I only meant I'm not the kind of guy someone like you would go for."

"But you thought someone like Luke was?" AJ held his breath. It was the first time either of them had named the jealousy between them.

"Yeah. He's a lot of things I'm not."

AJ didn't have an adequate reply. "And you're a lot of things he's not," he countered.

He could have listed all the things he liked about Adam, all the reasons he'd taken a chance on him, but he didn't. He knew he might be opening the wound again, but the only way he could think to answer Adam's confession was to take another risk. He turned onto his side again and pushed himself up until he was half hovering over Adam. Leaning down, he paused, hovering inches from Adam's face.

"Is it all right if I kiss you?" he asked.

"Yeah."

He descended, his mouth meeting Adam's. The kiss was gentle and hesitant; AJ didn't want to hurt him. Adam raised his hands to AJ's cheeks, pulling him more firmly into their shared space. They kissed for a long time, unhurried, exploring. AJ was pleasantly turned on, not enough to do anything but enough to feel good.

When he heard Adam's breathing speed up and the air catch, though, a ripple of desire surged through him. He pulled back.

"Are you all right?" he asked.

"Yeah." Adam groaned. "I want to keep going. My God, this feels so good."

AJ agreed, but there was something else he wanted. "Wait here," he said.

Adam's brow creased. "Okay."

He propped himself on his elbows, watching as AJ slid out of bed. AJ turned his back and stepped out of the room. He breathed slowly for a minute, gathering his thoughts, and ducked into the bathroom. He quickly shed his pajamas and underwear, exchanging them for Adam's gift, which he'd hidden in the drawer of the sink's vanity. Despite the fact that it was just the two of them, he felt strange about walking nearly naked back into the bedroom, so he snagged his bathrobe from the back of the door and put it on.

Back in the bedroom, he stood next to the bed. Adam looked up at him, eyebrows raised. AJ slowly untied his robe, and Adam's eyes grew round as he watched. AJ slid the robe off, letting it fall to the floor behind him. The cool air hit his skin, raising goose bumps, but he stood there anyway, waiting for Adam's reaction. When Adam sucked in his breath, AJ wrapped one arm around his own chest and used his free hand to cover his crotch. Embarrassment warred with excitement at Adam's hungry gaze, making AJ hot all over. Sure, Adam had seen him naked before, but AJ hadn't been putting himself on display, wearing something intended to arouse them both.

"Oh, God," Adam whined. "God, please. Let me touch you."

AJ stepped over to the bed and climbed in. Adam shifted and tugged on AJ until he straddled Adam, his legs on either side of Adam's waist and completely avoiding the site of Adam's injury. AJ knelt there, resting his sweaty palms against his thighs. Adam reached up with one finger and touched AJ through the fabric of the thong. When AJ hissed, he did it again, using more pressure.

"That looks so hot on you," Adam said, breathless. "I knew it would." His voice broke, surprising AJ.

"What is it?" AJ asked.

Adam composed himself, pressing his thumb and forefinger to his eyes. He looked up at AJ again and said, "I never thought I'd see you wear it."

AJ leaned down to kiss him, and the shift in position brought his bare ass in contact with Adam's straining erection inside his pajamas, hot and hard beneath the fabric. It sent a thrill up AJ's spine. He ground back against it, the friction on his own cock as he rocked forward bringing him to full arousal. AJ wanted more. Conscious of Adam's leg, he pulled back and looked down at him. When their eyes met, he saw a kaleidoscope of emotions written there—lust, gratitude, worry, and pain. AJ paused to lean down again for a reassuring kiss, then pulled back far enough to run his hands gently over Adam's chest.

"This might not be easy with your injury." He paused, his heart thumping at what he was about to suggest. It had been a long time—not since Garritt—but he was willing. "Do you want to fuck me this time? I can ride you."

Adam inhaled sharply. "Thought you preferred to top."

AJ chuckled, relaxing at Adam's concern for him. "Preference doesn't mean I'll never do anything else," he said. "I've done it before and would do it again, just not often. We're not playing the 'I'll only bottom for Mr. Right' game."

"Yeah," Adam said. "Yeah, I'd like to fuck you."

Unseating himself long enough to retrieve supplies from the bedside table, AJ returned in a moment. He stripped off Adam's pajama pants and then straddled him again, this time facing the other direction, offering himself to Adam. Time seemed to stand still for them as they took everything slowly. AJ remained motionless for a few minutes, looking at Adam's naked lower half. The wounds were no longer covered, but they hadn't yet healed into scars. They were an angry, red reminder of everything Adam had sacrificed to keep AJ safe. AJ's chest tightened, and he held back his sorrow. Would it have made a difference if he'd answered Adam's text asking to talk? He would never know.

AJ ran his hands lightly over Adam's skin, willing the lines to heal. Adam shifted under him, and AJ turned his head. "Okay?"

"Yeah. It...feels nice." Adam closed his eyes and tilted his head back.

AJ leaned forward, placing soft kisses all over Adam's belly and upper thighs, as though he could erase the pain with his lips. He brushed his fingertips over the coarse place where Adam's dark pubic hair had started to grow back in now that he couldn't strip it. Adam groaned when AJ's palm finally made contact with his semi-hard dick. They shifted together, and AJ felt Adam's hands on his ass, exploring every bit as slowly as AJ was. They had to find each other again, something different than they'd had before. Maybe something better.

"Can I suck you?" AJ asked, peering over his shoulder again.

"Yeah. Condom?"

AJ paused. "Do we need one?"

"I've been checked for pretty much everything, and you're the only person I've been with in almost three months."

"Good," AJ murmured. "Same here." He turned his head again.

He lowered his mouth, wanting to taste, to feel Adam swelling and hardening in his mouth. He closed his lips around Adam's cock and closed his eyes. He didn't hurry, drawing it out as much as he could. Adam gasped and squirmed, squeezing AJ's ass cheeks. AJ withdrew and made a production of applying the lube. Behind him, Adam recovered himself enough to gently move the string of the thong aside and work AJ's ass open. He started with his tongue, licking and then pushing it into AJ with little jabs, each one causing AJ to gasp and jerk. At last he slicked his finger and pressed in, waiting until AJ adjusted before adding another and moving them in and out. Everything was slow and sensual, both of them drawing it out until they were ready.

AJ turned around. He held himself open, Adam's hands on his thighs, and sank down at an agonizingly slow pace. It burned despite all their precautions, and he breathed through it. All the sensations were familiar, bringing out some of the memories AJ had tried to bury deeply. He held still, tensing both from the stretch and from the old wounds. But allowing access to his body in multiple ways had been how he'd healed after Michelle, and it was how he wanted to heal with Adam now. At last AJ adjusted, both body and mind, and sank down the rest of the way, settling himself and bending down for a kiss.

"Okay?" Adam asked. His expression was soft, inviting.

"Yeah." And AJ was, or as close as he'd ever been.

He moved, rocking on top of Adam and purposefully clenching around him. Beneath him, he felt the tension in Adam's muscles, fighting the urge to thrust up hard and fast—both for his own sake and for AJ's. His fingers dug into AJ's skin, gripping tightly and urging AJ to ride faster. Adam tipped his head back, squirming and arching up against AJ as he came with a series of desperate grunts.

AJ stilled his motion, enjoying the tremors running through Adam as he descended from his high. Once Adam slumped back against the mattress, AJ slowly pulled off his cock. There was no point in continuing; he'd never been able to come like that. Adam opened his eyes and looked up at AJ.

"You haven't finished yet," he said. "C'mere."

AJ slithered forward until Adam told him to stop, positioned so his still-covered erection was right at Adam's lips. Adam kissed him there, mouthing him through the fabric and making him pant a little. AJ raised his hips and braced a hand on the wall behind the bed. Slowly, Adam peeled the thong down until he'd uncovered AJ's thick, uncut cock. He ran his thumb under the foreskin, causing them both to groan, then toyed with it and slid it back to reveal the slick head. Putting out his tongue, Adam gave an experimental lick.

AJ groaned again as Adam teased, bringing him closer and closer to the limit of what he could bear. When he was sure he couldn't take it anymore, Adam closed his mouth around AJ and began to suck. AJ threw his head back and moved in rhythm with Adam. The pressure building in his balls was intense, almost more than he could stand. He was right on the edge, hovering, not quite there. It would only take one small push...

He needed it—needed to come, to let go in more ways than just orgasm. He reached between his legs with his free hand, touching himself below Adam's lips. There was no way he could take another minute without some relief. At the same time, Adam's hands rose, one to his thigh and one resting on AJ's ass. Adam once again moved the string of the thong aside. He probed with his finger until he found AJ's hole and applied gentle pressure.

That did it. Release hit him all at once, the pleasure of shooting his load and the intensity of his orgasm and the enormity of his emotions. He felt it all the way up from his toes, his hole tingling where it was in contact with Adam's finger and his cock throbbing against Adam's tongue. Everything went blank for a few seconds as he jerked and shook from the force.

The sensation faded, and AJ gasped for air. As soon as Adam withdrew his lips, AJ flopped onto his side, panting. All his joints felt loose, as though every bit of tension in his whole body had been let go at once. As he was beginning to recover, he felt a hand on his arm, rubbing gently, and the warm press of another body against his back. Adam placed soft kisses down his neck, undulating his hips against the swell of AJ's ass. Slowly, AJ opened his eyes and turned to look at Adam.

That one glance undid them both. AJ rolled over and drew Adam in, breathing in the scent of skin and sweat and sex, warm and real. They clung to each other, not exactly crying but shaking and pouring out the things they'd both held inside. Adam made slow circles on AJ's back, and AJ kneaded Adam's neck with his fingertips. Slowly, their breathing returned to normal and they eased up. AJ opened his eyes to look at Adam, running his thumb down Adam's cheek.

"Okay?" Adam asked.

"Yeah. That was...God. I haven't come that way in forever." One last tremor ran through him.

"Good." Adam kissed him.

Adam rolled over onto his good side, curling that leg underneath him and stretching out the injured one. AJ pressed up against him from behind. His body wanted to relax, but his mind was still going at lightning speed. He tried to tell himself it couldn't hurt to sleep a little, that Adam was safe and wouldn't harm him, but it was impossible even after what they'd just done and all the heaviness of the feelings between them. He rubbed Adam's arm gently, kissing his neck and shoulder, until he heard Adam's breathing slow and settle into a rhythm.

Once he was sure Adam was asleep again, he extracted himself and slipped out of bed, creeping from the room and shutting the door behind him.

CHAPTER NINETEEN

ADAM WOKE alone, the bed cold on the side AJ had been lying on after their middle of the night make-up session. He scootched to the edge of the bed and sat up, trying not to strain. Whether it was from the sex or simply one of those days, his leg hurt more than it had in about a week. He stood up slowly, testing his weight before limping out of the bedroom. At least it wasn't so bad he needed to go back to using crutches around the apartment, though it was bad enough he wanted something for the pain. He made his way into the kitchen to grab a glass of water so he could take the meds the doctor had prescribed. AJ was already in there, rummaging around in his cupboards and dragging out pans. When he straightened up to put it on the stove, he partially turned around and his eyes locked with Adam's.

"How are you feeling?" he asked.

Adam suspected there was more behind the words than a query about his physical health, but he only responded regarding the latter. "Sore," he admitted. "You really don't have to do that, you know. I'm better enough now I can get my own breakfast."

AJ shrugged and turned away from him. "I don't mind, and you should be resting."

The cooking was a screen. Adam stepped closer. "You should too."

"I'm fine," AJ snapped, not giving Adam so much as a backwards glance.

"You're not. You can't possibly have gotten good sleep on your couch." Adam crossed his arms.

AJ whirled all the way around. "I didn't–I mean–I–" He closed his eyes and leaned against the counter. "You knew?"

"Yeah, I knew," Adam confirmed. "You got up as soon as you thought I was asleep."

"I didn't want to disturb you. You're still recovering." AJ leaned back and rested his hands on the counter behind him.

Quietly, Adam said, "You weren't worried about that when we were making love last night." His chest tightened at the words. He hadn't said *fucking* or even *having sex*. He needed AJ to know it meant more, especially considering their conversation beforehand.

"Neither were you." AJ's knuckles were white where his grip on the counter tightened.

Adam decided to push him on it. "You never slept in bed with me. Not at my place, where you always left, and not since I came to stay here. You've always had an excuse, too. Even those nights you stayed with me when I was restless, you went back to the couch. The first time, you were up with the sun, and you passed it off as work, and one other time you said you'd been restless too and didn't want to wake me. Did you think I didn't notice all the other times?"

"I hoped." AJ dropped his hands and shrugged. "It doesn't matter either way. I don't sleep well, and I didn't want to keep you up."

Adam stepped closer. "Why?"

"So I don't interrupt your sleep, of course," AJ retorted.

"Not what I meant," Adam said, keeping his voice even. "Why don't you sleep well? Is it something you need to see a doctor for?"

"It's nothing, and a doctor won't help. I've been to one already."

Stopping short, Adam said, "It's not nothing. You spend so much time trying to fix everyone else's problems, but something is going on with you. When do you get to fall apart?" He reached out for AJ.

AJ flinched and jerked away. "I don't," he said, his voice flat. "It's not an option."

Adam inched closer. "Yes, it is." He put his hands on AJ's arms, feeling the tremor as AJ shook. "Talk to me. What the hell happened to you?"

"I told you—"

Leaning in, Adam rested his forehead on AJ's. "You can't deal with it by ignoring it. Whatever it is, we'll figure it out. We've been through worse already, right?" He backed up and searched AJ's face for a clue. "You still don't trust me."

AJ shook his head. "We've already been over that. It's not about what happened between us."

Adam scowled and made an angry sound low in his throat. "This is the same damn thing that caused us problems in the first place. You told me then you couldn't go away for the weekend, and you said whatever it was, you'd shared it with Luke. How can I help you if you won't even talk to me?"

"It's nothing you can help with!" AJ balled his hands into fists. "This is not the time. You're still healing from what Greg did to you. Let me get you breakfast, and you can go lie down." He turned around and opened the fridge, rummaging around.

Hobbling up behind him, Adam put his hand on AJ's shoulder. He pulled AJ gently away from the fridge and shut the door with his free hand. "*Mio tesoro*," he murmured, using AJ's term of endearment. "Tell me."

AJ leaned back against Adam and took several deep, gulping breaths. Slowly, he turned around. "I haven't slept right in more than two and a half years. Not since it happened. I haven't let anyone stay in my bed either, but I thought if I could trust you, it would go away. I would be able to lie next to you and not freak out. But I couldn't."

"You always have so many things going on in your head," Adam said. "You're starting at the end, not the beginning. Was it something with that asshole Greg? He's terrifying." Adam shuddered, his mind going to all the unpleasant dreams he'd had since Greg stabbed him.

"No." AJ's voice was barely audible. "It was my ex-girlfriend."

Adam nodded. He understood painful break-ups. "Okay," he replied then frowned. This was more than a heartbreak. "Go on. What happened with her?"

AJ sighed and crossed his arms and kept his eyes downcast. For a moment, he was silent, and Adam wasn't sure if he was going to answer the question. Eventually, AJ looked back up at Adam. "I lied to you," he said, his voice strained.

"Yeah, we both kind of managed that one. What did you lie about?"

"When we were talking about our courses of study. I was telling you the truth when I said my undergraduate degree is in Social Work, and I minored in Health Sci, but my other minor wasn't psychology." He cleared his throat. "It was art, and I never finished. I took incompletes for a semester and dropped all my art classes my senior year. That's why I don't do it anymore."

"I don't understand," Adam admitted. "Why?"

AJ twisted his lip with his fingers. "I wanted to help people. The plan was always to work with my dad at the shelter, and there were ways I could have done that. I'd been counting on going for my MSW and keeping up with my artwork, too. After Michelle, I couldn't do it. She was in half my classes. I decided I'd rather shuffle papers."

He stepped away from Adam and sat down at the table. He waited for Adam to join him then said, "We'd been going out for a while. At first, it was good, but it got to a point where it wasn't working." He folded his hands in front of him, taking a long time before continuing. "My friends didn't like her—she could be vicious, and I know they thought she was bordering on abusive." AJ looked up, and there was determination in his eyes. "This all started right after I told her I was bi and we had a big fight over whether I was going to cheat on her. She apologized and said she was worried I might be gay because we'd only had sex a few times before then and I was so reserved about it." AJ smiled, but it was sad, and he shrugged. "I used to be such a hopeless romantic. I always wanted sex to be special. I was raised Catholic but in a rebellious church that was dismissed for serving the Holy Eucharist to non-Catholics, among other things. I was welcome there, as were many other LGBT people. I never thought I had to be married to make love, but I did want every time to mean something. At least, I did before Michelle."

It explained a lot about AJ's odd vacillation between friends with benefits and holding off on sex. Adam nodded. "Go on," he encouraged.

"One night, we were at a party, celebrating the end of midterms. I was drunk—not my usual thing. I'd been buzzed before, but this was different. I'd lost track of how much I had, I think. Michelle let me crash in her room." He swallowed. "It's possible she was the one who kept giving me drinks, but I can't remember. I thought I'd fallen asleep on her beanbag chair. I don't remember how I got in her bed or how I ended up with most of my clothes gone. When I woke up, she was—" He choked then breathed steadily. "She was on top of me, and her roommate was watching us and masturbating."

Adam reached out and rubbed AJ's forearm gently. "What happened after you woke up?"

"It was a blur. I remember shoving her off me and asking her what she was doing. She was so pissed at me because I wasn't even remotely hard, and she took it as proof she was right and I was really just gay." AJ ran a hand through his hair. Softly, he said, "She told me it was over and that she'd never loved me anyway."

"Holy hell." Adam's fingers tightened involuntarily on AJ's arm, and AJ withdrew it.

"The worst part wasn't having her wake me up like that. It was the way she lied and distorted everything. The way the whole thing was staged to humiliate me, to make me feel small and worthless." He closed his eyes. "It worked. I doubted myself, blamed myself, wished I'd broken it off sooner. I hated her, but I hated myself more."

"What she did to you," Adam started. "You know it was—"

"Yes," AJ agreed, looking at Adam again. He wasn't crying, but his eyes were red. "I know. She assaulted me."

That hadn't been the direction Adam was about to go. "No, I was going to say it wasn't your fault."

"In my head, I know that. I tell other people all the time. But—"

"But what? A woman can't really do it to a man? You'd had sex before, so she thought she had permission to assault you in your sleep? You were drunk, so it doesn't count? You were in your underwear, so you were asking for it?" Adam's hands trembled with rage, not at AJ but at the woman who had done this to him. "Would you tell any woman who came into the health center that it was her fault for any of those reasons?"

"No." AJ frowned. "Of course not. Look, I do know about those things, but how I felt wasn't about any of them. One of the online groups I manage is for survivors whose assailants have been women. I was ashamed for continuing to trust her when I knew she was disgusted by who I am. If I'd been strong enough to leave her, she never would have had the chance."

"Did someone say that to you?"

"No," AJ repeated. "I didn't tell anyone."

"Why the fuck not?" Adam demanded. He felt like he was stuck in a loop of déjà vu, everything eerily similar to when he'd asked Connor why Luke didn't leave Greg.

The resemblance wasn't lost on AJ. "For a lot of the same reasons it took Luke so long to leave Greg—fear. She said if I tried, she would claim I had gotten her drunk and raped her, and everyone would believe her because that's how it works. Everyone had seen us together and knew we were both hammered. Her roommate was a witness, even though she sort of participated. Michelle said no one would believe she could do those things to me in my sleep. On top of that, she did this because I'm queer, and she would have made that a factor in her continued attack on me."

"No one at the college knows?" Adam asked.

AJ shook his head. "I thought they would either brush it off or demand I go to the sexual harassment and assault office."

"You should have," Adam said. "What she did was a crime."

"You don't get it," AJ said. "I don't remember anything else from that night. I was too wasted. It would have been her word against mine, and I couldn't take that chance." He sighed. "I kept it to myself, maybe for the wrong reasons. I'd worked hard to be able to go to college, and I didn't want my education or my future career ruined."

"You never even explained this to your friends?" Adam

frowned. AJ had seemed so close with all of them, and Connor had hinted at knowing something happened.

AJ slid down in his seat. "I told Luke, yeah, after Greg started in on him, but no one else. I didn't talk to Connor because he doesn't get what I see in women. He's not awful, but he can be weird about it. He'd have taken it as proof I should get over my denial or whatever. I let Donny and Piet think it was a bad break-up." AJ snorted. "I guess it was, really."

Adam shook his head. "You didn't give them enough credit. Connor knows there was more to it than you let on, and he said you're always assuming things about them."

"How would you know?"

"I talked to Connor when I was trying to make it right with you and you wouldn't respond to me." Adam reached out and took AJ's hand. "They all care about you, and they get it a lot better than you think they do."

"Maybe," AJ agreed. "I lost a lot of trust in everything that night."

"So, what did you do?" Adam asked, hoping there was a light for AJ at the end of this tunnel.

"When we were home for the summer, Piet asked his brother, Garritt, to set me up with people he knew so I would forget about her." AJ wrapped his arms around his waist and hunched up in his chair. "I wasn't lying when I said I'd had a couple threesomes. I already told you about Charlie and Neil, but the first one was with Garritt and his wife. When we got together to talk so he could set me up, he confessed they both found me attractive and asked if I was interested. Garritt and Tiff are the only people besides Luke who know the truth."

"You told them?"

"Yeah," AJ replied. "I really wanted Garritt—I'd crushed hard on him, and both of them have always been good to me. When I asked if it could just be him, they wanted to know why. After I told them about Michelle, I spent the summer hanging out with them a lot. They took me up to a cabin her parents owned—I told Piet it was to get a summer job, which I did, but it was mostly to be with them. We weren't having sex at that point, just talking and spending time together. Garritt and Tiff had a friend, a therapist, who agreed to see me. The whole thing was so healing. By the end of summer, I made love with both Garritt and Tiff, separately and together. God," he said. "It was so good. I don't think sex is the magic answer to fix a broken soul, but it was more about the way they cared for me than the physical. Everything they did was centered on making me feel okay again. Tiff had been through a similar thing, and she was amazing. Michelle's constant pressure about sex and my anxiety after her assault made me think she was right that I wasn't interested in women. Tiff took so much gentle care with me and gave me safe space to say it and then to relearn how to enjoy a woman's mind and body. She's also an activist, and she encouraged me to pour a lot of my energy into fighting biphobia." He sighed. "I guess I went a bit overboard, though, when it came to my friends."

Adam blew out his breath. "And you can't let anyone sleep in your bed because you don't take chances."

"Not entirely," AJ disagreed. "It's one of a handful of things which still trigger a panicked kind of reaction in me. There are others, like this one brand of perfume or certain sex positions, which do it too. I..." His brow creased with a faint frown. "I didn't want you to see me like that, and I didn't want to trouble you with everything."

"That makes sense," Adam remarked, reflecting back on some of the things he'd seen AJ avoid but hadn't questioned.

"There's more."

"More than you've already told me?" Adam gaped at him. "What the hell else could there possibly be?"

"I wasn't sure I liked you when we met, but I saw underneath your swagger all this potential. I wanted to bring it out." He lowered his voice. "Fix you, the same way I try to fix everyone else. Except I think maybe I'm trying to fix *me*." AJ rubbed his temples. "I'm sorry. This can't be helping you at all, listening to me go on." He shifted as though he meant to get up and go back to making breakfast.

"AJ." Adam put his hand out to stop him.

"What?"

Adam rose slowly and made his way around the table. He pulled AJ to his feet and drew him close, unable to form any more words.

He'd never been any good at all at dealing with this level of someone else's emotions, but with AJ it was different. He felt protective, as though he could erase it all by wrapping himself around his man and holding on for dear life. When AJ brought Adam home after Greg stabbed him, Adam felt whole, loved, and cared for. More than anything, he now wanted to absorb AJ's pain, to take it on himself so the person he loved wouldn't have to suffer.

The person I love, he repeated in his head. It had a nice ring to it.

"I'm glad you told me," Adam said. "Are you?"

"I don't know." AJ pulled away.

"I'm not angry with you." Adam cupped his cheek. "I want to tell you something."

"All right."

Adam pursed his lips then took a deep, cleansing breath. "How do you say, 'I love you' in Italian?"

AJ brushed his eyes with the back of his hand, and despite his anguish, a soft chuckle escaped. "That depends on who you're saying it to and why."

"To you," Adam said, and he trembled again. "Because it's true."

As he laid his hand on the back of Adam's neck, AJ said, "Well, if it were me, I would say, *Il mio cuore è solo tuo.*"

"What does that mean?"

"'My heart belongs to you.'" AJ pulled Adam closer. "Or maybe you mean, *Sono innamorato*—'I'm in love with you.'"

"I think that's the one I want," Adam replied. "*Sono inn-amorato.*" He said it slowly and without the graceful inflections AJ always had when he spoke Italian, even the dirty words.

"*Sono immamorato,*" AJ murmured into Adam's ear, "*mio tesoro.* And now, *ti voglio baciare.*"

"What does that—"

"Let me show you."

He stretched up at the same time he drew Adam's head down toward him. Their mouths met; it was not the thrill-inducing experience of their first kiss or the frantic lapping at each other they'd done the first time AJ had been to his apartment or the hesitant reacquainting they'd done the previous night. It was both sweeter and hotter than any other time they'd kissed, messily exploring each other's mouths but never venturing further. They let their lips and tongues say the words they couldn't speak in the wake of everything they'd been through.

At last they broke apart, and AJ said, "I love you too."

Adam didn't think he would ever get tired of hearing it. "*Sono innamorato.*" Nor would he ever tire of saying it.

Chapter Twenty

AJ WHISTLED as he put boxes away after stocking the front counter at the health center. He waved cheerfully to the undergraduate employees on his way out, ignoring their suspicious expressions. For the first time in a while, he felt lighter, and nothing they did was going to spoil his mood. Kira and the nurse practitioner on call could deal with whatever the pair of them dished out.

Adam had been able to return to classes that day, and Dr. Weinstock was still allowing him to do the bulk of his work for her from home. He'd been scheduled to start physiotherapy as well, and although AJ anticipated he would be tired afterward, he also knew Adam had been itching to get moving. Adam hated the feeling he wasn't doing enough no matter how many times AJ assured him it was all right.

AJ bounded up the steps to the apartment but paused outside the door. Something inside smelled delicious, and it surprised him. Slowly, he opened the door and peeked in, wondering what he would find. He almost laughed when he saw Adam standing by the stove in an apron, one hand balancing himself on his cane and the other stirring something in a pot. He was singing—off-key—with his phone. At least, AJ assumed that's what he was listening to through his headphones.

He didn't turn around until AJ was next to him. AJ approached cautiously, not wanting to startle Adam and have him fall or burn himself. When AJ tapped him on the shoulder, Adam pulled out his earbuds and turned to grin at him. He leaned in for a kiss. AJ would have liked to make more of it, but he didn't want whatever was on the stove to boil over because they were too busy in the other room.

"Hey, love," Adam greeted him.

"You didn't have to do this," AJ said. "You must be exhausted. Didn't you have physio today?"

"Yeah, but I zonked out afterward. Guess what I did?"

"Besides making my mouth water?" AJ smacked him at his wicked smirk. "From the food, you ass. Though now you mention it..." He shook his head, laughing. "God, what you do to me. Anyway, what did you do?"

"I drove!" Adam's smile reached ear to ear. "Since it's my left leg that's hurt, I figured maybe I could do it now that I don't have so much trouble getting in and out of a car. It's been really nice of the guys and Renee to take me everywhere, but it kinda sucks, you know? Doctor never said I couldn't drive, and I'm not taking meds that wreck my concentration anymore, so I did it."

"And?" AJ asked.

"Oh, my God. It was so fantastic. Makes it easier to schedule stuff like physio when I don't have to work around everyone else."

AJ gave him a gentle hug. "I'm excited for you." He waved his hand at the stove. "What are you making?"

"Some family recipe your Nonna gave me." Adam grinned.

"Wait...what? You talked to Nonna?" AJ's eyebrows shot up, but then he scowled. "How did you get her number? And just what did she say to you?"

"Oh, this and that," Adam replied airily. He gave AJ an evil smile. "When your mom called me to put me in touch with her friend about my case, I asked her for your Nonna's number too. You've been holding out on me, by the way. I can now use some very creative curses."

"She didn't!"

Laughing, Adam shook his head, and AJ swatted him. "No, she didn't. All she did was tell me how to make this soup and some kind of flatbread, which is baking now. Said it makes a lot." Adam kissed AJ's cheek. "I want to meet her in person, though. I think she likes me."

"Nonna likes everyone," AJ informed him. "Well, except for whoever she told to fuck themselves that one time. Hell, she probably even likes that person. So what's the occasion that you had to go to so much trouble?"

Adam cleared his throat. "I kind of have a surprise for you," he said. "We're having a few people over."

"Oh?" AJ raised his eyebrows, but he chuckled. "Is this our first dinner party?"

"Um." Adam licked his lips.

AJ frowned. "Tell me."

"I think...please don't get pissed...you and your friends need to talk about some things. I wanted to be here, like you've been here for me the last few weeks, and I knew you wouldn't do it on your own."

"What the hell?" AJ snapped. "Is this some kind of weird intervention shit? Like you think I need to give them all the private details I shared with you?"

"No!" Adam exclaimed, carefully backing up. "God, no. It's more about how you said you thought you were trying to fix everyone. Because they've all been driving me everywhere, we talk a lot. I thought maybe you'd like to catch up and get some closure on stuff." He sighed. "They're coming here to share with you how they're doing, and I'm making dinner as a way to thank them for helping me. Aside from that, you can tell them or not tell them anything you like—I can't make you talk about your life. It's just...between what you told me and what I've seen of your work, I got thinking about a few things."

"Such as?" AJ arched a suspicious eyebrow.

Adam came closer again and took AJ's face in his hands. "You love helping people, but practicing that skill set on your friends isn't always a good idea. They bring you all their shit because you *ask them to*, not because they're horrible friends who think you need to solve every problem. Why the fuck are you planning to go back and file papers—yes, I know that's what your non-profit job will be—when it isn't anything like where your passion lies?"

AJ closed his eyes. "Because it was all I could handle after Michelle." His eyes popped open and he looked into Adam's open, earnest face. "I can't make a living as an activist."

Adam did the last thing AJ had been expecting: he laughed. "The hell you can't. But why not go back to social work or community health education? What about your art?"

"I don't know..."

"I do," Adam said firmly. "You will end up miserable if you keep doing what you're doing." He kissed him, and it was a little rough. "Don't punish yourself for what she did to you."

"But my classes," AJ objected, searching for any reason Adam could be wrong. "I can't afford to start over."

"Look into it, that's all," Adam replied. "You have nothing to lose. If you can't do it now, then you finish up, work for a while, and figure out how to go back."

"All right," AJ said, hoping to end the conversation there.

"Promise," Adam growled, clearly putting it together that AJ was mostly humoring him.

"Fine." AJ acquiesced. There wasn't any point in giving Adam all the reasons it might be a terrible idea or not work out or cause more problems than it solved—at least not right before having company.

"Good." Adam brushed his lips against AJ's cheek. "Now, go get ready for dinner."

Everyone lounged in AJ's living room, taking up all the available space. Adam had carted the pillows out of the bedroom to make floor-sitters more comfortable, and AJ was glad he'd washed the sheets. Adam had outdone himself, or Nonna had—she was practically a miracle worker if she could get Adam to cook one of her recipes. AJ had tried to take care of the dishes afterward, but Dara, Luke, and Donny had jumped in before he had a chance. Now they were all comfortably full, spread out and talking in smaller groups.

AJ leaned over to Piet and asked, "How are you feeling?"

"Like crap," Piet admitted. "I'm okay—nothing has spread. But we're looking at dealing with this long-term." He looked up to where Dara sat on one of the dining room chairs, talking with Renee, and then back at AJ. "It's not fair to her." He tilted his chin at Dara.

"Or to you," AJ said. He pressed his palm on Piet's leg. His oldest friend, facing an uncertain future. He could have one more tomorrow or a thousand; it was anyone's guess.

Piet nodded. "I forget that sometimes." He looked sideways at AJ. "Like you."

AJ wanted to object, but he didn't want to argue. Instead, he nodded and stood up to get a glass of water for Piet from the kitchen. Sometimes, there was nothing else to do. While he was running the water into the glass, Luke came in.

"Thanks," he said.

"I didn't do anything," AJ replied. "Adam did all the cooking, and you and the others washed dishes."

"Not that." Luke shook his head. "Letting me crash here. Talking to me." He grinned. "Getting my mind off stuff with your weird boyfriend drama. You guys are together again now?"

"Yeah." AJ smiled in spite of himself.

"Good."

"What about you?" AJ asked. "Are you going to be all right?"

"I think so. I'm saving up again, and the family I'm with is really nice." His smile was rueful. "It's like after my parents kicked me out all over again, staying with a family. Only this time, I'm not planning on screwing shit up so bad."

"None of this was ever your fault, you know." AJ put a hand on Luke's arm.

"I know Greg wasn't my fault, but a lot of other things were." His expression turned amused. "Though I have to say, these last few months...what a hell of a lot of freaky shit."

AJ snorted a laugh. "Yeah, it has been."

"Did I tell you I've been texting with Jax?"

"No, you hadn't mentioned. That's great! They really need

someone to talk to."

"Yeah," Luke agreed. "And I feel...I don't know. Like someone needs me. I get it about their family. Mine always said I was listening to the Devil and I wasn't praying hard enough for a miracle." He tilted his head. "I never got one that way, but maybe they were wrong about what a miracle is in the first place."

"What do you mean?" AJ asked.

"I dunno, like...maybe we're each other's miracle, I guess. It feels that way sometimes after everything that's happened." He laughed. "That's so cheesy. Sorry."

AJ put an arm around Luke and squeezed. "No, it sounds about right to me. I'm still here if you need me."

Luke gave AJ a return hug. "I'm gonna be okay, I swear it. You and Connor and the others, too—you've all been so good to me. It doesn't take being blood to be family."

"Truth," AJ agreed.

He wandered back into the living room, handed Piet his water, and worked his way around a forest of his friends' legs until he reached Donny and Lauryn. She looked up and smiled, patting the floor next to her. AJ sat with his back to the wall.

"I didn't get a chance to talk to you after the health fair," she said.

"Sorry about that," AJ answered, grinning at her. "I got a little distracted."

She smiled. "Right. Well, I talked to Kira for a good long time. It wasn't only the protest—it was everything that happened, and she said it was proof we need to work harder to make the campus safe. I mean, Luke wasn't a student, but Kira said she's sure he's not the only one dealing with that kind of situation. A lot of students don't feel like there's anywhere to go when there's a problem."

Connor, who was on Donny's other side—when had they become friends?—leaned around him and looked pointedly at AJ. "Might have helped some when you were dealing with Michelle and the way she treated you."

"What happened?" Lauryn asked. "I always had the impression you got a whole lot of crap thrown at you for being bi and being so outspoken about it. Was she part of the problem?"

AJ's heart hammered. He hadn't expected Michelle to come up in conversation. He looked at Lauryn's concerned expression, Donny's confusion, and Connor's scowl. He bypassed them to where Luke sat next to Connor, his hand resting on Connor's leg. Only he knew the truth, and he'd kept his face neutral. AJ swallowed the bile rising in his throat.

"She assaulted me," he said.

Three mouths dropped open, and Donny said, "What?"

"AJ, you don't have to explain," Luke said quietly.

He hadn't planned on saying it, but now that the words were out, AJ didn't want to take them back or justify them or even explain them. He repeated himself, more loudly. "I said, she assaulted me."

The low buzz of conversation in the rest of the room stopped, and everyone's attention was on AJ. Adam hauled himself up from the couch and made his way over to AJ. Dara popped up and grabbed a chair for him. Once he was seated, Adam leaned down to put his mouth up to AJ's ear.

"Are you sure you want to do this?"

"Yeah," AJ replied. He moved so he could face out. "In case you were wondering, Michelle wasn't just giving me shit for being bi or for 'cheating' on her or whatever her issue of the week was. And now you all know. She...did things to me after a party once, when I was too drunk to stop her, and she did it because she couldn't deal with having a queer boyfriend." He took a deep breath. "Adam wanted me to see how you were doing because I've been busy with work and class and taking care of him. None of you hid anything from me, but I've kept this from all of you. It's time I told you the truth."

Lauryn reached out for him. "It's more important than ever what we're doing, working with Kira. We need to be believed without it becoming another way we can be hated for who we are. You're not alone, AJ."

"You never were," Connor said.

AJ looked around at all the people gathered there, every one of whom trusted him, believed him, and understood him. He brought his gaze to rest on Adam, who twined their fingers together and squeezed.

"You're right," he said to Connor. "I never was."

AJ and Adam sat down across from each other after carrying their order from the counter. Luke had thrown in a few extras, grinning at them and telling them it was his treat. Adam started in on the food right away, but AJ took his time unfolding his napkin and carefully arranging everything in front of him, the same way he mentally arranged what he needed to tell Adam. Eventually, Adam slowed down and looked up at him, his face twisting into a puzzled frown.

"Aren't you going to eat?" he asked.

"Yeah, of course," AJ told him. He took a bite, but it tasted like cardboard. He was too nervous. Setting it back down, he said, "I called my parents."

Adam followed suit and put his food down as well. "Ah, I see."

"I didn't tell them everything." Maybe one day he would, but that day had not arrived.

"It's okay." Adam reached across the table and took his hand. He rubbed AJ's knuckles, his rough skin comforting.

"I said I wasn't happy and that I didn't want to work at the shelter."

"What did they say?"

AJ sighed. "They were fine, actually. Dad said he'd been surprised when I suggested it in the first place—it was never what I wanted to do."

Adam nodded. "Okay. Then what are you going to do?"

"Well..." This was what AJ hadn't been sure how to tell Adam, in part because their relationship had taken so many convoluted turns. "I'm staying here for now. I'm changing my program, and it will take at least another year. Kira said she'll keep me on, since my work for her is relevant to my new classes. She's losing Carrie next year anyway, so I'm basically taking her place."

"What's your course of study now?"

"Social work, and I'm dropping the non-profit certificate." He looked down at the table, but then a slow smile spread across his face and he looked back up at Adam. "I might also take an art class or two."

Adam's eyes lit up, and it made the confession worth it to see how excited Adam was for him. To cover his combination of embarrassment and enthusiasm, he focused on his food and took a few more bites.

"And after that?" Adam asked.

AJ chewed and swallowed, thinking about how to answer. "After that, I don't know," he said. "I might just look for jobs and try to settle down, or I might figure out if I can earn a PhD." He took a couple of slow breaths. "I have no real idea, and I'm trying not to freak out about that." Adam laughed, startling AJ. "What's so funny?"

Adam composed himself. "Only that for once in my life, I'm very, very sure about a couple of things."

"Oh?"

"Yeah. While you're busy dropping your non-profit cert, I'm starting mine."

It was AJ's turn to laugh. "You'd be a hell of a lot better at the job I was supposed to do than I would have. Maybe I should call Dad back."

"Maybe you should," Adam said.

"What's the other thing?" AJ wanted to know.

"What other thing?"

"Whatever else you're sure about," AJ said. "You told me there were a couple of things, and you've only listed one."

Adam grasped AJ's hand again, lifting it and bringing it to his mouth to kiss the backs of his fingers. "You," he said. "I'm certain about you."

"Yeah?" The word came out breathy, and AJ's stomach twirled pleasantly.

"Let's see if I can remember how to say it." Adam straightened up. "*Sono innamorato, mio tesoro.* Did I get it right?"

"Yes," AJ told him. "Exactly right. I love you too, *tesoro.*"

Conversation drifted until they were talking about smaller, less significant things. They finished up and headed back to the parking lot, waving to Luke on the way past. AJ leaned on the car and pulled Adam in close, one hand on his hip and one on his neck. Adam rested his cane against the car and twined his fingers in AJ's hair. It was chilly, and their breath mingled in visible clouds as they hovered with their mouths inches apart. Adam closed the gap, pressing his cool lips against AJ's. He opened, allowing AJ to slide his tongue in. The kiss warmed AJ from head to toe, and when it ended, he sighed happily as he rested his forehead against Adam's.

"*Il mio cuore è solo tuo*," he said. "You have my heart—forever and ever."

"Want to go home and..." Adam whispered something hot and dirty into AJ's ear.

"Hm," AJ said. "Or maybe..." He whispered something equally filthy back.

Adam laughed and pulled away, clasping AJ's hand and swinging a little. He picked up his cane and stepped past AJ to climb inside the car. As AJ rounded to the driver's side, he reflected on Adam's choice of words: home. Yes, that was right where he wanted to be, with Adam beside him. He got behind the wheel and drove away from the restaurant, heading for home.

ACKNOWLEDGEMENTS

There are so many people without whose help this novel would never have seen the light of day.

First and foremost, love and gratitude to my colleague and friend, Adrian J. Smith, who asked me to write a story for Adam. He's not mine, but I've been graciously allowed to take him out and play with him for a while.

Grace, my excellent beta reader and fellow writer, rescued me more than once from the jaws of the wicked Plot Bunny. I'm grateful for her brandishing the Red Pen of Doom and slaying the beast.

Mountains of thanks go to Supposed Crimes for publishing my work and allowing me the freedom to infuse social justice and a whole lot of bisexual themes into my work.

I would also like to thank the board and the good folks at BiNetUSA for providing resources and information. These are some of the most kind, loving, witty, dedicated, and passionate people I've ever had the pleasure to meet, both in person and online.

A special thanks to Lynnette from the BiCast for her ongoing care and support and for some great conversations.

And finally, much love to my family for giving me time and space to let the words in my brain out onto the page.

Resources

For more information on bisexuality, please visit:

BiNet USA website: http://www.binetusa.org/ & Facebook group: https://www.facebook.com/groups/binetusa/

American Institute of Bisexuality: http://www.americaninstituteofbisexuality.org/

Bisexual.org: http://bisexual.org/

The Bisexual Index: http://www.bisexualindex.org.uk/

The Bisexual Resource Center: http://www.biresource.net/

For bisexual media, check out:

The BiCast: http://thebicast.org/

Bisexual Books: http://bisexual-books.tumblr.com/

Bi: The Web Series: http://biustv.com/

ABOUT THE AUTHOR

A. M. Leibowitz is a queer spouse, parent, feminist, and book-lover falling somewhere on the Geek-Nerd Spectrum.

Ze keeps warm through the long, cold western New York winters by writing about life, relationships, hope, and happy-for-now endings.

Hir published fiction includes hir novels, *Lower Education, Passing on Faith,* and *Anthem,* as well as a number of short works, and hir stories have been included in several anthologies.

In between noveling and editing, ze blogs coffee-fueled, quirky commentary on faith, culture, writing, books, and hir family.

www.ingramcontent.com/pod-product-compliance
Lightning Source LLC
Chambersburg PA
CBHW070938190726
48292CB00004B/1236